FOLLOWING YOU

FOLLOWING YOU

EVA LESKO NATIELLO

FINE LINE
PUBLISHING

Published by FINE LINE PUBLISHING
Printed in the United States of America.

cover design by Bianca Bordianu

Typesetting services by BOOKOW.COM

*For Margaux and Mark
when this began you followed me,
now I follow you*

CHAPTER 1

Lawrence

Wednesday, December 16, 2015, 3:00 p.m.

L AWRENCE slipped away from his desk, snaked down the hall, and ducked into the supply room completely unnoticed, while the detective bureau minions became transfixed by a candle-lit sheet cake bought to mark a colleague's occasion of some sort. He could literally teach a class in Everyday Stealth Techniques.

"Hey, Lawrence!"

Damn it.

Lawrence poked his head out. "What's up?"

"Did you get those photos?"

"Yeah, thanks."

Lawrence quickly barricaded the door with a tower of water-cooler jugs to prevent intrusions by the office underlings. That lame interaction just cost Lawrence solid time with Shae. Valuable together time.

He threw a ream of copier paper on the dirty linoleum floor so as not to soil his khakis and wedged his commanding physique between a stack of soda cases and a tower of ladies' products. Inside snug latex gloves, his hands glistened with anticipation sweat.

Lawrence's phone lit up with the most delectable image of Shae Wilmont—IShop's host extraordinaire—selling his favorite product line, Fruits&Flowers Ultra-Emollient Body Cream, on today's Beauty Hour livestream. With his nose pressed hard against the screen, he snorted her. Every pixel.

"Oh, *God*." He exhaled a hot burst.

Shae's snug azure sweater clung to her exquisite hills and valleys. The V-neck drew the eye not so subtly to one of her special areas, while the cashmere teased one's desire to touch. She stood behind a line of lotions. It reminded Lawrence of a border of heirloom tulips: impressive, gallant. Watching Shae without sound, he focused on her effervescent movement. The sway of her hips, the gleam of her green eyes, the lure of her knowing smile, the supple flesh of her décolletage, her fingers as they wrapped a bottle of lotion, but mostly, her lips as they formed words like "luxurious" and "sensual" and "velvety." Anything with an "l" exposed tongue. The "r" in "dreamy" and "creamy" required open puckered lips.

The camera zoomed in for a close-up. His cilia quivered. Gently, he touched his nose to the screen and breathed her in.

Mid-breath, he froze.

Had he locked his desk drawer? With the crime scene photos that had just arrived? He'd been waiting for Shae's body cream show—watching the clock, counting the minutes. It was easy to lose focus with Shae on his mind. But he didn't tolerate slip-ups or recklessness on the job—even from himself. Especially now. Lawrence was the new backbone of the Vista Verde Police Department Southern Division Detective Bureau. He'd stake everything on his professional reputation. Covering his ass had become a reflex. Shae had him doing things he'd never imagined, but leaving evidence on his desk wouldn't be one of them. He patted the front pocket of his khakis. A wad of disposable latex gloves in one, desk keys in the other. He sighed in relief.

He popped in an earbud, keeping the other ear free to detect if someone challenged the blocked door, which was, admittedly, not foolproof. If the men in the office didn't shit in repulsive stenches, Lawrence could watch the livestream without this covert effort in the privacy of a bathroom stall. But the odor would ruin everything.

Lawrence never missed IShop's Beauty Hour with Shae. Even if it was taped. But livestreaming on IShop's Facebook page was ideal viewing because one could comment in the moment. When it came to the lovely Shae Wilmont, there was plenty to say.

Shae chose the yellow bottle, SexyCitrus, closed her eyes, and inhaled deeply. Her chest expanded in a wonderful crescendo of flesh and cashmere. Lawrence imagined himself smelling it. He imagined smelling her.

Soon, he'd smell Shae in the flesh. Wedge his nose into her armpit—moist and hairy, he hoped. Two things women went to great lengths to avoid. If he knew Shae, and of course he did, chances were slim her armpit was anything but soft, shaven, dry, and scented like gardenia blossoms.

Shae fondled the bottle directly in front of her perfect set of balloons providing the loveliest tight-angle shot. Balloons, Lawrence noted, could sell anything. The cameraman knew that, certainly. That shot was held for a very long time.

If only Lawrence had a pair. What he *wouldn't* do with them. Girls didn't know how easy they had it. What a waste it was when a girl had perfectly bouncy balloons and didn't leverage their usefulness.

A pair of double Cs—or even young Ds—could coax the price of a new Toyota Corolla under list or fix a flat tire on the side of a freeway. An exasperated pair—with flounce and fervor—could grant entrance to a sold-out show without a ticket!

"Ba-*lloons*." Lawrence sighed.

His first encounter with this female secret weapon came when he was five, and an especially buoyant aunt (by marriage to Lawrence's uncle) visited for the first time at Thanksgiving. Her indiscriminate smiling and laughing more than put off his mother, who was devoted to stoicism and thereby kept the aunt at a chilly distance.

"I'll have another drink, Paul," Auntie smiled as she pressed against Lawrence's father. His mother shot her husband a look. He knew full well about the one drink rule in their house. But, sure enough, Lawrence's father glanced at Auntie's balloons and the snug dress that touted them and poured a second drink. As if under a spell.

When Lawrence's father brandished the electric knife to carve the turkey, Auntie gushed and launched from her seat. "I'll have a go at that," she said to his father.

Silence swept through the cramped kitchen. No one but his father ever carved the turkey. They didn't even dare touch the knife. The closest Lawrence ever got to the knife was after it was returned to its box, and he was told to put it away.

At first, his father seemed stunned. Then his saucer-eyes found her balloons again, and he slowly handed over the knife, trance-like, as his body relaxed into a massive grin that stretched his mouth out as wide as Lawrence had ever seen it.

It was brazen the way his aunt (by marriage) posed her desires as statements instead of requests. Lawrence's mother reminded him of this many times over the year that followed until his aunt and uncle returned. He did notice, however, her large balloons and asked innocently, "Why are your balloons so much bigger than Mother's?" to which his mother's eyes grew so large they took up most of her face, making them the largest thing about her in that moment. Everyone sucked in their breath. Except for Auntie. She howled with laughter while her balloons jounced in merriment along with her.

Now *there* was a woman who knew their power. More than that, she noticed things the average woman didn't. Maybe even the average man. She was a curious one, that generously proportioned aunt.

Over dessert, she leaned into Lawrence conspiratorially and whispered, "Don't let kids make fun of your buggy-eyes; you're putting them to good use. Being observant will get you far. So will eating your veggies, dear, so you can grow up big and strong like your daddy. You'll need something going for you."

That was Lawrence's first lesson on the rewards of being curious.

He rubbed his nose hard against the phone screen into Shae's soft balloons, and in perfect rows of rapid staccato snorts, he inhaled her. The rush of oxygen left him weak in the knees. He loved what snorting Shae did to him.

Having removed the cap, Shae curled her fingers around the bottle positioned in line with her cleavage, tipped her head down, nearly grazing her lips to the orifice, and breathed hungrily.

Lawrence ripped off his latex gloves. He cradled the phone in his bare hands—his skin as close to Shae as possible. The gloves made his skin sensitive, itchy, and irritated, but it was part of the job. He wasn't going to whine about it. Some part of Lawrence loved the suffering; the angry patches were reminders of his determination not to leave a single fingerprint—a veritable calling card—behind. Lawrence was a detail guy. Though unintentional, his gloves became his trademark, representing his seriousness and professionalism.

He shifted his weight on the floor, his long limbs in accordion folds—knees tucked under chin, arms wrapped around shins—as he peered through his knees at the phone. He loved it down there, shrinking into himself. Normally he towered over people and exploited his endowment. To shrink—to become invisible, even—was to wield a different power.

He pulled his phone close to his mouth and brushed his lips lightly against the screen, back and forth over Shae's soft sweater, careful not to get the saliva that pooled in the corners of his mouth on it. His tongue snatched the drool deposits. The last thing he wanted was the smell of his own breath getting tangled with the fantasy of Shae's.

He considered her breath. *The nastier, the better*, he mused. Mint disguised truth. Bad breath was intimate. Proximity, necessary.

Proximity was also necessary for the exchange of skin cells. Whose idea was it that shaking hands was innocent, platonic? Really? Having someone's skin cells and body fluids on one's hand was more than neighborly. For now, that was next to impossible. *Next to*. Those words rushed his blood.

Obviously, smell was the most anonymous of the five senses. One could smell someone without them knowing. Undetected. Unlike touching. People knew when they were being touched. Watching, yes, there was anonymity in watching someone under certain conditions—hovering from a distance online or in person with binoculars. People act differently when they think they're alone. Tasting was different altogether. Nearly impossible to achieve inconspicuously. *Near*-ly.

Lawrence pulled back from the screen. Shae pumped SpicyGinger onto her hand and massaged it in swirls. She brought her hand to her nose and breathed with her eyes closed. Would she call it "intoxicating?" Lawrence looked away briefly to grab his notebook. Last month she said "intoxicating" thirty-seven times. It aroused him each time. As if she said it to tease him. If she said it today, according to his notes, it would eke past "fabulous."

She looked straight into the camera. He loved the way she looked at him. Her lips parted into a mischievous smile.

"This is my favorite." She fluttered her eyes and exhaled. "It's intoxicating."

Lawrence jabbed the SHOP button. He arrowed up to five. Poked the SPEED BUY.

Success! The "Sold-Out" banner glided across the screen a moment later.

A murmur of voices grew animated outside the supply room door. He shook his head as if to erase them from his awareness. He needed one more untainted moment.

The doorknob cocked. Then a shove against the door. The water jugs shimmied.

Damn it.

He ignored the activity at the door.

Quickly, he propped himself on his knees. Lawrence logged into "Larry's" Facebook account so that "Larry" could comment on IShop's live stream. Lawrence's delicate touch typed "Larry's" love note to Shae.

"Your favorite is always my favorite."

He posted Facebook comments from "Larry's" account. Purchases and on-air testimonials were from "Lars." Instagram comments, "Lance."

Seconds later someone replied to "Larry."

"Don't be a fool, Larry, she changes 'favorites' all the time—the more favorites she has, the more she sells. Don't fall for it!"

Lawrence was livid. Who did Cynthia Nebbits think she was? Attention whore! Insidious comment troll! Accusing Shae of…of …insincerity, of…manipulative sales tactics!

Another shove against the door. Someone was dogged in their pursuit of supplies, and it pissed him off.

He lashed at his phone's keyboard, spitting out a reply.

A voice came from the hall. "Hey! Who's in there? Open the door."

Damn. It was Late Again—a.k.a. Joanne. The third time in as many days he couldn't avoid her. The supply room was an imprudent choice, but he was desperate.

He typed fast and hit enter. "Jealous much???? It's a woman's prerogative to change her mind!"

Shae had moved on to soaps—*without him.* Damn it. Dealing with Cynthia Nebbits cost him solid time! Of course, he could watch the DVR later, but he couldn't interact with Shae then. What if she said his name or read his comment on air? He wouldn't be able to respond! Not to mention, during the live show—for those precious moments—he knew precisely where she was and what she was doing. In real time. Later, while Lawrence watched the recording, she would've moved on. Out to dinner, talking to someone else. Looking at someone else. Not smiling at Lawrence. Not ogling him.

Lawrence—well, *"Larry"*—didn't comment every day, though willpower was not his strong suit. He knew he was getting closer, and he wasn't about to slip up now. No red flags. He had to be strategic about this whole affair.

"Why is the supply room locked?" someone shouted from the hall.

The knob twisted frenetically. Another *umph* of a shoulder against the door. The water jugs tottered. The imminent avalanche shot Lawrence to his feet.

"Hang on!" Lawrence sniped.

"I gotta get ink."

I gotta get ink. Damn buzzkill.

Lawrence steadied the tower, then shoved it away from the door. He slipped on a new pair of latex gloves from the stash in his pocket, brushed the seat of his pants, and pinched the pressed crease that ran down the front of his khakis to restore some decorum. He yanked the door open and attempted to temper his annoyance while he sidestepped Late Again.

"Oh, it's you," she said. "I knew it."

What was that supposed to mean? He could say the same about her. He almost fired back, but that's exactly what she wanted. He didn't have time for banter with the support staff. Especially someone with such disregard for workplace punctuality and obvious rancor for a new police department superior.

He strode into the hall.

"Did you drop this?" she called out.

Lawrence turned to look.

She held up a shriveled, clear latex glove. One of the fingers was inverted, and the wrist curled up to where the fingers branched out. A mutated hand. She pinched and waved it with great flourish, all pinky in the air. He had such disdain for her at that moment.

"You want it?" she said. Was she mocking him? "It's yours, right?" Her cheeks flushed.

He quickly shook his head. "No."

He wished he hadn't seen it. The twisted, pitiful thing.

"Well—" Lawrence fingered the sharp crease of his khakis and forced himself to calm down. He had to get along with these people. He motioned to something in the distance. "Better get back to it." Unlike her, he had actual work to do. He resumed the walk back to his desk.

At first, Lawrence deduced the reason for Late Again's aggressiveness toward him was disguised jealousy. Lawrence came from another precinct. He was offered the job over her, an insider. It was only a hunch—maybe a crazy one—because it was clear to him, and likely everyone else, there was no way an Investigative Assistant was qualified for his job. She lacked the skills, experience, and connections. And not to be sexist, but she was also a girl. He found out later she never applied for the job. Which left only one explanation for her antagonism. She probably wanted him.

Lawrence surveyed the room to see if anyone caught Late Again putting the moves on "the new guy." He didn't need that getting around.

He had little interest in the mundanity of the office staff and less interest in learning their names. They were drab, indistinct clones with their microwavable pork-fried-rice leftovers and lumbar pillows, cascades of dusty potted plastic ivy, and Valpak happy-hour coupons. He snatched the first and easiest identifying characteristic to separate them in his mind: Fruity Tums, Hangnail Biter, Late Again.

When the SpicyGinger Ultra-Emollient Body Creams arrived home, Lawrence would give one to Rita. She thought it was romantic when he bought her soaps and lotions. She appreciated his thoughtfulness. Boyfriends like Lawrence were hard to find.

Truthfully, it had been months since Lawrence's last gift to Rita. The Coco-Van Body Butter incident. Rita claimed coconut scents gave her headaches and stopped using it. Lawrence didn't appreciate her lack of appreciation for his spontaneous gift-giving.

But Lawrence came to realize that withholding from Rita was punishing himself. How else could he smell Shae? He was anxious for Rita to try SpicyGinger; it would intoxicate Lawrence as he'd imagine Shae. He was getting closer to Shae every day.

Closer.

Soon—very soon—he'd be close enough to smell her in the flesh. He was laying plans. Plans that were once next to impossible.

Next to.

Indeed.

CHAPTER 2

Shae

Thursday, December 17, 2015, 5:35 p.m.

ALL three stood shoulder to shoulder in IShop's hair and makeup room, facing the mirrored wall edged in lightbulbs protruding like pimples from the glass. They stood perfectly still except for their eyeballs pinging from one to the other. Shae looked at Figgy. Figgy at Val. Val at Shae. Alarm blazed across their faces—Shae, with a headful of Velcro rollers as big as soup cans, wearing IShop's *Today's Steal!*, Donna Karan's dolman sleeve knit with satin trim and ballet neckline in Midnight; Figgy with an eyebrow pencil tucked over an ear, a faded Minnie Mouse t-shirt snug across her wide frame, scooped low and revealing a swath of cleavage; and Val in her starched white button-down, a brown bob with bangs, no accessories, no makeup, no qualms.

A moment ago, Val sauntered into the dressing room, for the first time in three years since Shae'd been there, from the executive office. She detonated a quiet, unassuming verbal grenade—freezing Figgy, who was hunched over Shae, mid-stroke of the eyeshadow brush, with just enough room for Shae to leap from the chair. Now they stood like Rockettes in a kick line, however, still from shock.

A prolonged awkward silence filled the space. Except for an almost audible throbbing that traveled from Shae's chest to her throat and oddly, settled onto her bottom lip.

"The stalker's back…" Shae repeated Val's announcement in the soberest tone. Disbelieving the words as she said them.

Somehow discussing this in the mirror with their reflections felt less…grave. Less personal. It kept the unsettling news at a distance. Figgy mumbled something under her breath, put the brush down, and rubbed her hands along her thighs.

"The note—" Val found Shae's eyes in the mirror, then cast her gaze toward the floor in sudden realization, it seemed, that her voice and energy didn't match the fraught nature of the situation.

Shae shook her head in little jerky movements to settle her rambling thoughts. *So that's what this was about.* Val had been texting and calling her since lunch. Shae hadn't actually returned Val's calls. She should've called her boss back, *but* she imagined that Val intended to pull the Donna Karan show from her and give it to Bryan, the new guy. Yes, last-minute host changes were strictly done on an emergency basis, but Val had done that very thing— rare as it was—just that morning. Swapped Bryan out and Shae in. At the last minute. Without explanation. So maybe Shae became paranoid.

This wasn't that. Clearly.

"We called the police." Val said. "We had to." Her voice was matter-of-fact, like she was reporting on inventory projections. She fidgeted with her shirt, tugging the cuffs, swiping the sleeves.

Figgy plucked two tissues from the box on the counter and blotted her forehead and the top of her lip. She stuck the tissues into her armpits and left them there. Stuck another tissue into her cleavage. "It's hot in here," Figgy said. "Where's my cornstarch?"

Shae let this news congeal. The stalker was back. "The" stalker? Several months ago, she received a series of threatening letters. Then they stopped. The person responsible had never been found.

Shae was slightly embarrassed to think Val was calling to make a last-minute host switch. It wasn't so much the "last minute" aspect that bothered Shae about having to do Bryan's Sassy Mats show, because she was a professional and emergencies happened. But it was never explained as such; in fact, there was no explanation at all. Junior hosts, like Bryan who'd only arrived four months ago, worked with vendors like Sassy Mats. Shae was the top-selling host for the last fifteen months. She hadn't worked with that level vendor for years. Hearing about this bogus switch, another host said to Shae, "I call BS on that. Sounds like the beginning of a phase-out. You better get to the bottom of it."

It was unlikely Shae would "get to the bottom of it." She was more likely to "avoid conflict." Shae was a well-trained avoider of discord, taught by some of the most skilled evaders and deflectors around—her relatives. Reticence was ingrained. Mysteries and unanswered questions were part of her lineage and remained locked away like family heirlooms in a safe-deposit box. Shae had grown accustomed to navigating life while lacking information. Over time, she stopped seeking it.

Being told to cover the Sassy Mats show an hour before it went live felt underhanded. With no time to prepare, attend vendor meetings, or study the product, it could set her up for failure. She didn't trust Bryan, the smooth-talker, and she wasn't sure about

Val, either. Three years ago, Shae was hired to replace Val's friend, and she still wasn't sure what Val thought of her.

Hearing the term "phase-out" rattled her. Shae decided to be a team player, avoid conflict, and do the Sassy Mats show. It was perfectly reasonable to predict Val's texts this morning meant another host change was coming. So she ignored them. She wasn't giving up the DK show.

Now, part of her wished that was the reason Val was looking for her.

Figgy found her cornstarch, pulled open the elastic waist of her palazzo pants, and shook powder down there. When she let go, it snapped her skin with a muffled *thwap*, and a white cloud engulfed her, like Glinda leaving Munchkin Land. Figgy looked like she wanted to disappear, though the makeup room was where she held court.

Shae lowered herself back into the chair and faced Figgy, who patted her hand where it gripped the arm rest. "You'll feel better when you're on-air, cookie. That'll perk you up—always does. You'll be with your people. Don't worry." Figgy grabbed a bottle of foundation and shook it like a martini.

Figgy was right. Shae always felt better during a show. "Shae the IShop Host" was confident, happy, and exceedingly approachable—*on-air*.

Now, anxiety rose in Shae like steam from sauna stones. She tried to compartmentalize it. In her mind, she wrapped her nerves in a plush bathrobe so no one would notice, not even herself. She'd lived through a stalker before. Though it felt very different now.

She eyeballed the clock and launched from the chair. She should be on set.

"Jeez, Fig, I have to go—my show starts in ten minutes! You done?" Shae slid her handbag down the counter toward her and ransacked it. "Didn't I bring my cards in here? Where are my show notes?"

Figgy dabbed foundation onto her index finger. Shae held up her hand to stop her. "You did my makeup already. Hair." Figgy needed to pull herself together. Shae couldn't have Figgy fall apart. She was the cement of this place.

"My cards were here this morning," Shae said to Figgy in the mirror while tearing her rollers out. "Looking forward to a great show. This top's a winner," she said to alert Val of her intentions. Today's Donna Karan show would be Shae's third. Once a host had three successful shows with a vendor, she was locked in. No other host could work with them. Shae wasn't giving it up.

While Shae's mouth was on autopilot, her mind was thinking of something else entirely. How long had it been since she received that last letter? Months. Back then, the police claimed they caught the guy but later released him on insufficient evidence. Then the letters stopped. Three months had passed. The whole stalker thing *was over.*

IShop had been very supportive over those months. What would they do this time? Phase her out? Shae wouldn't let that happen. She had to do this show. *Had to.* It didn't matter how she felt on the inside as long as she didn't show it on the out-side—which had become the story of her life, really. How hard would that be? Shae couldn't lose this job. It was all she had. These people, this place, this job. To her continual surprise, she'd been very successful as an IShop host. In spite of herself, even. She wasn't naturally outgoing, self-assured, *or* friendly—qualities she thought necessary to be good on-air. She was the opposite.

But she could pretend to be anything. *That* she was good at. If someone said to Shae, "I think you'd be good at this," she just did it.

Everything, all of a sudden, came rushing at her. All of her misguided life decisions, her stupid mistakes along the way. No, she hadn't made the best choices all the time. Some still haunted her —but the past was the past. Was losing this job the way she'd pay for it? Losing the one thing that was right in her life?

"Uh, listen, Shae." Val studied Shae's shirt. She forced a stiff smile and wrung her hands. "I know you're supposed to be on set, and, well, I don't want to boil the ocean, but…listen, I realize the timing's terrible—"

"You know what, Val, I'm super late. Ed's going to kill me." Shae grabbed her earpiece and leaped toward the door. "I need to find my show notes. Sorry." Figgy grabbed a brush and spray. "Bring it, Fig—we'll do it on set."

Shae rounded the door as Val called out, "Security found the note in your car."

Shae stopped with her hand clutching the door frame. "In my car?" She spun around.

"Yes, the note was taped to a box. Security found it in your car." Val held her hands up. "Sorry. I didn't want to have to tell you." She paused. "That means—the person is—well…"

Shae turned to Figgy, who mirrored her shock.

"In my *car*?" Shae stuttered. "Figgy—" Her voice hitched.

Figgy grabbed Shae's hand and squeezed it. "It's okay, cookie. You're okay."

Shae swallowed hard. How did someone get in her car? She shook her head a hundred times. Maybe something would rattle into place. She was so confused. This wasn't what she—Shae palmed the wall to steady herself. Her head was spinning.

"Obviously, we wanted to ask you before we called the police in case it was a gift or something from a friend. But we couldn't find you." Val crossed her arms.

They couldn't *find* her?

"And honestly, the note on the box, it wasn't in an envelope. It was…anybody could read it. And, well…it justified a call to the police."

Figgy pulled her shirt away from her body to fan her chest with a copy of *People Magazine*, then her armpits. Alarm calcified on Figgy's face. It was unsettling to see her like that. All her natural bravado disappeared like powder clouds.

"We didn't want to take any chances—the detective said a package placed in your car meant the person was in close proximity. The sooner, the better for their chances of zeroing in on him. I stopped by an hour ago; I didn't want to spring this on you last minute. But Figgy said you were—" Val looked at her phone. "One sec." Her finger went in the air. "Hello?"

"Figgy?" Shae was incredulous. "Val was here looking for me? When? Where was I?"

Figgy's chin tucked into her chest, her lips pursed tight, and her eyebrows pinched together like someone had stuck her face in an eyelash curler. "What am I, a human Find My Friends tracker? I do hair and makeup!" She threw her arms in the air, then stuck another tissue in her cleavage. "Now look at the time! You think I'm a magician, too?" Figgy reached out to remove Shae's rollers. Figgy was perspiring everywhere.

Shae jerked back. "Figgy, seriously? You knew about this?"

Figgy turned away and pecked through her bottles. She closed her eyes and spritzed rose water onto her face, neck, and chest in big looping swirls. "If Val told me anything, it's not like I remember, cookie. I never remember anything that's none of my business." She avoided eye contact at all costs.

"*Seriously?*" Shae was shocked. Wow. If Shae didn't know how much Figgy cared for her and how scared she was the first time Shae had a stalker, this would feel like a betrayal.

Val finished her call. "The police asked if you received a gift from someone. They wanted to rule that out. Did someone give you a box of Laduree macarons?"

That nearly stopped Shae's breath. Laduree? Her favorite cookies from childhood. There was a Laduree shop a block from their apartment in Paris. Her father used to take her. She never told anyone about those. *Did* she? Only someone close to her would know that.

"No. No one gave me…a gift. There was no package in my car."

Val's demeanor became combative. "We didn't think so. Theo said you went out for lunch. He said you don't usually."

True. She almost never went out for lunch. Unless a vendor invited her out, like the rep from Donna Karan did today. But that was rare.

"I was only an hour. I parked in front of Murphy's. We sat at a window table. I could *see* my car. A cup of soup. A salad." Her mind reeled. "How could…I mean, it was only an hour, I had a cup of *soup*. I didn't see anyone. I never saw anything."

The blood rushed her face, scalding her cheeks. This energy was bad right before a show. How would she recover in a few minutes? *Compartmentalize.*

"I didn't search the car after lunch. I should have, now that I think about it," Shae mumbled to herself. That was their routine since the first stalking. Not that security had ever found anything in her car before. It was precautionary. Now they found something! "Why did I go into town? I never go into town."

"Did someone ask you to go? Who knew you were going? Did you tell anyone?" Val asked.

"Well, yeah. The rep asked me. So she knew, obviously." Shae tried to think. "Who else knew? Theo. Of course. He brought me my car. Figgy," Shae motioned to Figgy, "wanted me to pick up mascara—*oh!*" She stepped back into the dressing room and over to her handbag. She handed Figgy the mascara. "I forgot. Here. That's right. I went to the pharmacy, too." Shae slapped the side of her head.

"It's okay. No worries. I should've picked it up myself. I wasn't planning on going out." Figgy blotted the back of her neck. "Then Bryan ask me to lunch, so—"

Shae shot Figgy a confused look. "Bryan? He's here? How could that be? Why did I do his show?"

"I don't know," Figgy said, looking baffled, sneaking in a glance at Val, who was making notes on her phone. "He's got a show later?"

"No. He doesn't. He's not on the schedule," Shae said.

Figgy shrugged. "He told me he did."

Having Bryan on standby this afternoon was more than a little coincidental.

"Who else knew you were going to lunch?" Val interjected.

Shae's mind was buzzing. She racked her brain for any drop of sense. "I don't know. I think that's it. Unless they told other people?"

"We need to provide a list for the police. We need to drill down. They want to talk to you. The note wasn't like the others, there's that, too. It was handwritten, for one thing. I mean, yeah, it could be the same stalker, or…maybe I shouldn't use that word until we're sure." She checked the clock. "We need to decide about the show. The police will be here soon—it's not great timing. We didn't want you on-air without knowing. We don't expect you to do the show, of course. Bryan's here, so he could—"

What did Val mean, the note wasn't like the others? Was that good or bad?

"What did it say?"

"What?" Val said.

"The note. What did the note say?"

Val filled her cheeks with air. Then let go. She propped her hands on her hips and pressed her lips together, flat, as if she wasn't going to say another word. She tipped her head down.

"'You're so pretty. I follow you everywhere.'"

CHAPTER 3

Honey

Thursday, December 17, 2015, 5:45 p.m.

Honey slipped across a greasy patch of the black and white tiled floor, sailing past the server's pick-up window, and before she could stop herself, slammed into Enrique.

"Sorry!"

"In the bathroom again? Always in the bathroom." His spittle hit her cheek. She winced. "Better not be gettin' high!"

Honey was halfway into an eye roll when she caught herself. Classic Enrique. He knew nothing about Honey. Because if he did, he'd know that's the last thing she'd be doing in the bathroom or spending her hard-earned money on. She wiped her cheek with the back of her hand.

"Here's your tip from table eight," he said.

"Ten!" She snatched it from Enrique's hand. "That's so nice. On a turkey club and Coke."

"What'd you do for that, I wonder?" He sneered. "I got a pretty good imagination." Then a pervy closed-mouth grin spread like mold across his face.

Eww. Just when she thought maybe he was a quarter-decent guy, he'd open his mouth. The strip of silver roots that ran along the part of his dyed black hair told the world what they needed to know about Enrique. He was a skunk. There was nothing worse than a skunk with a little power. Just because he owned the place, he thought he could say or do whatever he wanted.

Honey ignored three-quarters of what Enrique said. Sometimes she had to play dumb around him, too. Whatever it took. A girl needed to protect herself. If she didn't literally need this job to survive, she'd tell Enrique what to do with that ten dollars. But she needed that, too.

"That's your omelet, Honey!" the cook called from the kitchen.

She stepped back to the window and grabbed the plate. "Supposed to be a deluxe," Honey yelled back. She returned the plate to the metal ledge.

"Clean up that grease." Enrique pointed at the floor before he walked back to the front. "You want someone to sue me!"

Honey took a napkin out of her apron and threw it on the floor. She swooshed it around with her foot while facing the bathrooms so she could take a quick peek at her phone. Still nothing from Marianne. She should've heard from her by now.

"Honey, your omelet de-*luxe* is up!"

She grabbed the plate and headed into the dining room. Enrique was seating a group of Honey's regulars in Gloria's section. She put the omelet down on table six. "Enjoy. Let me know if you need anything."

As soon as Enrique dropped menus, she whispered, "Why'd you give Gloria my regulars? I have a table. Didn't they ask for me?" She turned to the table. "Hi, y'all! Nice to see you!" She didn't want to challenge Enrique. But she knew if she didn't stand up for herself, people would keep stomping. Like Momma said, *What you don't change, you accept.*

Enrique balked. "Just because they ask for you, I can't put everybody in your station!" He was close enough to feel his hot breath, and she recoiled. "What do you expect me to do with the other tables? When you own your own restaurant, you can have all the tables!" He laughed.

LOL, Enrique. She ignored him. Honey wasn't spending the rest of her life in a lousy grease pit. That's for sure. Three more years and she'd have her dental hygiene license. Well, three and a half. She took off this semester to care for Momma and Mr. Moretti. Didn't turn out so well for Mr. Moretti. But as soon as Momma turned around, and she saved enough money, she'd be back at school. The tips at the diner were pretty good. That's because she knew how to treat people. How to make people feel valued and appreciated. Her regulars were generous and always asked for her.

The front door flew open, and Marianne stormed in. That was unsettling. She was a big entrance kind of girl, but fast was not her speed. She looked frantic—she didn't even have makeup on. Still, her hair looked good. Bad news was written all over her face, though. Marianne locked eyes on Honey and lifted her eyebrows. Honey thought she detected a subtle gulp, which concerned her even more. Marianne did nothing subtly.

Honey motioned to the counter. It would be easier to talk to her there while she filled the salt and pepper shakers. Enrique didn't like it when friends came by even though their money was just as green as anybody's. Did he think friends got extra pickles and free drink refills? He'd be right, of course. Behind the counter Honey lined up the pepper shakers and removed the caps, and waited for Enrique to walk into the kitchen.

"I thought you were going to text me. Don't you have class?" Honey said.

"Yeah." Marianne was out of breath. "I don't have a lot of time. But I wanted to tell you what my friend said. And the Medi-Clinic he works at is not far from here." She wasn't making eye contact with Honey, which gave her a bad vibe.

Marianne plopped down at the counter and threw her bag on the empty stool next to her. It wouldn't last long there once Enrique walked by: "This is a restaurant. Not a living room!" He didn't "have seats for people's crap."

"Looks like you'll need to pay the hospital bills, Honey. Your granny is sixty-four. You don't get help with medical bills until Momma turns sixty-five." Her eyes flashed up for a second at Honey. "I know that's not what you wanted to hear." She looked sheepishly at Honey.

"Why'd I bring her there? You know I'm scared of hospitals. All the beeping. I can't take the beeping!" She shook her head. "I don't want to know what my heart is doing. And the needles? No thanks. What did Mama get there that I didn't give her? An infection and bills. No fancy doctors. No cutting-edge treatments." She put the funnel in the shaker and grabbed the pepper jug from under the counter. "If I left her there—" She was about to say something she didn't want to hear or think. But she knew it was Momma's reality now. "I can't lose her, Marianne. She's everything."

"I know, Honey." Marianne reached for Honey's hand and patted it. "Have faith."

Honey twisted the caps onto the pepper shakers.

"I'm trying. But God isn't listening. Momma's suffering." Honey propped herself up on her toes to peer into the kitchen. Checking on Enrique's whereabouts. She lowered her voice and filled a glass with Coke from the soda gun. "I can't watch her in pain anymore." Honey moved her face closer to Marianne's. "I'm trying to make her as comfortable as possible," she whispered aggressively.

"I know you are." Marianne nodded.

"There's no limit to what I'd do for Momma. I would do anything! I'm not ashamed to say it!" Honey slapped the counter.

"Of course." Marianne gave her a weird look. "Okay." She put her hand up for emphasis.

Honey stepped back to look in the kitchen again. "I'm keeping Momma home from now on. Where she belongs. But that's another thing I'm worried about. How long can we live there?"

Marianne turned her phone over on the counter. "Now don't start worrying about that too."

"Start? I haven't stopped. It's been a month since Mr. Moretti passed away. Every time someone knocks on our door, I think somebody's coming to kick us out."

"You can't live like that, Honey. You need to find out. Who could you call? The cops?"

"Cops!?" Honey's eyes grew wide. "Are you high? I'm *not* calling the cops." Honey's pour got shaky, and salt went everywhere. "I can't believe you'd even suggest that."

Honey crouched over the counter closer to Marianne and whispered, "Hmm, let's think how that would go down, 'Hi, this is Honey Foster calling with a question. I live with my granny in a house that's not ours, exactly. My granny is the live-in caregiver for the owner, a ninety-six-year-old church-going dude named

Franco Moretti. Well, she *was* his caregiver. She's sick now with cancer so I'm *her* caregiver and Mr. Moretti's currently deceased. He was like family and we're mourning for him like crazy. His house has been our home for over four years and my granny is not well enough to move and she can't deal with any more sorrow or stress, so we're just wondering if we get to keep the house or if someone is gonna claim it anytime soon?"

"Yeah." Marianne shrugged. "What's wrong with that?"

"Okay, maybe I have police paranoia, but it's for good reason. Plus, we need a place to live, and it might not be a great idea to help accelerate our homelessness by bringing attention to this scenario. If your chin had a zit, would you circle it and write 'Don't look at this!' on your cheek with a Sharpie?"

Marianne sighed and threw her arms up.

"I don't know what to tell you. There's just no sense in you worrying in advance." Marianne opened the menu. She flipped the pages without really looking. "Wait a second." She looked up from the menu. "Call the church. They'd know about any family. They're the ones who asked Momma to take care of him in the first place." She lifted one brow. "Didn't Moretti have a sister?"

Honey had thought about the sister and didn't like thinking about her. Or the possibility of her showing up to the house unannounced. Chances were slim because she was in assisted living herself. In Arizona. Might not even be alive.

"She hasn't sent a Christmas card in a couple of years, so I don't know about her," Honey said over her shoulder, looking into the dining room at her tables.

"You think he left the house to you and Momma? Maybe no one's coming to kick you out. He always called you and Momma his family." Marianne's face brightened as if someone offered her a free blow-out.

That got Honey's attention. She liked the thought, but it seemed like a stretch.

"Honey!" Enrique appeared on the other side of the counter. "C7 yours?" He pointed to the guy sitting a few down from Marianne.

She twirled around to the dessert case and pulled out the apple pie. She cut an extra wide piece, added a gigantic squirt of whipped cream and two cherries on top, and pushed the plate over to the guy. "Enjoy." She grabbed the coffee pot and topped him off.

"Excuse me, Honey." Angel walked toward her with a rack of steaming glasses. She pressed herself into the counter to let him pass.

Honey reached into her apron and pulled out the flat powder puff from her compact to blot her chin. The free dishwasher facials would've been nice if she didn't have to touch up her makeup.

Angel leaned the edge of the rack onto the counter, and Honey helped him unload the glasses. "Hey, my sister loved that picture you drew of her," Angel said. "She hung it up. You're a great artist, Honey."

"Really?" Honey brightened. "Well, she's beautiful. It was easy."

Angel had the kindest face. Always smiling, like it was a birthmark, no matter what crap he took around here. He was the smartest one in this place. On his way to being the most successful. But they didn't care he was studying to be an engineer. Because when you're a dishwasher, respect was scarce. They stacked the glasses in unison.

28

"How's Momma doing?" he asked, glancing at Honey, who couldn't seem to respond. "You know, they made too much tapioca pudding this week. We need to get rid of it. Isn't that her favorite? I'll save you some."

He put his hand on Honey's shoulder before walking toward the kitchen, and she wondered how he learned to be so kind. How did he know a simple gesture like that had so much comfort? And didn't cost anything or take much effort. It was different than Enrique's opportunistic feels. She didn't know how to describe it, except that one was giving and one was taking. Honey didn't even know she needed it until she felt his hand on her shoulder. Between Mr. Moretti passing away nearly a month ago, and now Momma on the decline, Honey hadn't been her normal upbeat self. She was so busy caring for people, she forgot how good it felt to be on the receiving end.

One of Honey's customers waved for the check. "Angel," Honey took her pad out and ripped off the check, "do me a favor and put this on four, would you?" She handed it to him.

"I guess I'll have a burger," said Marianne. "Might as well eat now. I have Oral Pathology and a lab tonight, so I'll be home late." She looked at Honey. "Did you hear anything about the scholarship yet? I can't do another semester without you."

Honey shook her head. Marianne knew Honey wasn't going back to school unless she got it. It was a full scholarship and even covered room and board. She'd be set for three years. But she wasn't feeling hopeful. Honey wrote up a ticket for the burger and clipped it onto the order wheel.

Marianne got a text. As her thumbs texted back, she said, "Honey, I got some other news that's not so good. I talked to my brother." She lifted her head and rolled her eyes. Honey knew what was coming.

"It's okay, girl. I'll be fine."

"I told him the money was for you, and it's not like he doesn't like you, it's just he's not a big fan of mine right now. Some people with more money than God are the cheapest ones around. I'm really sorry." She exhaled, put her handbag on her lap and started to unload everything she owned onto the counter. "I'll help you figure this out. Don't worry. Everything will be okay. With Momma, too. She'll turn around now that she's home. If I know you, you'll have her jumping rope by next week!"

Marianne was back on her phone, scrolling as if her life depended on it. "Here are the earrings I told you about. My God, they're gorgeous, and they're on Ship now/Pay later!" Marianne turned her phone around for Honey to see. "Look at my girl Shae, aren't they beautiful on her?"

Honey closed her eyes and gave Marianne the talk-to-the-hand palm. "Want to get me fired? I'm working here, case you forgot!" Honey grabbed two meatloaf and green beans from the ledge. "I don't have time for your shopping sprees. I thought influencers got stuff for free? Why is it you're always buying stuff?" She headed to the dining room and served the old couple. "Enjoy, let me know if you need anything." She dropped a check on table five with the college kids.

"Honey," Enrique called out as Honey passed by him. "Your friend's starting tonight." He handed her a stack of menus to wipe down.

Honey blinked. "Jenna?" She took the menus and looked up at the clock. Yellow grease coated the glass and dust coated the grease, barely revealing the time. Honey side-glanced Marianne.

Her heart did a cartwheel. This was amazing news. She needed this news today. This was proof that God helped those who helped other people. Or something like that.

Enrique looked at her funny; she couldn't figure out what kind of look it was, but it made her uncomfortable. "You owe me," he said. Oh. That kind of look. No one ever wanted to be in that position with Enrique. Honey engaged her selective hearing.

"So you met her?"

"No. Hired her over the phone. If she's half as good as you, I got nothing to worry about, right?"

What the h? Enrique never said a decent thing about Honey. Ever. She always thought it would be nice to hear something complimentary from him, but now she had buyer's remorse. He was too cheap to give anything away for free. Even a compliment.

"She sounded young. She in high school?"

"Jenna? Nope." Honey shook her head. She wasn't now, but she would be soon. Not that Enrique needed to know. Like next week, in fact. Honey made an appointment with the high school principal, and she was going to take Jenna's sixteen-year-old ass back there and move her out of the monthly motel where she was living with her skank drug dealer boyfriend.

"Thanks, Enrique," she said without looking at him.

"She better not be trouble," he said, exposing yellow teeth coated in years of plaque. Honey wouldn't be surprised if there was a two-year-old burger stuck between his lower incisors.

"Welcome to Enrique's Grill," Marianne muttered under her breath.

A smile grew on Honey's face that filled her up like sunshine in a bucket, like Momma would say. "Text Jenna," Honey whispered to Marianne. "Tell her she can wear a t-shirt if she doesn't have a collared shirt. As long as it's solid white. See that, Marianne?" Honey smacked the counter. "You can't give up on people. That girl's going to turn her life around!"

Marianne texted while her eyes grew big as a boob job. "I don't want to be around when Jimmy finds out about this new side hustle of hers."

"*Side* hustle?" Honey threw Marianne a look. "Like she's got a main hustle?" She crossed her arms.

"Oh." Marianne's eyeballs flashed up for a split second to look at Honey, then back to her phone. "Thought you knew."

"Knew what?"

"About Jenna's...other job...with Jimmy."

"She's what?" Honey shook her head. *"Dealing?"*

"Uh...*no*..."

The front door swung open, and in walked Jenna.

Wearing a white shirt and a fat lip.

CHAPTER 4

Shae

Thursday, December 17, 2015, 5:50 p.m.

"I can *do this. I can do this. I can do this...*" Shae panted hot, frantic breaths as she tore down the hall toward Studio 3, forcing a lump the size of a macaron down her throat.

How did he know about Laduree?

She ripped the remaining rollers from her hair and chucked them to the floor. The inside of her cheeks trembled. Anxiety was best relegated to a place no one could see. Showing her nerves was out the question. Not that anyone cared if she was flipped out of her mind, as long as it didn't show up on her face, voice, or in sweat stains on the vendor's shirt.

"Where the hell is Shae?" Ed yelled from the control room soundboard.

"I'm here!" Shae shouted in vain—her mic wasn't hot yet. She could hear him, but he couldn't hear her.

She shot around the bend with her arms up at her sides like a toddler impersonating an airplane. Air flow under her armpits was crucial, far more embarrassing would be sweat stains on *Today's Steal!* (Donna Karan, Essence, $89 in Midnight—no, Moonlight. No—Midnight!)

The prop people spun around as Shae ran by, staring at her like she was the village idiot. Those two were the ones Shae overheard talking about Bryan yesterday. Something about him knowing the Donna Karan rep from F.I.T. where they went to school together.

The back edge of Shae's hairline was damp. She raked her fingers through the back of her hair to find the smooth patch of scalp. The feel of it soothed her.

"Does anyone around here know how to tell time? She's live in a minute—" Ed was bursting a blood vessel.

"I'm here, Ed!" she yelled, though futile.

A guy from inventory—standing between two rolling carts—whipped around to face her.

"What?" He pointed to himself. "Talking to me?"

"No!"

"Is Shae on set?" Someone else was in the control room now. A breathless Val.

"No!" Ed sniped. "What the hell's going on? It's time to go live. *Now.*"

"Go with Bryan, then," said Val.

"*Laura*—" Ed yelled for the stage manager. "Find Bryan, and mic him. He's on set."

Bryan's on set?

"Ed," Val's voice again. "Shae's stalker's back. He got into her car this time."

Shae tried to read the inflection in her voice.

"What?" Ed softened.

"He left a note in her car. With a box of cookies—to look like a gift. The security guard—Theo—found it. Apparently, she used to eat those cookies as a kid. We don't even sell them. Did she ever mention these things on air? The police want to know. You need to search the transcripts. We need it fast."

"Maybe it *was* a gift?"

"Uh...*no*," Val said. "Not if you read the note."

A bead of sweat shot down Shae's back.

Until ten minutes ago, Shae was feeling close to normal. Normal was riding the tide in. It was nearly at shore. Enough time had passed. Enough time in therapy. Was it naïve to think all would be normal again?

The banging in her chest wasn't normal. Val could've waited until after Shae's show to tell her. Couldn't she have? What harm would that have caused? In fact, Val had known this *breaking news* for hours.

Her timing was duly noted.

It didn't get lost on Shae that she was incapable of saying "Screw it—give the show to Bryan." Who the hell cared if Bryan got the Donna Karan show and sold more than her. Right? No. She couldn't do that. Why the hell did it matter so much? As pathetic as it was to admit, this place was more than her workplace. Her colleagues were more than colleagues. And her fans—were everything. On a daily basis, they somehow convinced Shae to like herself. No one in her life had ever done that.

In less than ten seconds, she'd be on set where she'd kick off her slippers, slip into shoes, tilt her face back for powder, close her eyes for hairspray, and watch the ticker count down to zero. Then a smile would emerge across her face with the predictability of a sunrise while she greeted her million closest fans who bought anything she was selling. In multiples. Stuff they didn't know they wanted or needed. And all would be right with the world. If only for an hour.

IShop viewers would call the testimonial line to talk to Shae on-air like they were old friends. They'd comment on Facebook pics of the beer-battered tilapia she posted from home: "Yum!" "What's the recipe?" And on her vacation pics: "You deserve it!" "Miss you!!" "Work that swimsuit!"

They were in Shae's life as much as anyone. *More* than anyone. There was comfort in that regardless of how lonely Shae sometimes (often) felt. Her fans believed they were Shae's friends. They believed they knew her. Were they friends? Shae knew the answer to that. She was also aware those fans didn't know a thing about her. If they did, they might not even like her.

It was much easier to endear fake friends. And keep them.

Shae peeled around a corner and body slammed someone on the studio tour. "Oh my gosh, I'm so sorry!" She kept running past the group.

"Shae! That's her! Oh my God!" a woman shouted with both arms stretched like goal posts over her head. People snapped pics. "Love you, Shae!"

Shae blew a kiss and ducked into the hall leading to the Fashion Studio. One of the product coordinators saw her approaching, dropped a handful of hangers, and pulled open the studio door. Shae feigned serenity and—two seconds later—was on set.

She shaded her eyes from the bright lights and searched for Ed, the associate producer up in the control room, and waved. "Hi, Ed. Good to see you!" She spotted Kaitlyn, the DK rep, talking to—*Bryan*—who was wearing a *mic*. And stroking *Today's Steal!*

Whatever he was saying had Kaitlyn giggling and throwing her head back. Jeez, some girls.

When did Bryan think he was doing this show—a minute ago or three hours ago?

They were thick as thieves, those two. Bryan knew what got a crowd to laugh or listen. And he wasn't even funny or interesting. All he had to do was smile, drop a "Hey, love" and wear his pants too tight. It worked like a charm. Some people were naturals. They breezed in. They breezed out. No evidence of uncertainty on their face. They laughed with ease. No side glance to check someone's reaction. They'd have a bad hair day and not even notice.

"Uh, hi," Shae said to anybody. "Kaitlyn—sorry, I'm—Bryan, what are—"

"*Shae!*" He shot around to face her and stepped in for a hug. His muscular forearms gave shape to his shirt sleeves. In a hushed tone, almost inaudibly, he said, "How ya doing?" Dramatically mouthing the question. He leaned his head toward her with faux discretion. "Are you okay? Are you up to this?" How the hell did *he* know? *She* just found out five minutes ago! He pushed his glasses up his nose—thin, angular—there were women who'd steal that nose off his face if they could. He moved closer, his mouth now inches from Shae's ear. "Listen, love," he whispered, "I know what's going on, and I don't blame you for being paranoid."

"Put in a promo!" Ed blustered to the producer. "You've got thirty seconds," Ed quipped in Shae's earpiece, startling her for a second. "Figure this out *now*." Only she could hear him. "It's you or Bryan. Let's go."

She pulled away from Bryan. "I'm fine," Shae said aloud—benefitting both Bryan and Ed, still processing what Bryan just said. Which of her current paranoias was he referring to?

"Hey, love, thanks for doing Sassy Mats." Bryan reached over to squeeze her arm. "Whenever I can make it up to you, say the word." He ran a hand through his hair—thick sandbar ripples. Then he straightened and said aloud to Shae, "You look great! That *top*!" Jazz hands. He reached out to Kaitlyn. "Am I right?"

Shae stepped closer to Kaitlyn, expecting Bryan to step aside. He didn't. Now the three of them stood awkwardly close to one another.

Bryan smiled and winked. "O-kay, looks like you're in good shape." He shot Kaitlyn with a finger gun, "Always great to see you, love!" He strode toward the wing.

"That color is amazing on you," Kaitlyn said. She scanned Shae in one swift sweep: hair, jewelry, top, pants, shoes. Their tribal greeting.

Figgy waved at Shae from the wing, holding the brush and spray in the air. Shae shrugged—and used her fingers to comb through.

"In nine—" Ed said.

"Oh, I almost forgot, here are your show cards." Kaitlyn handed them to Shae.

"Oh, thanks. Where were they? I looked everywhere."

"I don't know. Bryan asked me to give them to you."

Shae turned toward the wing as she took the cards. Bryan winked at her in slow motion.

"He's the sweetest," Kaitlyn gushed. "He came on set last minute when he noticed you weren't here. I told him not to worry, that I saw you at lunch. But he wouldn't budge until you arrived. Such a doll. He was ready to swoop in and save the day."

Do not roll your eyes.

"This place hasn't been the same since he arrived," Shae managed. Why do people always trust the good-looking ones? He didn't fool her.

She slid off her slippers and handed them to the production assistant in exchange for her shoes.

"In three—" Ed said.

Shae turned to the main camera as the LIVE light flicked on and greeted her fans: "Welcome to Shop Talk, IShoppers, it's So Chic With Shae! bringing you *Today's Steal!* One of my all-time favorite tops from one of my all-time favorite designers, Donna Karan!"

Shae greeted Kaitlyn with an exaggerated arm spread. "Great to see you!" They semi-hugged and air-kissed like they hadn't already greeted each other a minute ago. "We're so lucky to have you back today to help us spice up our wardrobe."

"Oh, definitely! For anyone still searching for the perfect top for New Year's Eve—we've got it for you on express ship!" Kaitlyn said.

Shae swiped her hand along the sleeve of *Today's Steal!*, displayed on a cascading rack in six colors.

"I wish you could feel this fabric. It's so sexy," Shae said. "I love wearing it. I feel instantly glamorous. And the little details—the silhouette—take this top to the next level. It's really special. The colors are a knock-out. Hmm—" Shae pulled the first one from the rack. "Now I'm thinking about this Cabernet..." She held it against herself.

"Isn't it beautiful?"

"Designers are clamoring to get in on this Cabernet craze, while you've had it for months. Donna Karan is always ahead of the trends. I love it. Need one. Right now. Why wait to wear it to a party?"

"Exactly, you'll want to wear this the day it arrives!" Kaitlyn grabbed the dark green from the back of the rack. "You know those ladies who wear that 'special top' wherever they go?" She punctuated with air quotes. "I'm always jealous of them. They don't save the special pieces in the back of the closet waiting for an occasion. They make it part of their everyday wardrobe."

"I love those women."

"Me too."

"I wanna be them," Shae said.

"Me too!" Shae and Kaitlyn grabbed each other's hands in solidarity. Sealing the pledge to become women who wear "that special top" any day of the week.

"Look at these details." Kaitlyn pulled the dark blue off the rack and held it against her. "Double-row stitching, satin trim!"

"And so slimming. The neckline is incredibly flattering. Everyone needs to show a little collarbone. Very sexy. Super chic. Great for travel. I can't say enough about this piece." Shae held up her hand. "Oh, wow, I'm getting word that we're nearly sold out of Nighttime. That's this gorgeous inky color. It's not quite navy, not quite black. Only a few extra small left in Midnight, which is the darkest, *darkest* black I've ever seen."

"Caller Amy with a question, coming now," said Ed in Shae's ear piece.

"We have Amy calling, hiya Amy!" Shae waved hello at the camera. "How are you, hon?" Amy was a power buyer. She had more clothes than the IShop fulfillment center. She was always given priority on the testimonial line.

"Hiya, Shae!" Amy enthused. "You look uh-may-*zing* in that top! This morning I saw it was *Today's Steal!* I couldn't wait, so I bought it online in Dazzle. For New Year's Eve. I bought Nighttime, too!"

"Oh my gosh, Amy, you'll look phenomenal in Dazzle." Shae pulled Dazzle from the rack. "Especially with your new hair color! The photo you posted on my Facebook page yesterday was gorgeous."

"You know me so well, Shae. You're so sweet. You're like my faraway bestie!"

"Spike." Ed, telling Shae there was a spike in sales.

"Well, I can't blame you for wanting this in multiples. I personally own three. Is that excessive?" Shae made a hope-you-don't-judge-me face at the camera. "This top, I daresay, is not for everyone. Right, Kaitlyn? It's for someone who wants to feel *special*."

Ed interjected in her earpiece, "Wrap up with Amy, a guy caller wants advice on buying it for his girlfriend."

"Amy, thanks for calling, hon. You always brighten my day. Leave a pic on Instagram and tag me, would you? Bye bye, Amy!" Shae waved and blew a kiss at the camera. Stu, the boom operator, blew one back.

"I sure will, Shae! You're so beautiful. Inside and out. You need to meet my brother. You'd be perfect together! He's single!"

Shae made a pouty face. "You're always thinking of me, Amy. So sweet." She waved goodbye to Amy. "We've got Lars on the line. Lars? You're a brave soul calling to talk blouses!"

"Hi, Shae. You look gorgeous, as usual."

"Thank you, Lars!" Shae spoke into the camera as if Lars were standing in front of her.

"I never miss your shows, no matter what you're selling."

"Aren't you sweet!" Shae took Cabernet from the rack and twirled it.

"In fact, I caught one this morning that wasn't even on your schedule. For floor mats. What a surprise!"

"Aww, thanks, Lars. Yes, you're right. I covered for one of my co-hosts." She traced the satin trim with her fingertip.

"I must say, you handled yourself with the utmost grace when the insensitive mat salesman asked if you were a dog person! Does he live under a rock? Who wouldn't be petrified of dogs after… the incident…you had?"

Without thinking, Shae slowly moved her hand to cover the scar on her left wrist. This call was taking a bizarre turn, and Shae couldn't get her thoughts and her mouth aligned in a way to veer him back on track.

"So, Lars," Kaitlyn interjected, "which of these are you buying your girlfriend?"

"Whichever Shae recommends. She has impeccable taste."

"Thank you, Lars." Shae smiled warmly, though reluctantly.

"You're so pretty," Lars said.

Shae's body tightened. The words suspended in mid-air, turned a brash neon orange, and pulsed along with her heartbeat. She forced a smile and walked over to the rack. She hung up the top trembling in her hand. Ed said something she didn't quite hear. She turned her back ever so briefly to the camera and took a breath. Her brain buzzed white noise.

People say that all the time. On-air. In fan mail. Tons of people. Stay calm.

The police were probably already connecting the package from her car to the letters she received in September. Especially since the first letter said exactly that: "You're so pretty." In fact, the comment was so commonplace, it didn't even raise concern until the follow-up letter arrived. It said, *"Just kidding. You're not pretty at all,"* and continued to explain how this "fan" would fix Shae's face with manicure scissors and a glue gun.

Kaitlyn patted Shae's hand, which gripped the side of the display table. Shae needed to get back in the moment.

"Right?" Kaitlyn asked.

Shae looked at Kaitlyn blankly.

"Aren't you nice, Lars?" Kaitlyn continued. She squinted at Shae. "Your girlfriend's so lucky."

"I always do what Shae says," he added.

Kaitlyn and Shae exchanged looks. Kaitlyn smiled and nodded, "Smart guy! Can't go wrong there. That's why Shae is 'America's personal shopper!'" Kaitlyn put her hand on Shae's shoulder.

"It would pair beautifully with the pants Shae wore for Fashion Friday," he said.

Kaitlyn's mouth dropped open. "Hello, super-fan!"

"Honestly, Shae'd look good in pants made of HoneyBaked Ham slices." Lars continued. "She'd smell great, too."

Kaitlyn laughed, but this guy was disturbing. Where the hell was Ed? Why was he keeping this freak on-air?

"Getting rid of Lars," Ed said in Shae's earpiece.

Finally. Shae could usually handle the rare weirdo, but that's what Ed was for. He controlled the testimonial line!

"Call one of the models out," Ed said.

Shae tried to block Lars' voice from her head. She could see herself on one of the monitors. It was scary how well she could disguise her unease.

"Let's see how Monica's wearing Dazzle," Shae said, forcing composure. "Ooh, with leggings and boots, what a fabulous look!

Thanks for calling, Lars." Shae waved at the camera. "Your girl-friend will love it." She did not wink. And she most certainly did not blow a kiss.

"How sweet was he?" Shae said. "Wanting to surprise his girl-friend. Wow. Listen up, ladies out there! You want one like Lars!" As shaken as she was, Shae was on autopilot—IShop talk reeled 24/7.

Ed cut Lars off even before the model appeared. Shae continued to talk to him like he was still on-air.

"Sorry, Shae. We're checking him out now," Ed said. "No more callers today. My bad."

That was unexpected. Ed rarely apologized for anything.

After the show, Figgy met Shae in the dressing room with a cup of tea. "Maybe they should shut down the testimonial line until you get information from the police?" She squeezed Shae's hand and handed her a mug. "Funny how it was Theo who found the note. No?"

That surprised Shae. "No. It's part of his job to check my car." If Shae sounded defensive, maybe she was.

"Okay." Figgy patted Shae's arm. "Well, I never trust security guards, you know. To me, he looks like somebody security should keep an eye on."

Shae let out a heavy sigh. She didn't want to argue about this with Figgy.

Figgy shuffled over to the hair station. "Strange how Theo never talks." She plugged in the curling iron. "Just to you. Nobody else. Strange." She shrugged.

"Speaking of strange, what was Bryan doing on set wearing a mic?"

Figgy cocked her head. "What's your problem with him, any-way?"

"Problem? I don't have a problem." Shae didn't like Bryan, but she wasn't about to tell Figgy. Truthfully, she didn't exactly know why. If she tried to explain, it would no doubt sound childish and petty.

Shae was suspicious of vigorously self-assured people. Some people knew who they were with such conviction; he was one of those people. The flashy smile, the arm squeezes and air-kisses. Never a sliver of self-doubt.

Who *were* you if you didn't know who you were? How did that look on the outside? Shae stared at the makeup station. Lost in thought. The sponges and brushes, glosses and shadows. A trans-formation in waiting. But identities weren't created with a smoky eye and fake lashes, a microphone, and a job description. Or were they?

It had always been easier for Shae to be who others expected her to be, rather than to decide on her own.

Perhaps she wasn't suspicious of confident people. Perhaps she was envious.

"He's nice to you. He's nice to everybody." Figgy threw her arms in the air. She brushed through a wig resting on a Styrofoam head.

"You know what he asked me yesterday?" Shae said. "He stuck his face close enough to mine that I could smell the mint on his breath. He said, 'Do I make you uncomfortable?'"

Figgy tucked her fists into her waist. "Well, everyone knows *that*, cookie!"

Everyone knows that?

"The way you act when you're around him. Maybe you have a crush on him?" She elbowed Shae. "Close your eyes, I'll take your lashes off," Figgy said. "Why do you want to wear these, anyway?"

"I don't know."

"You don't need them. Look at your real ones!"

Something flashed across Shae's mind—Capucine—the eccentric cleaning lady who lived in Shae's house when she was a child. Shae's father kept a revolving door of staff to manage the home and take care of Shae in the absence of a mother. But Shae had a particular fascination with Capucine, who was, in hindsight, unapologetically flashy. She'd tell Shae that being pretty was a blessing. "Natural beauty is God giving you gold." Capucine would say, "Use your beauty, little one. Squeeze out everything till it's dry as a heart."

But beauty was a red herring. Plain-looking people were the blessed ones. Nobody looked at them wanting something in return. Nobody had lofty expectations of *them*.

While Figgy peeled off her lashes, Shae's hand fished through her handbag for her phone. Shae scrolled down her Facebook feed for her most recent livestreams and stopped on yesterday's Fruits&Flowers Body Cream show. "Nine hundred twenty-seven likes. Seven hundred forty-six comments—wow."

Figgy laughed. "They love you, girl."

"Yeah, they liked the girl I replaced, too, don't forget. Why'd they get rid of her?" Shae muttered.

"Are you serious? She's been gone for three years! You're competing with someone who doesn't work here anymore? What's wrong with you? I can't believe you're still talking about her!"

Figgy threw her hands up. "They didn't get rid of her—she moved. To Michigan. She got married."

"They *didn't*? She *did*?" Shae stared at Figgy. "You never told me that!"

"You never asked." Her head jerked back. "All those mysteries swirling in that head of yours. You make up half the things you're worried about! Go easy with those books of yours." She pointed to a stack of books Shae kept in the makeup room. "You don't need to fuel your paranoia!"

That word again.

Figgy looked at Shae in the mirror. "Get your head straight, cookie. Concentrate on all the good you've got. Feel the love from your fans."

How *did* Shae get so lucky? What was she doing right? Why did they love her?

Shae looked back at her phone. "Wish I could answer them all," she mumbled. "At least I need to get back to my regulars... Amy—wow, that red hair suits her. Cynthia, Delores, Larry, Susan. They never miss a show." Shae typed out replies, then dove back into her bag for tomorrow's show cards. "That's weird. My cards for tomorrow's show aren't here." That reminded her, how did Bryan end up with her DK cards? "I can't confuse the colors again."

Figgy laughed. "You got flustered. Give yourself a break. Nobody's getting on you for that." She put down the curling iron. "Val's all bark, no bite. Trust me—they wish you could do all twenty-four hours of shows. They even named one for you—nobody else has a *So Chic With Shae* show! Why'd they give you spiral hams last week? Because nobody can sell them like you. Not even Bryan." Figgy shook her head. "Did you see him in those pants today—*cookie!* Yeah, he's hot—but he don't got what you got. You could sell facials made of bird poop. *And* you'd sell them out!" She laughed with her whole body.

"You'd convince everyone that you discovered this great bird poop invention. Sure it'd smell like poop, but that wouldn't matter. Your fans would see the glow!" Figgy clapped.

Shae couldn't help but laugh too. Figgy was probably right. She was probably being paranoid. If they planned on phasing her out, what would they tell her fans?

"By the way, you're staying at my house tonight, cookie. Like last time. Your room is waiting for you." Figgy swept Shae's hair off her shoulder.

Shae stared at Figgy. "What about your sister?"

"What about her?" Figgy talked into the mirror. "I'm not too big to share a bed with that skinny thing." Figgy winked. "No arguing. That's that. The boys can't wait to see you." She smiled wide. "You always have a home with me. However long you want. Until they have some answers."

Shae could feel her breath catch in her throat. She didn't want to get teary. How embarrassing. But her ability to stow away emotions was being tested today. To Figgy, this was a small gesture—something she does all the time for people. But to Shae, well, she never had someone in her life like Figgy. A true friend. Someone who treated her like family. Shae didn't even have family like that.

She wagged her finger. "But no gifts. You've spoiled us for life already."

If only Figgy knew that buying gifts for her family brought Shae immense joy. It made her feel like she was part of a family. What else, if not that, could she do for them?

Shae couldn't imagine what it was like to be Figgy. To have a sister by her side when she needed her. An aunt who FaceTimed her every Sunday. Two young brothers she took care of. A real family. Shae had a father. That was it. No mother, siblings, cousins. A father whom she hadn't spoken to in years.

A text sounded on Shae's phone from Val.

"I need to meet with the detective, Fig. He's here."

CHAPTER 5

Lawrence

Saturday, December 19, 2015, 6:30 a.m.

WHILE the shower heated up, Lawrence peeled the plastic seal from the new cleanser he'd saved for this occasion. Leaves&Twigs Body Wash for Men. The perfect blend of bergamot and sandalwood. A scent that smelled confident, capable, masculine. It should've been called *Lawrence*, for that matter. In his plush gray bathrobe, he whistled merrily as he darted from closet to bed, laying out clothes to wear.

Nothing could bring Lawrence down today. Today, Shae was hosting a live audience show with Emeril to debut his new stovetop grill pan, What's Sizzlin', to which Lawrence *had a ticket*.

As euphoric as he was at the certainty of proximity to Shae in a few short hours, a pesky inkling gnawed at him. Lawrence detected something amiss coming from IShop's airwaves. In the last thirty-six hours, Shae had become noticeably inaccessible. Keen observation skills were crucial in his line of work. Evidenced by his recent fast-track job change. Perhaps her unavailability was innocuous, however, he had an unshakeable suspicion it was not.

First, Shae's testimonial line was closed. Then she stopped posting on Facebook and Instagram. In fact, she even stopped replying to comments. Lawrence had been cut off. Well, everyone had, but none felt the sting as brutishly as he.

Ignoring his gut, he focused on the positive. This day was finally here! Larry, Lars, and Lance had the day off—it would be all Lawrence today! Today, he'd be so close to Shae, her energy would be palpable. He'd meet her flirtatious glances *in person*. With ears perked for her off-camera banter, he'd experience the stripped-down, real Shae. Above all else, his fantasy was to be the audience member chosen to ask her a question.

Before showering, he quickly scanned his emails.

His eyes skidded to a stop. "URGENT—FOR TICKETHOLD-ERS OF TODAY'S IShop LIVE EVENT."

He swallowed hard and felt his heart sink into his stomach and slosh around the bile in his gut.

*"To all ticketholders for today's IShop Live Studio Audience Show with Shae Wilmont and Emeril, please note this show has been **CANCELED**. This show will be rescheduled at a future date to be determined. Original tickets will be honored for the rescheduled show. We apologize for any inconvenience this has caused."*

"Are you *fucking* kidding me!"

"Lawrence!" Rita called from the kitchen. "Language!"

He flung his phone across the bed. He was livid.

It took some wrangling to come by a ticket for that show. And all the *planning*—what he'd wear, and what he'd say on live TV if chosen. What he'd do if the opportunity presented itself for more …*interaction*.

He grabbed the khakis Rita ironed, crumbled them into a ball, and threw them against the wall.

No explanations?

What would he do now?

He never told Rita about his plan to visit IShop. Instead, he said he was going to the office to "put in some extra hours" even though it was a Saturday. "When you're the new guy, you need to go above and beyond." "Earn your stripes." Blah, blah, blah. He had to tell her something—obviously, he still needed his khakis ironed—without instigating an endless tedious interrogation. The prospect of her veritable cross-examination sprouted a phantom headache above his right brow. No matter how meticulous his answers, Rita's suspicion always mushroomed from thin air.

He was determined to avoid drama, inquiries, and participatory interest, at all cost.

It wasn't as if Lawrence regarded himself a true relationship expert, but some things he knew. Namely: never reveal everything to a partner. That's what kept a relationship fresh and exciting— the titillation of kept secrets.

The mystery of Shae's social sequester throbbed at him even more. It was clear something was askew at IShop, and he was the man to sniff it out.

He showered, shaved, unrolled and patted down his khakis, poured a cup of coffee into his travel mug, said goodbye to Rita, and got into his car. With unfettered determination, he proceeded to the IShop Studios, where he decided he'd take the All Access Backstage Tour.

Lawrence would turn lemons into a soufflé if anyone could.

He took the ramp to Freeway 695 and headed south. The nav had his arrival time at ten. Precisely the start time for the tour—a five-hour behind-the-scenes tour of IShop's inner workings.

To be in the bowels of IShop meant an errant left turn, peeling away from the assemblage of tour-goers down the "wrong" hall-way, could put him face-to-face with her. Even though the live show was canceled, Shae had other shows today, which he was apprised of compliments of the website programming tab. He also had the map of the place in his pocket. Plan B was looking just as promising as Plan A.

Acquiring the studio map took a smidgeon of investigative ef-fort, as it wasn't public information. The whereabouts of the prep kitchen, green room, hair and makeup, prop room, wardrobe, con-trol room, etc. were at his fingertips.

The bite of Shae's inaccessibility felt all too fresh. Only three months ago, Shae was similarly cloistered. Worse, even. She was completely removed from on-air appearances. Last September, for twenty-two days, was a very dark time. It had gone on for so long that a Facebook campaign galvanized, aptly named "Where's Shae?" Lawrence's—well, "*Lee's*"—brainchild, of course. If IShop wouldn't provide answers, he'd find them independently. No one needed to remind Lawrence slackers were never crowned a hero.

Her absence was torture. During the first week, there was a ru-mor she had been sent on a last-minute "Venetian vendor visit." Lawrence didn't buy it. There wasn't one speck of evidence she was in Italy. If legitimate, Shae would've posted a Facebook video of a gondola ride, flirting with the stripe-shirted boatman, flashing her brilliant smile, giving him a knowing look, fluttering her long lashes. Or at least a stunning Insta photo dressed in a fabulous Italian designer gown—hugging her bottom curves and lifting her top curves—while standing mid-bridge as the sun set behind her. Or, if her fans were truly lucky, a YouTube video tutorial of Shae blowing glass at a factory in Murano.

But no. None of that. Not a lousy crumb of Parmesan. Not an espresso cup lipstick smudge.

Lawrence couldn't loll around waiting. If he made enough noise on Facebook by getting her fans to question her absence and demand her return, IShop would need to fork over some information.

The page had 4,653 followers in less than forty-eight hours. Lawrence combed through the spate of comments as they came in. Many predicted she was "getting work done." Some idiot claimed she was fired. The majority, like Lawrence, pined for her.

The comment from Nodda Chance stood out among the others for its alarm: "No one has said the obvious. She's been kidnapped."

Lawrence reported Nodda Chance to Facebook, hoping they'd alert IShop about this guy. Instead, Facebook suggested Lawrence block him, but he'd do nothing of the sort. Never silence a squealer. First thing he learned on the job. This guy might have more to say, and Lawrence wasn't about to shut him up. Any detective worth his salt knew that.

Shae returned after twenty-two days, discrediting the "fired," "face work," and "kidnapping" teams. During her first show back, Lawrence called the testimonial line. He was desperate to talk to her, to welcome her back, to tell her IShop wasn't the same without her, not to ever leave again. All he got was a recording that said the testimonial line was temporarily closed. Another red flag was confirmed when Lawrence called a few hours later during Bryan's crockpot show. Unsurprisingly, the testimonial line was open.

Several weeks later, the truth was revealed: Shae had a stalker.

Lawrence couldn't imagine to what extent this unbalanced deviant had gone to force IShop to send Shae on a fake spontaneous "trip" for an unspecified duration until said stalker was apprehended.

Alarmingly, to this day, no one had been apprehended.

Now, three months later, the smell of foul play had returned. Lawrence would bet every Summer Showers Linen Sachet he owned that Shae's social isolation would reveal something distressing. If so, IShop's decision to keep her on the down-low until things were sorted out was prudent. One could never be too careful. These days, there were unhinged whackos masquerading as upstanding citizens at every turn. It was possible to pass a psycho on the street multiple times a day and never know it.

Lawrence arrived at the studio, parked, and sat quite still, taking in the moment. This would be a day to remember. Today, he'd make something happen. Palm to palm, he rubbed his hands as if willing a genie to come forth. There was something forbidden about skin on skin, even if it was only his own. The patch of eczema had grown by a barnacle or two, now creeping into the tight crevice between fingers three and four of his left hand. Rita would know what to do. A side benefit of having a nurse in the house. He pulled on a new pair of gloves.

Through the passenger window, he studied the studio entrance. This was where it all happened. His body buzzed with excitement. No doubt feeding off Shae's energy. He knew she was in the building. He felt her presence. He practically smelled her.

All was oddly still at the lobby entrance until someone materialized from the circular door. Presumably a security guard, judging from the uniform. Judging from everything else—sleepy eyes, sorry shoulders, unsure stride—he could've been a ten-year-old who lost his puppy. The prospect of this guy taking down a stalker, if the need presented itself, was slim to none.

Lawrence strode past him to enter the lobby. There was nothing unsure about Lawrence.

He sidled up to the front desk. "Hello, I'm here for the studio tour—"

"Sooo sorry," said the receptionist, who was peeling off strips of nail polish using her teeth. "The studio tours have been canceled for the day." She was the sort who ended a statement as if it were a question. She smiled wanly. "It was posted on the website." Another question. Punctuated by the ascent of her eyebrows. She dove in for more nail polish.

"*All*—" Lawrence stuttered. "*All* the tours?" He was practically flatulating from the mouth.

A "yes" leaked from the side of her lips.

His nostrils swelled with barely concealed outrage.

He sputtered, "Wh—why? What's the reason?" He was frantic.

She hoisted a nude fingernail in the air to put Lawrence on hold while answering the phone. "IShop, join us 24/7 for the products you crave for today's lifestyle. You never shop alone at IShop. Hold please," she said to the caller, slowly returning to Lawrence. "Sorry. Can you repeat that?"

"I'm asking what the reason is for the cancellations? And why I—*we*—weren't alerted!" Lawrence gestured with his arm to indicate the legions of others who had arrived for the tour. Oddly, there was no one there but him.

"Oh." She curled her bottom lip and pondered. As if for the first time. *How is it that these people hold jobs!*

"They didn't say." She shrugged. "Sorry." Her pursed lips curled upward in concert with her shoulders.

Lawrence retreated, adrift.

"But the Studio Store is open!" she called out.

With sullen shoulders and dragging feet, Lawrence found himself wandering the Studio Store. Unwittingly, he stopped directly in front of a sign: Shae's Favorites. An entire corner dedicated to the products Shae adored.

"Your favorites are always my favorites," he muttered.

He fondled the Scrub Daddies—Shae'd convinced him to buy several sets of these sponge marvels (for the garage, kitchen and bathroom) for which he awaited delivery. The Dyson Hand Vac, which had changed his life in recent months. The Lovely Linens Hand Cream Sample Set, Shae's favorite handbag—the leather supple like a baby's bottom, and from the corner of his eye, the Smokin' Hot! Electric Smoker with Remote for ribs, chicken and sausage. It was *impressive*. As luck would have it, they were sampling just-smoked sausages. The aroma was, quite literally, intoxicating.

Lawrence hadn't considered buying the smoker since he'd recently succumbed to Shae's urging about a ricer, sous-vide, *and* pressure cooker. "How many cooking methods do we need?" asked Rita. She didn't get it. Rita wasn't a shopper, which irked Lawrence. She reminded him of a girlfriend he once had who didn't understand that bras—at a certain stage—were meant to be *thrown away*. There was no shame in getting rid of a bra that had developed a gray patina or had sprouted tendrils of elastic from every juncture. Whose metal hooks were twisted with scoliosis and lace pocked with holes. These symptoms signaled the end of a bra's life. She didn't see nor act upon any of these telltale signs. Though Rita's undergarments were much nicer and she understood the concept of "wear and tear," she didn't enjoy the act of shopping. The thrill of a new acquisition.

Lawrence found himself face-to-face with the massive—sturdy —*strapping*...smoker. His defenses waned. What with the smells and the tastes (and the frustrations and disappointments of the day), he needed this.

No propane was necessary. One simply plugged it in. It functioned by remote at a distance of up to twenty-five feet, *even through a window.*

Lawrence had little in the way of willpower for the fantasy of sitting in his media room with a remote in each hand, smoking his favorite meats while watching Shae, live, selling Body Shapers.

Lawrence pinched the skin between his thumb and forefinger to get his head back in the game. How easy it was to get lulled and lost in Shae's world. Everything felt soft and plush and warm in there.

He called out to someone stocking Emeril's grill pan—the very one from this morning's canceled show. "Excuse me, do you know when Shae Wilmont's Emeril show will be re-scheduled?"

"No idea." He shrugged. "You could ask Shae." The guy looked around.

"*What?*" Lawrence's body tensed. He whipped his head around. "*Where?*"

"She was just here." He shrugged. "Guess you missed her." He shoved the last few grill pans onto the shelf and walked away.

Lawrence dropped the Hand Cream Sample Set. It hit the floor, and two creams popped from the box and rolled away. He quickly scanned the room and searched the lobby. He inhaled through his nose; maybe he could smell her. He stuck his head out the front door and scurried over to the hall leading to the restrooms.

She was nowhere in sight.

How close he'd been! The universe was sending him a message. Shae Wilmont was clearly within reach. It wouldn't be long now.

When he arrived home, the house was empty. He could use the bathroom without Rita talking to him through the door. Bathroom time was sacred. Some people didn't understand that a closed bathroom door was not meant to have discussions through.

When Lawrence emerged from the bathroom, Rita was standing there. Waiting. Her arms crisscrossed and pinned to her chest. He was surprised she could breathe.

He was shocked to see her there but didn't let on. She hadn't made a peep. It was strange not to hear the gurgle of the garage door, the jangle of her keys, or the sound of her handbag being thrown like a shuffleboard puck across the kitchen table.

They didn't exchange pleasantries. It was rather awkward.

Lawrence didn't like the vibe he was getting. It was never a good thing when Rita met him at the bathroom door. An accusation was not far behind.

She took a step back to let him into the kitchen.

"Where were you today?" she asked.

He didn't like her tone. He didn't like it at all.

"What do you mean? At work. Where do you think I was?"

He advanced into the kitchen, which forced Rita to step backward. Another power move in his toolbox of power moves. *Don't cower, use your power.* He focused straight ahead on the Zwilling Block Set. He grabbed a toothpick from the drawer and poked between his teeth. It splintered in half, causing more harm than good.

"Don't pull that crap with me. I called your office. No pickup."

Lawrence whipped around to face her. He straightened his back, lifted his chin. He used every linear foot—*inch*—he owned.

"Jeez, Rita! I told you not to call me there. I don't want people picking up my phone if I'm in the bathroom or something. I told you to call my cell."

Her face was cold as stone.

"Nobody picks up your phone, Lawrence. Nobody. So don't worry." She tweezed her phone from her jeans pocket. "I called seventeen times." She held her phone in the air like a rat by its tail. "You can see right here."

Whoa. Lawrence was flustered. He needed to ground himself. He narrowed his stare and inflated his chest. He pinched the skin between his thumb and his forefinger before folding his arms in front of him.

"Seventeen times? Are you demented? Something's wrong with you," Lawrence scoffed, blowing aggressive swaths of air.

"I kept asking myself why no one was answering your phone." She dropped her arm to her side. "Don't they want to know if hot tips are coming in from bystanders? Important calls could be coming in. People with evidence. But not one person picked up your line. Here, count 'em."

At this, she cast her arm out again and shoved the phone at him. He could see his reflection in the screen. It was horrifying. He looked lost. Like every fiber of power had been drained out of him.

With gritted teeth, he shook his hand out in front of him. "No, thank you." This discussion didn't deserve a modicum of respect. He wouldn't indulge her a single moment more with this ridiculous line of questioning.

He straddled his feet. Propped his hands on his hips. Yeah, he saw that TED Talk. A big stance equals power. He prepared for moments like this when power needed wielding. He loved putting the Power Pose Ted Talk into practice. Rita wasn't getting anywhere with her meek little performance.

"Thanks, but I don't want to see that you're a crazy, insecure stalker."

"I'm not insecure, Lawrence, if all the evidence points to you lying." Her cell phone swung back and forth from her pinched fingers like a noose. This was some kind of show for her. To be the lead, center stage. Too bad she didn't get that part in high school like she wanted. Maybe all this could've been avoided.

"All the evidence?" He tilted his head. He needed to use the interrogation stare on *her*. Turn the tables. What the hell was she talking about, anyway? He leaned back and puffed out his chest to make himself bigger, giving him time to think in the Power Pose.

"That's right, Lawrence. I got a nose for stuff." She put her arm down.

He recoiled. *"You* got a nose?" He jabbed his chest repeatedly. *"I* got the nose, Rita. I got the nose! We both don't have it, I got it!"

"You sound a little crazy yourself, Lawrence." She didn't move. She was calm.

"Really? You sound a little crazy. You should know that's how *you* sound." He chewed the toothpick.

"Your odometer this morning read 34,545. Your odometer five minutes ago read 34,889. So, where's your office, Mexico?"

"Jesus. What the hell? Have you lost your mind? Now you're reading my odometer?" He swiped at the air. "Rita, I'm not going to dignify your accusations, but do you even know what I do at work? Do you know where I go to do my job? Why don't you ask yourself those questions?" He shook his head slowly. He brought his hand up to his nose to smell the faint aroma of latex left behind on his skin. That always soothed him.

She tapped her right foot. If she thought that would intimidate him, that was laughable.

"Okay, I'll bite. What is it you do?" She glared at him and tightened her grip around herself, but Lawrence could detect a slight softening around her mouth. Like maybe she was willing to reconsider her allegations. Maybe she was hoping she was wrong. Women. That's what they wanted deep down. They didn't want to be right about this stuff. Ultimately, they wanted to be wrong. They wanted the guy to prove that he wasn't up to any shenanigans. They wanted him to have proof he was true-blue after all.

"By the way, someone *did* pick up your phone, finally. The eighteenth time." A flicker flashed across her face.

Lawrence narrowed his gaze and top-stitched his arms across his chest. Who the hell could that have been? It better not have been Dale, that arrogant, smelly little prick. He girded himself for that possibility.

"I asked if you were out on a case. That got a hardy laugh, 'Yeah, a case of Coke!' What does that mean, Lawrence?" Her ponytail bobbed.

Lawrence let out a brusque laugh. "Oh, it was good 'ol Ant! He's a funny guy. That's code, Rita. That's code we invented—classified. I can't tell you what it means. Sorry. You wouldn't understand, anyway." Lawrence chuckled. "What else did he say?" He shot Rita a look.

"Your friend said you might be delivering mail."

"Ha! Good one! I have to hand it to Ant, he's one helluva funny guy. 'Delivering mail'—that's code for pissing." Lawrence laughed again. "Work would be pretty dull without him around!

He probably didn't know it was you calling. What else did that wiseguy say?" Lawrence laughed some more.

"That's it." She straightened the glasses on the bridge of her nose. "But his name wasn't Ant."

"Wasn't Ant? Anthony?" His shoulders sank. "Then who the hell was it?"

"It was a girl." Rita put her phone on the table. "Joanne."

"*Late Again.*" Lawrence seethed, hissing her name through clenched teeth. "That incompetent—I'll have her insubordinate ass fired. She's pretty plucky when I'm not around. She didn't think it would get back to me. Those worthless clerks; they'll never amount to anything."

"She said she didn't see you all day."

"Really? That's because her head's up her ass on a regular basis. You can't see a *Mack truck* from in *there.*"

He punched the air. Rita jumped.

Lawrence had to remind himself that Late Again was the lowest rung on the ladder, for God's sake. He could squash her like a mosquito, with two fingers.

"For your information, since you're so interested for a change, I didn't even drive my car today, Rita. Other than to and from the office. Ant needed it. For a meeting at Southern Division. His car's in the shop. So he took mine. Jeez, Rita, I thought we were good. I don't know now."

"The same Ant you thought answered your phone?"

"Yeah, that's right." What was her point?

"You smell like a girl, Lawrence."

Lawrence thrust his hands out in front of him, shocked. "What's next, Rita? Huh?"

Was he an absolute moron? *Idiot!* He should've pumped the lotion onto a tissue and then smelled it. Lovely Linens was about to do him in! Why the hell did he rub it on his hands? Why in God's name did he slather it on his neck!

Rita drew closer and sniffed his neck.

"*Rita*—" Lawrence shrunk back. He shouldn't have done that. Nor should he have rebuffed her with aggressive arm wielding. Big mistake.

She curled her tiny fingers into a palm and shook her walnut fist at Lawrence.

"You can't tell me you weren't with a girl today, Lawrence!" Her fist was a gnarled stump at the end of her arm, all bumps and grooves beating the air. It would've been humorous except her face morphed from anger to something else.

"I smell her all over you!"

Her eyes became glassy. Was she about to cry?

This was officially out of control. The minute the waterworks started you could kiss the power techniques goodbye. Her top lip, so thin it was nearly nonexistent, completely disappeared, her close-set eyes got even closer, and her ruddy cheeks turned bright red. The color traveled to her neck. Every frizzy end of her hair sprung from its ponytail and curled into a fuzzy halo.

Lawrence reached out for a bottle of seltzer on the counter. He wrapped his fingers around it to ground him, but to his dismay, the bottle didn't support his grasp. It wasn't hard as he expected. It was limp. It gave way.

"I hate flat seltzer!" He pounded the seltzer bottle against the counter.

"This is not about seltzer! Give me a break! Nice try. But I'm not falling for it!"

Lawrence stormed through the kitchen to the garage and slammed the door behind him. He popped the trunk and rummaged through a bag. He snatched a box and marched back into the house.

In the kitchen, he threw the box on the table. It slid until Rita's handbag stopped it.

"VaLavender Body Souffle. Combination vanilla/lavender. Supposed to be a Christmas present. But you ruined that now."

Rita, ungratefully, gave it the side-eye.

This was not the time to bring in the Smokin' Hot! Electric Smoker with Remote. If ever.

When Lawrence returned to work the next day, he was on high alert for Late Again. He avoided her at all costs. A confrontation with her—seeing her smugness or worse, listening to her insidious taunts—wasn't going to happen on his watch.

Lawrence had made a grave misstep. The trip to IShop to sniff out his theory about Shae was the wrong move. Major developments were occurring at the office—opportunities that surpassed his wildest dreams—while he sampled smoked weenies and slathered body butter. He'd never been the passive type, waiting for things to come to him. Though some opportunities appeared to manifest by chance, Lawrence knew it was always something he'd done that ultimately created them. He engineered all his success.

Proof of that was waiting on his desk.

CHAPTER 6

Shae

TWO WEEKS LATER

Thursday, December 31, 2015, 9:30 p.m.

SHAE waited in the studio lobby with her palms pressed against the glass door. Through the door, she could see Theo round the front of her car. He leaned into the wind to keep his footing. His pants flapped wildly around his ankles. Hopefully, this storm would blow over. Theo opened the back door and flashed a stream of light on the floor. He stuck his head in to look under the front seat.

Everyone going to the New Year's Eve party from the studio was already in their car, lined up in a chain. They liked to travel in packs. They were waiting for Shae to have her car checked. She didn't get in until one of the security guards searched it first. It was routine.

She'd never been a fan of New Year's Eve, an opportunity for suffocating self-examination. It always pulled back the curtain on what was lacking. This time, the last day of the year couldn't come soon enough. Good riddance, 2015. She couldn't wait to put some space between her and the twelve months she'd like to erase. Typically, December 31 was to the calendar what a juice detox was to the colon; you only needed to get through it. This year, she'd celebrate the fresh start that awaited on the other side. New Year's Eve was an annual guaranteed absolution. Control, alt, delete.

In the door's reflection, Lexi and Kayla from Merchandising approached. Lexi wore a black bustier trimmed in ostrich feathers. Kayla had on a strappy sequin dress. Shae looked down at her own clothes to evaluate. She couldn't be more than five years older than these girls. Even at their age, Shae never had the confidence to dress to be noticed. Unless she was on-air.

"Hi," Shae said, smoothing her hair. "Heading to the party?"

"Yeah," Kayla said. "Are you waiting for someone?"

"Ooh, love those earrings, Shae," Lexi interjected. Her breath came at Shae like a dagger. "Could I borrow them, I mean, since you're not going. Shame to waste them." She clutched Shae's arm to steady herself.

Kayla swatted Lexi's arm.

"What do you mean?" Shae glanced from one to the other. "I *am* coming." She fingered her earlobes to remember what earrings she had on. Didn't she look dressed for the party? Shae would never wear an iridescent top, black satin pants, and these heels to go home and watch a *Bachelorette* rerun.

"To the party?" they asked in unison.

"Yes."

"Oh, right." Lexi winked. "You *say* you're coming. Then don't show up. Like last time."

Kayla threw an elbow into Lexi's side. "Lexi, *seriously*. Don't listen to her, Shae. Are you driving with Figgy?" Kayla looked down the hall.

"No, she has to cover the next shift. Someone called in sick," Shae said.

"Wow." Lexi shook her head. "On New Year's Eve? Super bad karma. Even I wouldn't do that." Lexi reached out and stroked Shae's bag. "I tried to get that Tory Burch bag. Couldn't find it anywhere."

"You actually can't buy it in gold." Shae looked down at the bag. "It's one of a kind. Tory made it as a thank you for the sold-out show we had. She signed it, too." Shae opened the bag to show Lexi.

"Yeah, well, I was supposed to be a host," Lexi slurred, "but I'm not into stalkers—"

"*Lexi*, what the hell!" Kayla turned her back to Lexi. "She's been drinking. Obviously."

"What? She's got another stalker," Lexi said to Kayla. "Bryan told me. All I'm saying is if a stalker left a note in my bedroom that said 'I follow you everywhere—'"

"It was my car. And it wasn't a stalker. It was a fan; she left a Christmas gift in my car. I know—it's screwed up. What was she thinking? But it was very innocent." Shae wanted to change the subject. "Anyway, security checks my car." Shae motioned outside. "It's no big deal."

"Shae—" Kayla pointed to Shae's hand. "The nail polish on one of your fingers just turned pink! Are you wearing Intuition, the new nail polish line?"

Shae examined her hand. "Yeah. Val asked me to test it. But this product is a joke. I was going to take it off, but I love this color. It's like the color of brand new pennies. It's called *What Happens In Vegas*." All of her nails were a shimmery copper except for one. The fingernail on her index finger had just turned bright pink. "No surprise it failed Product Testing. Don't tell Val I said that. Her sister-in-law is the rep. Val did her a huge favor getting it into Product Testing. But she can't seriously be considering a nail polish that claims to be an intuitive radar." Honestly, Shae wished it worked. Her natural instincts failed her regularly.

"But it just worked! You'd sell tons of them," Kayla said.

"The nail polish on your index finger is supposed to change color depending on what it 'senses.' Like color coded gut warnings." Shae rolled her eyes. "Different colors mean different things. When it turns red it means: your secrets are safe; purple is: someone's lying to you; white means: tell the truth. Blue, from the product fact sheet, says: buckle up—you're in for a wild ride. Green means: don't go—work things out. Etcetera. The concept is ridiculous. We'd be overrun with returns." Shae wasn't going to risk her reputation selling a bogus product straight from a YA fantasy novel.

"I want to try it! What does pink mean?"

Shae laughed. "Leave him before he leaves you." Shae didn't even have a boyfriend.

Lexi leaned on the door letting an urgent swoosh of air leak in. "Too bad it doesn't warn you when a stalker is following you. Your other stalker is still out there, right? They never caught him." Lexi shook her head. "You couldn't *pay* me to go to a party. I'd never leave my house. But I have a boyfriend to hang out with, so it's different."

"Okay, time to go!" Kayla opened the door and pushed Lexi out. "We wouldn't blame you, is all, if you didn't come," Kayla said quietly.

"I'm coming!" She wished everyone would stop treating her like a china doll.

"Want to jump in with us?" Kayla said.

"No thanks. I want to have my car." Shae pulled her keys from her bag. "I'm *fine*."

"It's okay," Lexi yelled back into the closing door. "I don't need your earrings!"

"See you there!" Kayla slipped through while the door lagged open.

They teetered away, and Shae's face became hot. Prickles needled her scalp. She didn't want to be reminded of the other stalker. For months Shae had endured her colleagues' curled shoulders, furtive eyes, awkward semi-grins as they passed her in the hall. The same people who moments before were laughing or smiling. She'd grown accustomed to the hang-in-there face. Figgy insisted Shae move in with her for a month. Others were so uncomfortable, not knowing how to act or what to say, they pretended not to see her at all.

She'd become an expert accommodator of her fears. An outward oasis, an internal disaster. She compartmentalized alarm and anxiety. Tucked them away. But paranoia always leaked out.

She was determined to silence any doubters tonight. Anyone who thought she was too fragile for "real life." Her friends would see the old Shae when the ball dropped tonight. No, a new Shae.

Theo slammed the trunk and faced Shae with a thumbs-up.

CHAPTER 7

Shae

Thursday, December 31, 2015, 9:40 p.m.

THE party-ready studio people were behind their wheels, engines purring, like jockeys on horses at the gate. Jim, one of the cameramen, knew the guy throwing the open house party on Laguna Crescent. Jim claimed his friend threw the best parties and spared no expense. "Everyone will be there."

Theo opened the driver's side door for Shae and rested his hand on the frame as she crouched to get in.

He asked again, "Sure you don't wanna wait? Two hours, tops." He slouched down to face her with his sad Basset Hound eyes. "You know Jim's probably lit already, right? He's crazy behind the wheel even before he drinks." His hair was thick and rumpled like he had been endlessly running worried hands through it.

"Right," Shae agreed. "That's exactly why I'm driving *myself.* I'm a big girl, Theo." She patted his arm. "What's the worst that could happen? I'm just *following* him. I don't want to change my mind. If I wait for you or Figgy, that might happen. Plus, I have directions, thanks to you!" She waved her phone in the air, then dropped it in the cupholder.

He gave her one of his looks. "You're not going, are you?" He didn't wait for her to answer him. "It's okay. I only want to know so I won't worry." He really was kind. Why did Figgy distrust him?

"Of course I'm going! Who wants to stay home on New Year's Eve?" Shae grabbed the door handle and closed the door.

"Did you get your nav fixed?"

"Not yet. Next week."

"Well, you have the address."

"Yes."

"I texted you directions."

"I know. Thank you." She smiled warmly.

"Stay behind him, anyway. Don't go off on your own."

"I will. I won't."

"You have Jim's number."

"*Yes.*" Shae huffed and immediately regretted it. Theo was being very thoughtful, albeit chattier than usual. She'd never admit it, but Figgy was right. Theo rarely talked to anyone but her.

"You want to use Google Maps?"

"Yes, I will. Theo, please. They're all waiting. See you there."

Theo walked in front of Shae's car and stopped to look at Jim's rear fender. He retraced his steps and walked to Jim's driver's side window.

"Your taillight is out. On the left. You gotta get that fixed," Theo yelled into Jim's car. Then he shrugged and walked away.

None of them thought she was going to the party. *None of them.* Why? She was completely confused. Shae thought back to some of the recent parties she was invited to. Well…now that she thought about it…she didn't go to them. She never thought people noticed.

Honestly, she didn't think they'd miss her. She didn't think they actually *wanted* her there. Not that they didn't want her there. But she couldn't imagine she added anything to the experience. They had fun together in ways Shae didn't feel like she belonged. Was that just in her head? She thought they were always being nice to include her. So she wanted to return the favor by not going. Geez, that was screwed up. What the hell was wrong with her?

Well, Shae would show them this time. She was going to this party. She honked to alert Jim, and the train of cars pulled out of the lot.

Some studio people had obviously started partying already. A postponed Holiday Entertaining Show with Emeril left the studio with enough stuffed lobster tails and petit filet mignon to cater a small wedding. It was classic how the shows leading to New Year's Eve were about indulgence and excess, and once the New Year gonged, it was all Nutri-System and Total Gym. The two sides of the New Year's Eve hypocrisy: if you have friends to celebrate with, then drink and eat! If you don't, start your diet and exercise early so the same thing won't happen next year.

The cars ahead of Jim zipped toward the freeway, shuffling into the congestion going north.

Shae turned on the radio, then quickly turned it off. The story about the missing mom from San del Sol had taken over the local news. The latest report was about her "popularity" with her son's high school soccer team. Shae didn't see how reporting the way a woman dressed for her son's soccer carpool was going to help find her. This woman's disappearance seemed to entitle people to gawk, a free pass to expose.

When someone went missing, her unmentionables were strung on a line for the world to see. Disguised as an attempt to find this person, everything once kept private was dug up and sprung from its most intimate vault. Nothing was off-limits. A perky newscaster's eyes would sparkle while exposing some closely held secret. *It could lead to her discovery.*

Shae needed to stop following this story. It made her physically ill. This woman's poor children and husband had to hear this gossip about her. And their friends were reading this stuff. It was heartbreaking and humiliating.

The car procession broke up not too long after they hit the freeway. Not that anyone seriously expected it to stay together. Jim didn't need to follow anyone; he knew how to get there. But Shae didn't want to lose Jim. She'd never been to that area, and her sense of direction was abysmal. Honestly, she'd have trouble getting out of her own driveway, if not for her house at one end. She was about to start the nav when she noticed Jim's blinker flashing.

That wasn't bad at all. At the end of the ramp, they made a left and drove underneath the freeway toward the coast. Jim said his friend had a pretty nice house. Shae assumed he was exaggerating, not being modest.

A few blocks west, the traffic slowed. A strobe light swooshed over the cars. Orange signs sprouted up every twenty feet announcing a lane shift. Jackhammers. A water main break.

Cars began to leave their lanes—clogging into a knot of metal. All of them jockeyed for a chance to slip through, like sands of an hourglass. Jim was much farther up. She kept her eye on the left corner of his roof. The car beside Shae's was filled with girls dressed to party. Their car pulsated from the bass of their radio. They all bobbed in their seats at lopsided intervals, looking like a bunch of preschoolers in a bouncy house, except for their lip gloss, dangling earrings, and fancy clothes. "All the single ladies!" They shouted their anthem. One girl slapped the window to the beat.

Shae crawled along with the others. She never realized how many silver cars were on the road. Every other car, practically.

The strobe was right outside her window. The intensity of the swirling lightsabers, dipping in and out of her car, was blinding. She pressed her eyelids together to clear the white spots floating on the inside of her lids.

Was it 4715 Laguna? Or 7415? It didn't matter. Theo texted it. She grabbed her phone from the cup holder. Should've done this when she was at the studio like Theo said.

It would take forever to move this mass of cars, and she was nowhere near the light. Jim was closer to it in the right lane. Shae tapped the nav when she spotted his car zip out of the lane and into McDonald's. What the *hell*? Then he darted around the drive-thru lane toward the side street. What was he *doing*? What if she hadn't seen him?

She banged the wheel. Now she'd have to do the same. "Damn it, Jim!" Her car inched right, but no one would let her in.

If only the car in front would scooch. It didn't budge. Shae pounded the console with her fist. This was costing minutes! She honked. "I need to make a right!" Shae shouted at the car. Someone behind her leaned heavily on their horn. Shae blocked two lanes now. Halfway in the right, halfway in the left. "Where do you want me to go!" she yelled in her rearview mirror.

Finally, enough room for her to squeeze into the right lane. She shot out the other side. Into the shoulder. Into McDonald's. She snaked through the parking lot, passed the drive-thru, and careened onto the side street.

Jesus!

Now to find that asshole.

Shae pounded the wheel. "What the heck, Jim!" She accelerated as the street curved to the right, heading inland now. *Follow the detour signs and keep calm.*

She jabbed the home button to light up the phone screen. Google Maps could've been on the whole time. The *whole time*!

Shae pushed dark thoughts from her mind.

Stick with this, Shae.

It was New Year's Eve. If there was ever a time to turn over a new leaf, or, in her case, replant the tree, this was it.

Shae slid closer to the steering wheel as if that would get her closer to Jim. She pushed down a creeping sense of anxiety. *Compartmentalize it, Shae.* Half of her wanted to pull over and forget about Jim, get the nav going. She skimmed the phone to tap Theo's directions. Her screen was ablaze with messages. What the hell? Why didn't she hear anything? What about Bluetooth!

Missed call from (669) 619-4338.

Missed call from Val.

Text from (669) 619-4338.

Missed call from Figgy.

Text from Val.

Text from Figgy.

What. The. Hell.

Whose number was that?

She went to her texts.

(669) 619-4338: *Hi Shae. This is Sgt. Tramball. I've replaced Sgt. Clemson on your case. Please call me.*

Her case? Her case was wrapped up. There was *no case*. The note was from a fan. Not a stalker. A stupid fan who left a box of macarons. A midwesterner. A Christmas gift.

Val's message: *Tried to call you but no answer. Please call. There's a new detective on your case. His name is Sgt. Tramball. He needs to talk to you. Not the new case. The old one.*

Figgy's text: *Why aren't you picking up? Call me. ASAP.*

CHAPTER 8

Honey

Thursday, December 31, 2015, 10:10 p.m.

Honey was a nervous wreck walking this part of Fernando Boulevard by herself at this time of night. Everyone knew only specific people did that, and she didn't want the cops mistaking her for one of them. This street buzzed with all kinds of sunny business during the day. But now, the only transactions being made were with drug dealers and sex workers. Honey had been warned about cops trolling here to bust the girls. That's exactly why Honey was there—to find Jenna. Tragically, she was moonlighting on the Boulevard. Honey was certain Jenna didn't arrive at that business decision herself. Jenna was hanging out with the wrong guy, and Honey was doing her best to undo that.

To think Honey and Jenna met at church only six months ago. They were the youngest by far in the congregation. It took only one week of exchanging glances across pews for them to start chatting after services. There was something tragic-looking about Jenna even back then. She had the look of a baby girl who aged a whole generation from bad luck and circumstance. They became fast friends. Honey told Jenna she could live with her and Momma, that she had to ditch her pimp boyfriend. Honey had a plan to take Jenna back to high school like Momma did for her. When you're sixteen, the only guy you should be doing is the one sitting next to you in Algebra.

They discovered they had something in common: they were both runaways. Now Honey was trying to track her down at the Boulevard and pry her away from her scumbag boyfriend.

But seriously, did Honey expect Jenna would be lounging at the curb in a beach chair checking out her Insta feed, waiting for Honey to drop by? Wasn't the first time Honey didn't think things through.

A car coughing an old man phlegm ball drove up behind her. *Don't look at that car. Don't turn your head, girl. Keep walking. One foot in front of the other.*

Parking at the opposite end wasn't smart. Did Honey really need to park legally? Cops didn't hover around this neighborhood to give parking tickets. She should've driven up to the girls like the johns do. She could've stayed in her car! Instead, her legs were shaking, trying to get her scared ass down the street without attracting the wrong kind of attention. *Good Lord, watch over me.* The car behind her was huffin' and puffin' like an old man spit snort. She prayed it was dark enough he wouldn't see her.

Honey's head stayed so straight, her neck hurt. *Please don't stop. Please. Don't. Stop.*

The car slowed. She kept up her don't-mess-with-me walk. Knees high, head high, heels hitting the ground hard. This was her look-don't-touch walk in other scenarios. Hopefully, it translated.

The horn blasted. Honey jumped like a wuss. The sleazebag cackled, and she jumped again.

"Hey, girl! You new?"

Honey waved like she was dusting him off the road. "Move along! Move along!" Without turning her head, she kept walking. "I don't work here!" Some kind of braveness filled her at that moment. Her left hand swept over the smooth skirt of her uniform that she ironed this morning. It felt safe, like home. But she was trembling like a doe that lost its momma.

She kept laser-focused on her car only thirty feet away, waiting on Honey like some kind of hero.

"Drive your beer can somewhere else. Shoo!" Why couldn't she keep her mouth shut?

Honey's nerves were sizzling like a cheeseburger on the grill. She picked up speed and started jogging while pretending to pull her phone from her bag to fake a call to the police. Only she was so nervous she didn't pull out her real phone. She used her hand —talking into her pinkie with her thumb in her ear! What kind of idiot?

"Bitch!" The nasty sputter of his car morphed into a zoom. Music to Honey's ears. She galloped to her car, fumbled with the key, jumped in, and locked it behind her. Safe at last.

She sat very still. Paralyzed with fear. What the hell was she doing? This place scared her senseless, and she wasn't the one being lured with an endless supply of drugs from a pimp "boyfriend" to work the Boulevard. How the hell was someone in the last licks of childhood doing this? Honey must have channeled Momma's strength in order to come here looking for Jenna, putting her fears behind her to save Jenna. Honey said a quick prayer for Momma in case Jesus had an opening and was taking calls. She hoped she didn't make a mistake leaving Momma tonight, even if it was only for an hour. She'd never forgive herself if this was the wrong night to leave.

Honey focused on Momma's words: "You can't save everybody. Sometimes you've got to make tough decisions."

With the key in the ignition, she tore out of there. Pebbles kicked up from her tires and hit the side window, making her yelp like the wuss she was.

Honey passed the girls but didn't look, even though she heard a lot of commotion. She blocked them out. She didn't want that image cemented in her memory. Girls lying on a collapsed chain-link fence like it was a hammock in Acapulco, their asses squeezing through like waffle batter. She didn't want to think of Jenna there. How scary it was when the cars came lurking. She needed to erase it from her mind. This excursion didn't pan out the way she wanted. No Jenna. Nobody had seen her in days. One girl said, "Look for Jimmy, and you'll find her." Honey already knew that, and she was intentionally avoiding him like bad news.

In the side mirror, the group of girls got smaller. Once she was around the bend, past the crumbling old buildings, she'd be close to the ballpark and the bodegas. Nearly there. Thank you, Jesus!

Then, like a mirage, a figure emerged from the side of the road and walked into the street toward her car. Honey was forced to slow down to avoid hitting her. The girl was taller than anyone Honey'd ever seen. She took two long strides like a flamingo in high heels. Honey pressed the brake and kept her foot there, though she didn't want to.

"Girlfriend," the girl purred and pointed to Honey.

She rapped her knuckle on the passenger window. Honey leaned over to open it.

The girl folded at the waist like a giraffe trying to lick its toes and leaned on the window frame. She stuck her head in and looked around. "You the one looking for Jenna?" The way she moved her yardage hypnotized Honey.

"You know her?"

"Yeah, I know her." Everything about this girl was slow motion tree sap. Even the way her words glided off her tongue. "She's with Jimmy. You know him?" She was not in a hurry. "He drives a blue car. Nobody likes Jimmy. He's planning on taking Jenna to Texas."

Honey's mouth fell open. Oh no, no, no. Honey did not just hear that. No. That asshole loser was not taking her girl. She was not going to lose Jenna. Uh-uh.

"He needs to leave town. I wouldn't get mixed up with him if I were you," warned the flamingo-giraffe.

Hell no, Honey already knew that. She'd been avoiding him and his derelicts for the last three days. Miraculously, she'd eluded confrontation with Jimmy and needed to keep it that way. Him leaving town was good news. She owed him a lot of money, and available funds were replenishing at a slow trickle. Maybe he'd leave without it. But he better not take Jenna.

The girl fluttered her long fingers like a wheat field swaying in the breeze, putting Honey under a spell if she stared too long. "Something's up with that girl. She doesn't look right to me."

Honey gulped down every fear she had about Jenna. When you're relieved your girlfriend's alive and not in juvie-jail, it was a low bar indeed. Now she had new fears. Honey was about to divulge her plan to grab Jenna by her silky brown hair, drag her to Honey's place where she'd sober up, straighten out and stay living with her and Momma, now that they were down one with

Mr. Moretti gone. But Honey stopped herself from disclosing too much and silently praised herself for exercising discretion.

Honey wasn't judging anybody. Dropping out of school—been there, done that. Honey didn't dare judge those girls on the Boulevard, either. If not for the grace of God, who knows, she might've been standing around their water cooler right now. That's probably what got her shaking. If not for the grace of Momma, more like it. Honey owed every minute of her straight and narrow to that glorious being. Momma was an angel in an apron. She told Honey sometimes you have to move on to save the people who stand a chance. That's what Honey was doing.

Honey wasn't getting high and mighty about the Boulevard girls. This was a stepping stone to survival for a lot of them. But Jenna was a baby and clearly not in charge of her own thinking. When you let a sleazebag dealer-pimp make your decisions, you're in trouble with a capital T.

"Tell her Honey's looking for her. Tell her to call me. She's not returning my calls."

Once the girl collected her arms, neck, and head from the car, she glided back into the night. "Happy New Year!" drifted through the dark like the coo of an owl.

Honey couldn't wait to hear the rattle of her under-car parts, and once she let her foot off the brake and put it back on the gas, that clatter sounded like a rusty knight in shining armor.

At the light, she'd turn off the Boulevard. She couldn't get there soon enough. She drove faster—ignoring her police paranoia in the process. She tried convincing herself that cops around here weren't after speeders. They were shaking down Jenna's colleagues.

Just like that, a car appeared in her rearview mirror, so close he could've been sitting next to Honey in the front seat. Where the hell did he come from?

"You can't drive faster than someone you're behind! Unless you're in front!" Honey yelled in her rearview mirror. And picked up speed.

All the loose car parts jiggling didn't sound so good anymore. Sounded like the car was about to give up. Every time Honey sped up, the car behind edged closer. She made a quick left and regretted it. It was the wrong way.

He made a quick left, too.

Damn it. She tried to take comfort in someone driving these empty streets with her. At least she had company, right? But dark thoughts kept creeping in. People driving around here were johns. Or cops.

Something one of the girls said flitted through her head. *Cops prowl the Boulevard looking for girls to bust.*

Honey didn't work the Boulevard, but history proved that being in the wrong place at the wrong time could change your life in an instant when cops were involved, no matter where on the guilt spectrum you hung out. Honey's mother, Denise, was proof of that. She went to jail for drug possession and distribution. She claimed it was a setup. Maybe it was. She had been associating with the wrong people for as long as Honey could remember. But if Denise was innocent before she went to prison, she certainly wasn't after. It didn't take long for Denise to slip back into her old ways. Out of a job, always high, never home. When she did come home, she came with a boyfriend. Honey didn't like how uneasy Momma seemed when this happened. They were always looking for something, and the boyfriends were never the type you'd want to say no to.

They say prison changes you for good. It changed all of them and not for the better. Maybe if Denise never went to jail things would've been different for them. Better. There's no way to see that rerun. Honey always felt guilty about being happier when Denise was in jail. It was less scary and unpredictable.

Another possibility wedged its way into Honey's swelling paranoia. The guy following her could be one of Jimmy's guys. To collect from Honey. Or scare her. Like the guy who came to the diner two days ago. Sat in Honey's section. But he wasn't there for the lemon meringue pie. He accomplished what he set out to do. After conveying Jimmy's "friendly" reminder that her payment better be on time, Honey had the runs for the rest of the day.

Honey made a quick right onto El Centro, where there'd be a lot of people around. Enough of this no-man's-land. She'd been spooked enough for one night.

Nothing in the rearview mirror. Thank the good Lord. Almost home. Everything would be better there.

Lights flashed in her mirror. There it was again. That damn car. Like a zit, back as soon as you thought it was gone.

She shouldn't have gone downtown. Wouldn't be the first time she was in the wrong place at the wrong time. Honestly, some places were wrong all the time. She should've gone straight home to sit with Momma—how many more days could she do that?

Finally, Honey's street. She parked in a hurry. No other cars drove up the street, but she ran anyway around the side of her house to the back door and locked it behind her. Honey's paranoia polyp burrowed so deep, she felt it fester. She turned up the music from her boom box in the living room to drown out her thoughts.

She was so terrified the cops picked up Jenna, she didn't consider them coming for *her*.

Honey walked back down the short hall to Mr. Moretti's old room off the kitchen where Momma had recently moved from the basement. She opened the door and stood in the doorway. Momma hadn't moved an inch, it seemed. The sheet covered her body but looked like there was hardly anything under it. Honey swallowed her fears and tears. She didn't want Momma seeing her like this. That woman's radar could detect anything no matter how deep you hid it. Honey needed to be brave. She sat down and slipped her hand underneath Momma's hand, paper-thin and light as a whisper. "Momma, how you doing? You look good," Honey lied. "I went looking for Jenna. You would've been proud of me. I was scared, but I did it anyway. Couldn't find her, but I'm not giving up. She'll be moving in soon. Can't wait for you to meet her."

Honey leaned over, kissed Momma softly on the head, and breathed in the smell of her. "I hope I got what it takes—" Honey choked up. Momma flinched and groaned. "Because it's just you and me, so without you, it'll just be me." Honey stroked her wispy hair which fanned out on the pillow like a crown. If only Momma would open her eyes and look at her. "That's okay, I'm not scared. If you need to go, it's all right." She gulped. "I promise to do my best. You're my hero, Momma. You know that?" She bit her lip hard. "Say something, Momma," she whispered. "Please, say something." Hot tears pooled around her eyes. But Momma's mouth was folded shut like the edge of a pie crust.

Momma hadn't said a word in days. Honey begged God to let Momma say something before she left. Honey needed to hear her voice once more. She needed to heed her words. Honey needed every morsel of Momma-sense she could soak up.

Honey picked up the plate of food she left this morning, which was hopeful thinking at best. "It's almost time for your chemo." She gave Momma's hand a little squeeze. She went to the kitchen to get the new package of Depends. Honey's favorite song was on the radio. That was good luck, right there. When your favorite Rihanna song came on, it was a good sign. "What Now," indeed.

Honey walked into the hall to put her earrings on the table under the mirror. She pulled off her wig—long, black and straight—her version of a rabbit's foot and her disguise for the Boulevard rolled into one. She took a long look at her reflection. Worry lodged in her eyes. Funny how life keeps pelting stuff at you with no time to breathe in between. At least her own hair—long and blonde— was looking good. Honey raised her arms to smell her armpits. Not that she needed to. Nervous b.o. hits you in the face like a cast-iron frypan. Lord, it was vile. Way worse than regular b.o. She needed a shower and bad. Right after this song was over and she changed Momma. She unbuttoned her shirt, pulled her arms from the sleeves, and let it hang from the waist.

Honey expected to feel better once she got home, but her nerves were spitting like onions on the flat top. Even Rihanna didn't help. Something felt strange. Like someone was watching her. Honey sure could scare herself. Probably her nerves working her over, but she would bet every sad song on the radio that out of the corner of her eye, something just moved in the living room.

CHAPTER 9

Shae

Thursday, December 31, 2015, 10:11 p.m.

Wﾡ her eyes on the road, Shae pressed the button for Siri. "Call Figgy."

"There are two numbers for Figgy. Which would you like? Figgy New—"

"Yes, *yes*. Jesus! I only call the *new* one."

"Please don't call me Jesus, Shagreen. Calling Figgy New Number." Siri with a freaking attitude.

The call went immediately to voice mail. *Crap.* "Figgy, what's going on? Everyone's calling me. My phone is on; I don't know why it's not ringing…"

Shae felt for the volume button with her thumb. "Shit!" she said mid-message. "The volume was off. Somebody named Sergeant Tramball called me. Who's he? What happened to Clemson? So did Val. What's this about? Good news? Bad? I'll try Val now. Call me. Jim's being an asshole."

She threw her phone onto the passenger seat. "Jim, I swear I'm going to kill you later!" If she ever found him. She had lost focus on the road and couldn't see his car anywhere as others sped by.

She untwined her tight grip from the steering wheel to reach for her phone. *Calm down. Don't worry about the detective. Or Figgy. Or Val. When you get to the party, you'll call them. You need to get your nav going, stupid. And calm the hell down. Enough with Jim and his idiotic games.*

Peace of mind was a few taps away. Her hand searched the passenger seat to retrieve the phone. She pressed the home button.

The screen was black. *Stay calm.*

Nearly at the light. Straight or right? *Make a decision.*

She jabbed the button again. Then a hundred more times.

"I don't know. I don't *know!*"

No power. The phone was dead.

She banged the steering wheel with the heel of her hand and unintentionally slowed nearly to a stop in the middle of traffic. A rush of honking horns bleated obscenities from behind. Just then, a single car made a right turn. It darted so fast she almost couldn't tell it was *silver.*

At the last possible second, Shae yanked the steering wheel right. The car screeched a skin-crawling cry.

With her right hand, she dumped the contents of her handbag onto the seat. She raked through the pile for her charger. Comb, makeup bag, change purse, sunglasses, gum. That's okay. She'd stop at a gas station. 7-Eleven. Whatever. Get directions. This wasn't Mars!

This following Jim thing was over. *Over!*

She whipped open the console door, drove her hand to the bottom, and surveyed the contents for a charger. Hairbrush. Chap-Stick. Tissues. Floss. Mints.

There were no cars in sight. *None.* Where the hell did he go? She was a minute behind him! Less. This was the scary part of Fernando Boulevard. She'd *never* drive here—alone—in the middle of the night, passing a group of girls who looked like prostitutes. She couldn't imagine anyone voluntarily hanging out here. What a terrible place for a car to break down.

Shae scratched at both palms where her nails dug a row of deep indentations from her tight clamp of the steering wheel. She was in her safe place. She loved her car. The quiet. After a long day of nonstop talking, she could be silent here. It was a luxury not to speak. Sometimes she couldn't take the chatter from her own mouth anymore. She loved the feel of the door sweeping shut. The weight. The strength. Like a pair of strong, muscular arms wrapped around her. One swift sweep of the door and the whole world was shut out. Nothing could go wrong in the protective womb of her car.

A sound came from the back seat. Something moved.

Shae froze. Her breath caught midway up her windpipe. She slid to the edge of the seat. Her eyes bulged.

"Who's there?" Her voice cracked.

No way someone was back there. This whole time. *No way.* Theo checked the car. She watched him *check the car.* Shae's head was rooted into her neck, unmoving, while every other part of her trembled. Through the rearview mirror, she could only see outside.

Another sound from the floor. She jumped. "Who's there, I said!" Her eyes flicked with tears. "What do you want?" She choked out.

Silence.

She punched the light on—snapped her head around. Her round brush—stuck to the rug—ripped off at every jerk of the car. A book, her wallet, slid from her tote bag, now strewn across the floor.

Jesus.

She siphoned her anxiety into her right foot and laid hard on the gas. Around the bend in the road—a glow of lights. A car!

It was Jim! Even in the distance, she could see the car had only one brake light. His junky car was the most beautiful sight in the world.

His car slowed, then stopped in the middle of the road. Was he waiting for Shae? Before she was close enough, he took off again. What a freakin' loser. What an absolute ass.

A figure coalesced in the street, walking away from where Jim's car stopped a moment ago. Walking toward the curb. Strange. This place was deserted.

As Shae approached, she could make out the girl. The longest legs Shae had ever seen. The highest heels. The shortest skirt. Who was she? Why would he drop her in the middle of nowhere?

Oh no. No, no, no. A prostitute? What the hell, *Jim*! He picked up a hooker? Figgy'd never believe this. Retract. Yes, she would.

Right before the girl evaporated into the darkness, she turned to look at Shae and waved. Her long hair swirled upward like Dairy Queen soft serve, making her appear even taller. Shae'd never been that close to a prostitute. Ever. Unless what she had heard about Capucine was true. She once overheard her father accuse Capucine of being a prostitute. It always stuck with her. Mostly because it was the first time she had heard that word. She didn't know what it meant. It was a terrible memory to hold onto.

She turned her head to focus on the street and sped up. She wanted out of there. She didn't want to think about hookers.

Shae raced along the dark stretch, passing a half-demolished building on a dirt lot where vagrants lived in a cardboard box village. Weeping clothes hung from a chain-link fence, lifting in the wind, waving in surrender. Guilt rumbled in Shae's stomach, wrestling with the other unwelcome emotions of the last twenty minutes. It was only hours before that she touted button detailing and darts that flattered curves and hand-embellished sequins. Not here.

The wind was nuts. Something flew at her windshield, a white plastic lid, like a frisbee. It smacked the glass.

"*Jesus!*" She jumped.

This was insane. All of this. She was just going to a New Year's Eve party. A simple declaration of being "back in the world of the living." Moving on from being holed up in her home, locking doors and windows, having her car checked for random stalker notes and mysterious packages. Then this lunacy had to happen!

Shae exhaled a round of short bad juju breaths. *Get ahold of yourself. See this through. Get to the party. They'll never believe your intentions if you cop out now.*

Her thoughts were a tangle of conflicting pleas. She wanted to believe it wasn't Jim dropping off a hooker. But that meant she was following the wrong car. She didn't want to believe that either. She knew it was Jim. Why did he have to be such an ass?

Jim made a right turn. So did Shae. A bodega appeared. Then another. Civilization! The street quickly became cramped. Cars parked and double-parked. People loitered in the street, blowing into noisemakers. A man walked right in front of Shae's car and grinned a toothless grin at her. "Happy New Year!" He waved.

Shae shuddered. How do you lose every tooth in your head? It reminded her she was late for a cleaning.

Jim made a left onto a street with no lights. If not for his head-lights, and now hers, she wouldn't have seen the row of bunga-lows, cramped like a mouthful of crooked teeth, on both sides of the narrow dead-end road. Jim slowed and pulled over to park.

This was the place?

How?

It was awful.

Shae called this one! She took no pride in that now. Of course, he was exaggerating about his friend's house. By epic proportions.

Several cars were parked along the curb on one side of the street. She scanned them for Donna's. Could Jim and Shae have arrived first? Jim parked up ahead, in front of the only house with lights on. Shae found a space down the street on the other side of a fire hydrant. She turned the car off and leaned forward to rest her forehead against the steering wheel. Her whole body shook. That was crazy.

Jim, though a shameless liar, and by all accounts, irresponsible —and likely drunk—got her there. Shae would see this through. She'd find a phone charger, have a drink, and get the hell home. She needed to clear her head before Jim got to her. She dug deep for "bright" and "festive," attempting to conceal "raging" and "homicidal."

Shae slugged some water. Then noticed the nail polish on her thumbs turning blue. Thumbs weren't supposed to change color. *You're in for a wild ride.* Thanks.

Too late for that now.

CHAPTER 10

Shae

Thursday, December 31, 2015, 10:43 p.m.

ANOTHER light flicked on in the party house. Bright yellow filled the window on the side facing Shae. It was impossible to see inside from her angle. But something was immediately visible: bars. Security grills covered the windows of all the houses. Except for windows covered in plywood.

Shae knew Jim embellished the description of his friend's house, but this was a bald-faced lie. They all got suckered. Shae didn't know neighborhoods like this in Vista Verde. These were not her people. Vista Verde people lived here for the glamour, the fantasy of the place. Maybe that's what drew Shae here. Implausible balminess, relentless sunshine, sparkling beaches, never-ending rose gardens, smiling people. A real-life fairy tale.

But the night revealed something else of this place: where the others lived and slipped through darkness unseen. Part of another mechanism the sunny people disregard.

For a split second, Shae considered not leaving the car. She wanted to go to the party, but she didn't want to be there.

Forget the party. What had she come for, anyway?

She quickly abandoned a probe of deep thoughts. Shae had already dealt with the worst of this. She didn't want to be snob-shamed. What did the others truly think of her anyway? She needed to make an entrance. Show them indeed she came. Charge her phone, have a drink, leave.

Jim was taking a long time getting to her. She leaned over the passenger seat to look up the sidewalk. She expected more people around. Cars, even.

There he was.

Shae turned the light on so he could see her "one-minute" finger. She grabbed her makeup bag and swiped on some lipstick. She dusted her cheeks with blush, then swept everything back in her bag. An envelope leaned against the back of the seat. She peeled it away. Figgy's phone bill. Damn. Shae had promised to mail it. Now it would be late on account of Shae. She stuck it in her bag and turned off the light.

She popped three Altoids, pulled the door lever, and slid her leg out. From behind the door came a low, sinister growl. The kind of growl vicious dogs make.

The growl grew louder. And closer.

Shae didn't move. A snout jutted out. Then a head.

A violent image flashed through her mind of the last time she was this close to a dog.

She yanked her leg back. Slammed the door.

Eyes glowed. Ears pricked. Slowly, the dog crouched its shoulders and snarled.

Shae didn't budge or breathe. She couldn't if she wanted to. She stared out the windshield without seeing. Every fear she ever had for anything in the world, and there were plenty—rodents,

loneliness, carbon monoxide poisoning, singing, relationships—
had slipped away. Except for one. That dog.

She grabbed her wrist and thumbed the scar tissue. A raised
slippery blade of skin. It felt all too recent. What the hell was she
doing here? Afraid to get out of the car, on a street, in *daylight*, she
wouldn't be caught dead on, going to a party thrown by a stranger
—and from the looks of things, not someone she'd ever hang out
with—led here by a reckless drunk asshole and possible hooker
solicitor. To say this was out of her comfort zone was the under-
statement of the year.

Without turning her head, she detected a second dog. By the
sound of it, they weren't friends. Their growls crept under Shae's
skin and manifested in an outbreak of goosebumps. Shae hummed
to drown out the feud.

Her palms were slick with sweat. She locked the door. Nothing
could go wrong if she stayed in the car. She slid her hands under
her thighs, tipped her head low. Maybe they'd kill each other.

Silence.

That didn't mean anything. They could be lurking. Shae
worked up the nerve to turn her head and inspect. They were
gone. Swallowed by the night.

Her body buzzed from head to toe. The sidewalk was empty
now—where the hell was Jim? What an ass! He said he'd walk in
with her.

Music wafted through the air, shoving the quiet aside. It was a
throbbing noise, but oddly comforting, knowing her friends were
near.

Another car drove onto the street. Maybe someone from the studio. The driver eyed Shae looking at him. He pulled over in a
spot across the street. Shae didn't recognize him, but if he walked

toward the party, she was getting out. She grabbed her bag and moved quickly before he was gone. She opened the car door cautiously and listened for the dogs. Someone yelled something up the street. Shae jumped out of the car, quickly got to the sidewalk, and walked up the path toward the house. The guy made a U-turn and drove away.

Jim told the props girls to just walk in when they arrived. "It's an open house," he said.

"What do you mean, walk through the front door?" Shae had asked. Everyone stared at her like she was an alien.

"Yeah." Jim repeated. "It's an *open house.*"

Shae let it drop. She didn't want to embarrass herself. No one else thought it was odd. This was all part of her New Year's resolution. *Relax. Don't worry about how to act. Or what to say.*

Closer to the front door, she took inventory of her courage. Could she walk into a stranger's house? She glanced at her fingertips. All of them glistening copper. Some encouragement would've been nice.

With gnawing unease, Shae peered at the large picture window —the only window on the entire front of the house—trying to see anything through the drawn blinds.

Nope.

Uh-uh.

Not doing it. There was no persuading her gut. None of this felt right. Sorry. She didn't need to prove anything to anybody. Not even to herself. She pivoted on her heels and made an about-face toward her car. New Year's resolutions could start tomorrow. In fact, that's when they were supposed to start.

Finally—she'd come to her senses! Not going to this party didn't say anything about "who she was" or if she was "ready" or "one of the them" or "fake," "uptight," "paranoid," or "terrified."

Her pajamas, a glass of Cabernet, and any one of the three books she was currently reading was, all of a sudden, New Year's Eve perfection.

Why was she always testing herself? Why was she always testing *others*? Did they honestly like her, did they care, were they sincere? That was over. It was time she liked herself for a change. *Trusted* herself for a change.

She could deal with being lost in this neighborhood. As long as she had gas, what else did she need?

A heavy weight lifted with the mere decision to retreat. Shae took two amazingly confident strides down the path, back to the car. God, it felt incredible. Like someone had unbound her wrists. *A hot bubble bath. Ginger salts. The Italy part of Eat, Pray, Love.*

Something rustled in the shrub alongside the path. It burst from the hedge. A mangy, bony something. Shae could count its ribs. Her heartbeat went ballistic. Thigh muscles tightened. Feet leadened. Knees locked. Something dropped from its mouth. And hit the ground with a thud. Shae pleaded with herself to do something. She was halfway to the car. Not really. Closer to the house. Much closer. The dog panted. Staring her down. She considered dog-radar. Would she test this dog's ability to sense her unmitigated fear?

With a decisive pivot, Shae took one long stride *away* from her car, her home, her bliss, toward the house. She grasped the lever, opened the door, and, against her instincts, she slipped inside.

CHAPTER 11

Shae

Thursday, December 31, 2015, 10:58 p.m.

SHAE stood trembling in the middle of the living room. Her back pressed against the door to iron down her shakes, then sprang from it when the dog's nails gouged the other side.

The house was *empty*. Shae followed the lights, the music, *Jim*. Where the hell was everyone?

The music blared and shook the flimsy walls of the tiny bungalow. Deafening her thoughts. Confiscating her ability to reason. Vibration oozed up from the floor, buzzing her feet.

The figure of a girl loomed in the dark hall. Her back to Shae. She was dressed from the waist down. Facing a mirror. Her unbuttoned shirt hung around her hips, revealing her bra. *What the hell*. Shae needed to get out of here.

She was in the wrong damn house.

The girl was shouting a song at her reflection. Shae could leave unnoticed.

With her back pressed to the door, hand on the knob, she twisted it imperceptibly. With painstaking subtly, Shae opened the door a crack. Strains of a song leaked into the house from outside, competing with the girl and Rihanna. *The party house?*

Jesus. She picked the wrong house. And walked right through the damn door.

In the corner of the room, something moved. From under a chair, the hairy, pointy ears of a German Shepherd inched out.

The rest of it followed.

A pool of saliva collected in the well of Shae's tongue. It tasted like fear.

The dog's eyes locked on Shae's. Its jaw clenched. Revealing the teeth too big for its mouth. The dog readied itself to lunge.

The inside of Shae's cheeks—along with the rest of her—drummed with panic.

Subtle moves, Shae. No need to alarm anyone—or anything—by being assertive.

She shifted her weight, ready to rotate. Her hand cramped on the doorknob.

The girl spun around. And shrieked.

She shielded her chest with folded arms. "Who the hell are you?" A wig hung from one hand. "What are you doing?"

In a flash, she became unhinged, a spastic whir. She threw the wig at the couch, a brush at the wall; she pulled up her shirt, shoved arms through sleeves, shouted over the music.

The dog sprang to its feet. Barked brutally. An urgent threat. On a loop. Every bark launched the dog into the air.

"I said, who the hell are you?" Her eyes pinged every which way. "How'd you get in?" She surveyed Shae up and down.

This was nuts. She was nuts. The dog was nuts. Shae's teeth rattled.

The dog stretched its legs on the rug in that I'm-about-to-rip-your-face-off way.

The girl paused briefly. "You work for Jimmy?" She nervously buttoned her shirt.

"You know him?" Shae muttered, astonished. She never heard anyone call him Jimmy. My God, this *was* the place.

"Seriously?" The girl slammed her fist on the back of the couch. Shae popped off the floor. The dog howled like a wolf. "You work for that scumbag? Jesus. Dressed like that? Now I've seen everything! Well, I don't have his money!"

What the hell was happening? Why did Jim bring her here? Shae was going to *kill* him. She trembled uncontrollably—the keys in her hand clanked like a wind chime from a horror movie.

"No—" Shae shook her head wildly. "I don't know what you're talking about. I'm not looking for money—"

Shae was surprised by her own voice. It didn't sound like her. She momentarily forgot why she *was* there. The dog didn't stop once for air.

The girl spotted the keys in Shae's hand.

"*Wait.* How'd you get a key?" Her mouth dropped open. Fear shot across her face. If only Shae could keep up with her. The girl dropped her head and fluffed the pillows from behind the couch, moving quickly, smoothing cushions with her palm.

"Is this about Mr. Moretti?" She strode to the side window and misted a plant with a sprayer. "Are you related?" She wasn't looking at Shae. "I don't know what to tell you. He was old!" All her focus was on the plant, pinching leaves. Spritzing.

This was the time to bolt. If only the dog wasn't inches from Shae's knees.

The girl plucked some leaves and shoved them in her mouth, "His basil's doing real nice."

Shae blinked to erase this scene from her view. She tried not to see her. She tried not to hear her.

The girl slammed the sprayer on the windowsill. "Momma did her best! For years she took care of him!" the girl shouted. "People get sick! He was ninety-six! We loved him! It wasn't our fault!"

Oh my God. Stop talking. Please.

The dog yowled. Shae could barely keep herself together; she was unspooling by the second.

"Mooch!" the girl yelled at the dog. "I can't think!" She clapped her hands like cymbals. The girl jerked her head twice to look at the boombox. She reached her leg over to the cord plugged into the wall and stomped on it, making it spring from the outlet.

Silence.

The quiet was terrifying.

Shae started to talk without thinking. "I don't know…I mean… Mr. Morti…I'm here because I followed…" Shae was dizzy with confusion. "I was following—"

The girl spun around.

"I knew it!" She jabbed her finger at Shae. "I knew you followed me!" She was enraged. "Jesus, a girl cop—how pathetic!" She laughed. "Why should I be surprised?" She paced the small room. "That's how you get your kicks." She clapped again, like a deduction. "You have a respectable job, so you lock up sex workers. That's shameful!"

What was happening? What did Shae say?

"You can't lock me up! I know my rights! And you're breaking and entering!" Her arms flew around like a flock of birds.

The dog's ears soared to the moon.

"I got it now. Makes perfect sense. The Boulevard girls think they can trust a girl. You get dressed up and lure them into your sticky web with your blow-dry, perfect manicure, fancy jewelry. Flash your bleached teeth, then your badge." She folded her arms at her chest, fluttered her fingers.

Hostility whooshed in like the wind. "Where's your badge?" This cued the dog. It barked without breathing. Shae's ears rang. Blood drained from her head. She was about to faint.

"You can't arrest me! I didn't do anything!"

Arrest her? Shae wished she could laugh—she wished the girl knew how funny that was. Shae stared at the girl's features, her perfectly arched brows, almond-shaped eyes, slender nose. Long wavy blonde hair. She tried to comfort herself by believing pretty girls wouldn't hurt each other. Like a silent pretty-girls honor code.

Tears puddled in the sharp corners of Shae's eyes. She dug a fingernail deep into her palm to stop herself from crying.

The dog sat on its haunches and yelped. Sweat beaded under her arms, and for a split second, she panicked about sweating through her top—but she wasn't wearing Donna Karan. And she wasn't on set. If only.

"No, *me*? I'm not a cop!"

The dog drew closer still. A menacing gurgle dripped from clenched teeth.

"I'm not going to jail! Who's gonna defend me? Nobody! Who's gonna believe me? Nobody! Only rich people have that luxury. We're easy targets. Just another disposable. Well, one Foster is enough!" She paced in short snaps behind the couch, her fury escalating. Arms flying in a riot of gestures. "Look at Denise now —a damaged, drug addict dealer. You think people come out of jail ready to dazzle Fortune 500 companies? After Denise got out, she tried one scheme after another. One of those schemes involved me! I was a kid!" She gripped the back of the hands. "She told me if I didn't do what she said, I better move out!"

Didn't she hear Shae? She beat her fist on the couch. Not listening to a word. They were having two separate conversations simultaneously.

"So here I am. A million miles away from her doing my best. But trouble finds me anyway. Right in the middle of my living room! That's b.s.!"

Shae couldn't listen to her. She needed to ration her focus. On the dog. She needed to get out. Find Jim. The music outside grew louder. He was probably looking for her.

Shae eyeballed the dog's throat. She judged her ability to kick it if necessary.

"What exactly do you have on me? You saw me talking to a guy?" She drummed her long fingers on her forearm. "I told him to blow off." She shuddered. "I wasn't there to *do* the guy. I was looking for someone. Why did you follow me home? Why didn't you pull me over?"

Wait.

What?

Something started to crystallize in Shae's mind. Like brain binoculars dialing in.

Shae shook her head. "*No.* No, no." Shae stammered. "I didn't follow you. It wasn't me. I followed *Jim*." Warm tears leaked out. She couldn't stop shaking her head. "*Jim.*" Her brain was thawing. "Not you." Shae was adamant. "God no."

She shook her head a few hundred times. "I work with Jim," she babbled. "He's the new cameraman. They wanted me to follow him. I didn't know how to get here."

"Wait. You *work* with the guy in the car? That asshole's a *cop?*" She smacked her hands together and whirled in a circle. "Jesus! He was gonna take photos?" She stabbed her finger at Shae. "I never got in his car!"

Shae's brain tried to send her a message. She ignored it.

"No...good. Yeah, I...I didn't get in his car either. I don't trust him—he's a drunk. Practically. Well, I don't *know* that...but he drinks...a *ton.*" Shae lost her point.

They both talked aloud to themselves.

Shae cracked her head to the side. Glimpsed out the window. "He's outside—with the others. Somewhere." Her feet were cemented to the floor. She couldn't muster the guts to turn around. To turn her back on Jaws in the process. She crouched a tiny bit to look out the window again to see if Jim's car was still there. Somehow she already knew.

"He was driving like crazy, of all of the people to follow," Shae said. "Why would they have me follow him?" Shae tasted salt on her lips.

"I was looking for Jenna," the girl said, quieter. "She's caught up with the wrong people. I'm getting her off the street. I got her a job at the diner."

"Theo said not to follow him. Theo looks out for me. Figgy thinks he's strange. But he's a decent guy."

"I'm not looking for a medal from you. What do you know about needing money to survive? You got a job. You got a place to live. Fancy clothes." The girl stared at Shae's handbag. Shae pulled it closer. "Jenna's holed up at a motel with some pimp drug dealer. Why don't you go after him? I'll give you his number." She stomped, and the floor shook. It cued the dog into machine gun yelps. "Don't you have anything better to do! Isn't there a violent gang or drug traffickers you could shake down? Or murderers on a day off? You're a lady—whose side are you on?"

The girl raged at Shae, whose thoughts reeled like a combination lock. Spinning right, spinning left. The floor shifted under Shae's feet as she grew dizzy.

Oh God.

She shuddered at the chain of events. Lined them up and pulled the shackle.

She hadn't followed Jim.

She'd followed her.

CHAPTER 12

Shae

Thursday, December 31, 2015, 11:06 p.m.

Laguna Crescent? Was Shae delusional? Of course this wasn't Laguna Crescent!

What the hell was wrong with her? How long was it going to take? The party? It wasn't next door. Jim's car? It wasn't Jim's car. When did it stop being Jim's car? Who knows! Jim's car wasn't on this street now or *ever*. Wherever her friends were, they were together. Shae was alone. They were laughing and drinking. Shae was shaking and sweating. Shae's friends were nowhere near here.

Nowhere. Near. Here.

In the ten minutes Shae had been in this house, she'd amassed enough triggers for a lifetime.

"That's okay," Shae offered, both of them oblivious to each other. "These things happen, right? You're clearly busy—I mean, I'm obviously—this isn't Laguna Crescent."

Did she say that out loud? Or to herself?

Herself.

Out loud.

It didn't matter. The girl ranted on. Her anger escalated. She wasn't listening to Shae anyway.

Shae needed to get the hell out of there. Her friends would be looking for her soon. Worried sick about her. Theo would find her. Or Figgy. Someone.

"So if you're a cop, how'd you get the key?" A chilly gaze eked out of her. "Moretti's sister? She still alive?" Her nostrils flared. "That's still breaking and entering!" She wiped her forehead with the back of her hand. "Everybody at church knew about Mr. Moretti. Father Joseph—everybody! It's no secret! Momma took care of him like he was family." She leaned on the back of the couch. A look of deduction washed over her face.

Her voice dropped to a whisper. "I know who's in on this! *Him!*" She swung her arm toward the side of the house, with an accusing finger as taut as a tightrope. "Big *Marty*, that *wretched* busybody. What did he tell you?" She darted about the room. "That he hasn't seen the old man's caregiver? That's because she's sick! That he hasn't seen the old man?" She was talking to herself. She spun around. "That's because he's dead!"

The outburst triggered the dog as if they were some kind of performance duo.

Shae scanned the room. It was sparse and smelled of old people. An ancient braided rug, a turquoise couch from God knows what era, a boombox, a plant. A drooling four-legged monster that could devour her whole. She needed a plan. The girl wasn't focused on her right now. She was in her own world. Shae's gaze stalled on the skinny table in the hall under the mirror. On top were a lace doily, an old telephone, a lipstick, and a gun.

Shae's eyes grew like a bee sting. She tried to find something else to look at. The curved back of the stiff couch. Gray damask floor-to-ceiling curtains, out of place in this room. The boombox on the side table. The wig. Anything. But that gun was an eyeball magnet. The girl followed Shae's gaze. Then whipped her head back at Shae.

She quietly walked backward toward the hall, careful not to turn away from Shae. Her hand fished around for the wall so she could navigate without looking. She stopped at the skinny table.

"He doesn't know anything," the girl said in a measured tone. "He's a lazy busybody. In his muumuus. And plastic beads. Like he's on some year-round Mardi Gras float. And all those crazy cats —at least *twenty*. You're going to listen to him?"

The girl fidgeted with the table's drawer, using her body to block what she was doing, keeping an eye on Shae. With her back to Shae, she walked to the wing chair in the corner of the room. Now was Shae's moment. *Now.*

The dog's chin jerked up, as if reading Shae's mind.

The girl twirled around. "So Moretti's not here. He died! Okay? There's nothing illegal about us living here. Moretti wanted us here." She dusted off her clothes.

Jesus. Please stop talking. Shae didn't want to hear a single word more. She couldn't listen to another utterance from this possible hooker/squatter. Maybe worse.

"I get what you're doing. The intimidation game. That's your MO. It's pathetic. That's how somebody like Denise gets arrested."

The dog turned to sit next to the bowl—both sets of eyes glued on Shae.

Every third word seeped into Shae's head. Prostitutes and prison. Dead people and disappearance. Pistols and pills. She didn't have a single lint ball of brain space for the girl's ramblings.

"If you don't control your dog, I'm slapping you with a summons," Shae blurted.

Where the hell did that come from? Was that a thing?

That shocked the girl. She pointed and yelled, "That dog's not mine!"

"Doesn't matter. That dog jumps me and—and—" And what? "You'll be joining your mother." Shae was stunned that these words escaped her mouth.

That silenced the girl, at least for a second. She stared at Shae's neck. At her necklace. The platinum and diamond circle pendant. She wouldn't put anything past this girl. She was probably a thief, too. Shae subconsciously fidgeted with the pendant. If only she could distract the dog somehow.

The girl walked back to the table, about ten feet away, to the gun. Her back was turned.

The dog, at the same distance in the opposite direction, sat by the water bowl.

Shae's left hand disappeared into her handbag hanging from her shoulder. But not before she noticed her fingernails. Green, white, copper. *Seriously?*

Her fingers searched for the car remote.

She tucked the remote in her palm and concealed her hand inside the bag.

In one swift move, she tore the necklace from her neck, hurled it over the dog's head, yanked the door open, and pushed "unlock" on the remote.

Shae lunged over the threshold. And ran.

"Oh my God! *Noooo!*" the girl yelled from the house. *"Mooch!"*

A shot rang out.

The sound of the gun stopped everything.

It sliced through Shae's ears. It silenced the night. It severed the cool dark air. Air that felt odd to Shae as she gulped it. It tasted of escape. Freedom. It was shocking how amazing and strange it felt.

Shae dropped hard to the ground. Her head whacked the edge of the path. Her *ankle*— it was in the dog's mouth. In the grip of its teeth. The dog tugged wildly. Dragging her body in short spurts. Scorching pain ricocheted up her leg. Shae wailed. Another crunch, teeth piercing skin, cracking bone. The dog crushed Shae's leg in its mouth.

Waves of shrieks filled Shae's mouth. Choked her ears. They came from her and at her. The dog released Shae's leg. There was a struggle beside Shae, moaning and crying as the girl wrestled the dog.

Then they were gone.

Shae couldn't move. Hard to breathe. Her head heavy, face pressed into the gritty ground. Gravel studded her gums. Waves of heat pinged up her calf, searing veins, singeing nerves. She whaled a horrific sound. Kaleidoscope colors whirled in her eyes. Blood flooded her mouth. Leaking to the ground, joining blood from her head and blood from her ankle, all streams meeting at a river. To take her home.

She made it. She was outside.

She was free.

CHAPTER 13

Honey

Thursday, December 31, 2015, 11:11 p.m.

"Mooch!" Honey shrieked. "Oh my God, *no!*"

She dove at the dog. *"Get off her! Get off!"* Honey dropped the gun and grabbed the ungrateful fool's collar with both hands. "She's a cop, you idiot!" With every ounce of strength, she yanked at the thin strip around Mooch's neck. The dog practically gagged up a lung.

"You stupid animal! Get inside!" Honey dug her bare heels into the dirt. She pulled his collar and fell backwards to the ground. "Jesus! Help me!"

She scrambled off the ground, grabbed the collar with one hand and used the weight of her body to pry the dog away. He was choking, gagging, gasping for air, but Honey didn't give one crap. At that moment, she would've killed that dog if she could.

"How stupid can you be! You think I need this? You think I need more trouble!"

Honey couldn't look at the cop, couldn't take the sounds and blood coming out of her. Mooch tore her leg to shreds. Little remained of that ankle. The bone popped out like a turkey timer. Everything was falling out of that leg. Honey could practically see up to the cop's kidneys.

She heaved her body toward the front door and the dog with her. She should've left him on the street where he belonged, begging for food and a home. What was she thinking, trying to rescue a street dog?

Honey's heart banged in her chest. She dragged Mooch across the living room floor and into the bathroom. She slammed that door with twenty-one years of bad luck. "Exactly where a piece of shit belongs!"

Back at the front door, against her will, Honey eyeballed the cop on the ground. No screaming. No squirming. Could've been passed out. Or dead. Blood everywhere.

Honey was screwed. This was an almighty disaster.

She picked up the gun, stepped back inside, and quietly closed the door. She needed to think. She patted down her hair. Smoothed her dress.

"Think, Honey! *Think!*"

She rushed to the kitchen with her head swirling. The first thing she spotted were her car keys on the counter next to the sink and took it as a sign. Honey swiped the keys, grabbed open the back door and bolted around the side of the house. Up the street, she jumped in her car. And took off.

Damn, damn, damn. She hit the wheel with her fist. Her bare foot pressed against the gas pedal. "Momma, I need you right now. I gotta get a dose of sense in me fast."

The dead-end street forced her to make a U-turn and drive in front of her own house. Past the cop. Damn dead end.

Wasn't *that* the truth.

"Nice one, God." She shook her head. "I'm seriously wondering whose side you're on."

Honey kept her eyes on the road. No way she wanted to see the front of her house. She started whistling a made-up tune. Minding her own business. Going for a nice drive.

At the last second...she couldn't help it. It was eerily still over there. A front yard that had a whole lot of whooping and barking and biting and shooting and howling and screaming a minute ago, now had nothing. No evidence of gunfire, dog attack, or possible cop death.

Except for the body lying there. And a puddle of blood.

The cop wasn't bringing any attention to herself. Not even a peep from Mooch, though he was probably sounding his alarm at being stuck in the bathroom, which always pissed him off.

The sign of a prize neighborhood, when *all that* doesn't bring a lick of attention. When even Big Marty was out on New Year's Eve, it was time to worry about your social life. Honey was worried about a lot more than her social life right now.

Honey's busted exhaust pipe clanking under the car was the only thing she could hear. It was comforting in a strange way. It sounded like old times. It reminded Honey of her life before a cop followed her home to bust her ass for doing nothing, and her goddamn stupid shit-for-brains dog mauled, and possibly killed, this cop.

Jesus, only a few hours ago she was just worrying about Momma dying and a friend in trouble. It was not possible for this day to get worse.

Honey headed to the bodegas on El Centro. Seeing humanity would be good. Seeing how people without a care in the world act on New Year's Eve would eclipse what just happened. She'd be cleansed by the sight of kids drinking slushies and old men smoking cigarettes.

An image of the cop's ankle flashed across Honey's mind. She shouldn't have looked at that revolting thing. Would this happen for the rest of her life? When she least expected it? When she was living her ordinary hard-working life, would she see the cop's anklebone popped out in her mind's eye? A river of blood and leg guts on the ground?

Why was this happening to her? She was already over her head with Momma. She was close to losing the only person in the world who loved Honey unconditionally. And now this.

If Momma never got cancer, if Honey never rescued that foul dog thinking she could turn its sad life around, if Momma never agreed to take care of Mr. Moretti, if Momma never took that job at the church to begin with, if Momma never came to California looking for Honey, this never would've happened. If, if, if. If Honey was going down the *if* highway, this was all Honey's fault. It started with Honey running away from home and coming out here in the first place.

Who knows where the fault started? Actually, the fault was with Denise for giving birth to an "ungrateful, selfish kid," which was how Denise referred to Honey. She never wanted a kid, and she made Honey pay for that. She wouldn't even let Honey call her Mom. She was always trying to erase Honey in one way or another. Until Denise discovered it would be useful having someone around to expand her foothold in the illicit drug market. She tried to recruit Honey to sell dope to the middle school kids and at the high school. She told Honey if she didn't, she better find a new place to live. That, and the presence of a few of Denise's loser boyfriends, was the final straw that pushed Honey to leave home. To California and homelessness. Let's blame it all on Denise. That actually made Honey feel good for the first time today.

If Honey learned anything about being grateful, it wasn't from Denise. She was as selfish as they came. Honey didn't want to start pitying herself, but it sure would've been nice to have a father in her life when she was growing up. Someone who would've stood up for her. Protected her. Maybe even someone to do stuff with. Someone who liked her. Who she could depend on. There was no guarantee he would've been any of those things. He might've been just as scary as Denise and her sleazy boyfriends. Honey didn't know who her father was. She was never convinced Denise knew either. One thing was certain. Honey always had Momma.

But Momma wouldn't stand for whining about the cards they were dealt. She wasn't one to complain about her lot. She never blamed Honey for making them homeless. And she never threatened to take Honey back to Louisiana where they had a home. Instead, Momma chased after Honey, snatched her up, and brought her to church by the scruff of the neck like a lion with her cub. The church gave Momma a job and both of them a place to stay. Then Momma took Honey to the closest high school and told the principal Honey's story of running away from home, hoping to live her life without shame or fear. Momma told the principal, "Honey's a smart girl. She's got talent. Wait till you see her drawings." Honey never heard anyone talk about her like that, least of all to a stranger. "This girl's got purpose," Momma said and turned to Honey. "Don't let your life be a movie nobody came to see. Starting over won't be all fried-chicken-picnic. It's going to take work. That's okay. You can handle it." Momma fixed her eyes on Honey with one pair of glasses perched on top of her head, another pair on the slope of her nose. Those glasses must've been good for something, because Momma saw right through her.

That principal didn't know Momma was actually Honey's granny. She said, "Honey, you're lucky to have such a loving mother."

That's when it occurred to Honey how mommas were supposed to behave. What they were expected to do for their children. Sitting next to Momma, Honey beamed with pride. Her heart filled up like a soup pot. So full of love it nearly suffocated her lungs. It was the happiest memory she had.

She owed everything to Momma. Most of all, her example of always being grateful. Grateful to the church for giving Momma a job and letting them live there until they got on their feet. Grateful when somebody at church asked if Momma would move in with an ailing parishioner and take care of him. An old Italian guy who lived by himself and was housebound. Mr. Moretti.

"That's God's hand, right there," Momma told Honey. "He found us a home and a purpose. Never let anyone go invisible in this world."

And Honey was going to start pitying herself now? Momma wouldn't stand for it. "If you make a mess, Honey, clean it up." Momma was usually talking about Honey tracking mud inside the trailer when she was little. But the sentiment worked now, regardless.

Moving into Mr. Moretti's was the first time Honey ever lived in a house. It was a sign of good things to come. It opened her eyes to what could be. To how other people lived. And how she could live, too.

At a red light, a young kid ran up to Honey's passenger window. An old guy limped behind him with bags of noisemakers. "Happy New Year!" the kid said, leaning on the open window. The old guy blew into one, and the bright foil unfurled like a lizard's tongue. "You need some noisemakers!" It wasn't a question. "Three bucks for eight!" the kid said with a big smile.

Honey got choked up. "No, thanks." She could barely get the words out. Something about this kid and the old guy sharing a New Year's Eve together.

Honey waved the kid off. "I don't want any."

She was breaking her own rules right then. Namely, the "Don't let self-pity seep in or seep out" rule.

This driving around like old times was pointless. She couldn't keep driving for the rest of her life.

She made a U-turn. When Honey pulled back onto her street, the cop was still there. Honey hoped she'd be gone. As stupid as that was.

Honey's heart started up again. Pounding loud. She was going to have to deal with this, and she had no good ideas.

There were no signs of life coming from the cop. Honey could feel for a pulse but didn't want to touch her. She squatted and held her hand above the cop's mouth. Barely anything. She couldn't tell if it was a breeze or a breath. Honey kneeled on the ground beside the cop. If only she could text God. She didn't have too much faith He'd answer, but she had nothing to lose trying. She clasped her hands.

Dear God, it's me, Honey. I know I haven't been in touch since my pleas for Momma, and well, maybe you've been busy but you're really letting us down here. Momma's spiraling fast, and we haven't seen any evidence of your help. Seems like my prayers have pretty much gone unaddressed. My prayers for her to stop hurting. My prayers for you to take her home. My prayers for you not to take her home. Maybe you were like, girl, make up your mind. I don't have time for this.

So, if I'm being honest, I had it in me to break things off with you. So maybe it would free you up for some other unfortunates. But I'm back. And I need help like never before. Not for me, well maybe for me, indirectly. I hope I'm catching you at a better time. For the love of all things holy, please help me take care of this mess. Please don't let this cop die—if she hasn't already—for I'll surely go to jail. I can't go there. I'm scared of jail almost as much as I'm scared of hell—which I can't go to either. If I end up there, I'll never see Momma again—because we both know where she's heading. I don't mean that as a threat, I'm just saying.

Back to this current predicament. Let's focus, together. You have to trust me, Jesus. I will do right by this cop. I'll fix this. I promise. She didn't deserve this, I guess. Even though she busted into my house and was about to lock me up for doing nothing. If I save her life, I promise to think before I act next time. Please help me not screw up. I'm going to need to be a hero. It's the only thing that'll save me. Thanks for listening.

Honey dropped her face in her hands and unraveled fast. She pressed her eyes tight, rocked herself back and forth and wept until she had nothing left.

Honey heard something. A grumble. Her eyes flung open. She could've sworn the cop's fingers moved.

"You're alive!" Honey jumped to her feet. The cop's arm was outstretched on the ground like she was raising her hand. Her fingers wiggled. Crawling, like. Something was twinkling in the weeds, beyond the cop's hand. The silver metal of keys sparkled as they caught the moonlight.

Honey ran to the keys and snatched them off the ground. This was a sign from God. He was trusting Honey to clean this up. It was clear what she had to do. She had to bring the cop back in the house. Honey shook her head.

"I don't appreciate the irony, Jesus."

Honey kneeled back down on the ground at the cop's waist. Before she picked her up, she had to negotiate a few things with the cop. For the record.

"Okay, listen. That effing dog is not even *mine*. I already told you he's a stray. It's a long story. Maybe I didn't think it through, but that doesn't matter now. I planned on getting rid of him— that's obviously moved to the front burner.

"So, these are the options: I call an ambulance, and they take you to the ER. I made that mistake with Momma. She nearly died. If you die at the hospital, they'll come for me. I have no illusions about that. And I know what they'll do to me. No. You're not looking good from where I'm standing. And neither am I. Momma and God expect me to make things right, so you're coming with me."

Maybe it was Honey's purpose to make things right with the cop.

In the house, Honey put her on the sofa. She had no prayer of keeping the cushions from staining. Yeah, that sofa was old twenty years ago, and Mr. Moretti wasn't around anymore. But. He was proud of his stuff and shared everything he had with her and Momma. Honey didn't want to be the one ruining it. She found a few plastic bags to put under the cop's bleeding areas, but the damage had been done.

Honey kept checking the cop's pulse and hoped she didn't spot Honey feeling up her wrists. They were petite little things. She was a real puzzle, this cop. Sort of fragile-looking and pampered-pretty. Nothing Honey would've expected an officer to be. But life throws you some curve balls you can't always duck.

The leg would need cleaning. Right now, though, it was gushing like a hole in a sugar sack. A rag tied tightly around her knee was all Honey could do to get it to stop.

"As you know, I fully intend to get you back on your feet. So I was thinking, if you're feeling any sense of gratitude, perhaps you'll look beyond things you may consider infractions."

Nothing.

The cuckoo clock on the wall said it was almost eleven, which meant it was almost midnight. The clock didn't keep precise time; it was off by an hour and six minutes, which was close enough. Apart from winding it once a week, which already made Honey uptight—it was a Moretti family heirloom—she wasn't going to mess with time.

"It's almost midnight!" Honey slapped her lap. "The ball's about to drop." It was hard to get excited under the circumstances, but it never hurt to lighten things up. Honey grabbed the remote. Maybe some good old-fashioned New Year's Eve merriment would help them both. "Might as well. This is the last show we're going to watch together."

Ryan Seacrest and Jenny McCarthy were laughing up a storm. They'd make a decent couple if she wasn't married already.

"Only twenty-three seconds?" That cuckoo was more than a few tweets off.

"Nine! Eight!" Jenny shouted, bopping up and down in the crowd, her hair flying everywhere. "Five! Four! Three!"

"I guess we need to look on the bright side," Honey said to the cop. "We'll never have another New Year's Eve as bad as this one. At least we got *that* out of the way."

If only the cop would stop bleeding. Healing wouldn't start until that happened. When you lose that much blood, you have to replenish fluids. Honey jumped off the couch.

"Water okay?" Honey called from the kitchen, not expecting a response. She grabbed her favorite glasses from the cabinet—thick glass with air bubbles inside. Honey's stand-in for bubbly.

She returned to the couch carrying a tray with two glasses. One had a bendy straw she found in the back of a drawer. She placed the tray on the cop's chest to make it user-friendly.

"Better drink up."

Honey took her glass from the tray and tapped it lightly against the cop's glass and sighed a squall. She composed what she hoped looked like a smile.

"To us."

CHAPTER 14

Shae

Friday, January 1, 2016, 2:23 a.m.

"SWEETIE, you have to rest. You need your strength." The girl bent over and snatched Shae's car keys from the dirt, inches from her fingertips. "You don't need these," she laughed. "You're not going anywhere!" She cackled like a cartoon.

Two steps closer to the curb, she pointed her gun at Shae's back tires. A shot rang out. Then another. The tires gushed, and the car sank to the ground.

"Thank your lucky stars! If anyone else found you chewed up like this, they would dump you at the hospital. They would never take care of you like I will!"

The girl struggled to yank off Shae's shoes. "I'll take care of these for you." One shoe was blood-soaked. "We can't leave these nice shoes looking like this." She brought them into the house and dunked the clean one into a bucket of blood. "That's better."

She grabbed a pillow from the wing chair. "Where're my manners? That's no way to treat a visitor." Back outside, she fluffed the pillow and shoved it under Shae's head, so her face wasn't in the dirt. She returned to the house and wrung the blood out of Shae's handbag into the pail. "Come in when you're finished bleeding!"

Shae was burning up. Out of nowhere, her father, Peter, stood over her with suspicious eyes. He didn't believe Shae had a fever. He never believed her.

"I'm not lying," Shae insisted. "Here—look at the thermometer!"

She thrust the thermometer at him. "Here, look!" But instead of a thermometer, she handed him her leg.

"You don't need Capucine," he snapped. "The girl will take care of you. Capucine doesn't know anything." He was irritated. He hated looking for Capucine.

He took Shae's leg, grabbing it by the ankle, still bleeding. "You better not be faking!" And left in a huff. The front door slammed shut. Shae recognized her childhood bedroom.

How could her father trust the girl? She was stealing Shae's blood. Capucine would know what to do. Maybe she'd bring Shae a gift. A bunny. Or chocolate. Or car keys. Yes! Capucine was scrappy like that. Then Shae could drive away from here.

Shae's bedroom door was ajar, letting a sheet of light slip through. Shae smelled that smell. It was Capucine! She'd recognize it anywhere. The scent of her clothes. They might be dirty and old, but they carried souls of queens and starlets who wore them before her. That's why she didn't clean her clothes. She wasn't going to wash precious souls out of them!

There was no chatter between Peter and Capucine. What was taking so long?

Capucine! Shae's head thrashed back and forth against the pillow. But she couldn't move her body. She couldn't move her leg.

The *pain*. Circles of heat. Wildfires shot up her hip. It was real fever, not pretend. If only Shae could open her eyes. They were stuck closed. Her lashes were claws, locking her lids shut.

She heard a terrible, frightening moaning. The moaning grew louder, more desperate.

"*Rose?*"

Who was *Rose*? Where was Capucine?

"Rose, are you listening?"

The voice got louder, closer, clearer. It wasn't Capucine. Yet…it sounded familiar. Shae's mind was playing tricks on her. Was she home in France? Of course not. She hadn't been there in years. She thought Capucine was with her. Another trick. What was wrong with Shae? Her eyes were heavy. Her lids were leaden. Her lashes clasped together. Shae plied her lids apart a crack. *She had been dreaming.*

The moans grew louder. My God—the moans were coming from *Shae*.

"Rose?" someone called again.

Oh, no. Shae knew who it was. It was the girl. *The girl with the dog.*

A tremor rippled through her—and fixed on her left ankle. The iceberg in her mind thawed around the edges, sweating icy drops of recollection. The fever worked to melt her frozen brain. She was burning up, but somehow a chill seized her.

The girl's face floated in and out of Shae's mind. The girl had picked her up off the ground; Shae remembered that. Where did she bring her?

She heard—felt—a repetitive thumping. It was in perfect synchrony with her heartbeat. It thumped a foreboding message; she felt it in her throat. It was the rhythmic terror of a waiting dog.

A tiny sliver of light seeped through her lids, slipping between the bars her lashes created.

Was she coming out of anesthesia? Going under? She had a sense of not being there. Or anywhere. Of floating above her body. Of looking through a window at herself.

Something was terribly wrong with her. Her ankle. Her leg. Parts of it—all of it—were on fire. Pain pinged up and down. The bone sizzled. Her knee was a siren of throbbing circles.

Then...everything went...blank.

CHAPTER 15

Honey

Friday, January 1, 2016, 3:03 a.m.

AROUND three in the morning after she got the cop to stop bleeding, washed the bloody towels, and dumped some water outside on the blood-soaked ground, Honey went to attend to Momma and give her some chemo. After that, she'd say goodnight and go to sleep on the bed downstairs in the basement. Honey was exhausted. She sat in the chair next to Momma's bed with a heaviness she thought would crush the chair's creaky, fragile limbs. Momma and Honey joked about the chair having osteoporosis, like Momma.

"Sorry if it got a little crazy earlier. Uh, it's nothing to worry about, Momma." Honey gulped. "I got this under control. Gonna take care of everything, just like you taught me to do." She patted the tissue paper skin on Momma's hand and crooked a finger to stroke Momma's cheek with a feather touch. Her hair was long and thin and usually up in a bun, making Momma look regal. She hadn't worn her hair like that in over a month. Now it lay in long fingers across the pillow. Just then, Momma's eyelids fluttered, and she looked at Honey. Honey gasped. Momma's eyes were a fuzzy gray color, but seeing her eyes was a sign from God. A blessing. Momma gave Honey's hand the slightest squeeze. "Thank you, God, for this miracle!" Honey exclaimed. Momma's lips twitched; she was trying to open her mouth.

"What is it, Momma? What? I'm listening—I'm right here." Honey stood up.

Momma slowly closed her eyes and opened them again, just as slowly. It looked like her eyelids were waving. They took twice as long to close this time. When they did, Honey waited. She waited to see Momma's hazy eyes again. "Come on, Momma. Open your eyes. Say something. I'm listening!" Honey gagged on her plea. But that was it.

Momma was gone.

"Momma!" Honey cried. "Momma! No!" Honey put her ear to Momma's chest, but she already knew. She clutched Momma's sides and held her. Screaming. *"Momma—you can't go—please, no!"*

The unraveling came quick and fierce. She gasped through sobs. "No, Momma! You gotta come back!" Trying to get air, but choking on her breath. She sank to the floor. Transfixed with grief. Paralyzed with fear. With loneliness. Everything came at Honey in that moment. Every effed-up thing in her life, new and old.

How would she survive alone?

How could you prepare yourself for losing the one person in the world who loved you? Who'd do anything for you. Who *did* everything for you. And never expected anything in return.

Honey's body was a mound of loose rubber bands. Her mind was a lump of soggy cotton balls that leaked out her eye sockets. The worst night of her life was seeping into the worst day.

One minute Momma was there, the next she was gone. No take backsies. No JK-ing. No do-over.

Honey was pissed at God.

CHAPTER 16

Honey

Friday, January 1, 2016, 9:50 a.m.

I⸀ᴛ was barely ten a.m. on New Year's Day. The last twelve hours felt like weeks. Honey was spent. Emotionally and physically. She walked through the house, Mr. Moretti's loving home, gliding her fingertips across the walls of the hall, pressing her cheek against the basement door, caressing the upholstery and the satiny floral sprigs on the curtains. Like she was communing with the house. She fell to the floor and genuflected on both knees, tipping her head to the rug and stretching out her arms as far as they'd go —the rug in her grasp—as if to cling to as much as she could of this place. This precious place. She was so lucky to live here with Momma and Mr. Moretti. He loved Honey and was always happy to see her. He told her a story, and repeated it often as he became sicker, about his regret of never raising a family in this house. His wife wasn't able to have children. He'd say to Honey, "It's up to you to have a family here." It was a nice thought. One that she tried not to get too attached to. She always wondered if he knew what he was saying and if he meant what she thought he meant. It was nice thinking of Mr. Moretti's house as permanent and not temporary. Eventually, the grip of senility clenched his memory so hard, he didn't exactly know who Honey was. Or Momma.

Everything had changed in the blink of an eye.

Going to work was the last thing she wanted to do. She didn't want to experience one hangry customer or her slippery boss. Honey didn't have that kind of backbone today. Today, her bones were a pile of kindling.

Wasn't everyone just a pile of skin and bones? That's all, really. Everybody was made of the same stuff. The only thing that separates people is what they bring to the package: stuff you can't see or touch, but you can feel. Momma brought *everything* to her package. Everything. Goodness and light and happiness and trust and truth. And her peach pie was damn good, too.

Honey wished she could hit the pause button today. Life didn't go away on the days you needed to check out. How could she check out? The people in her life were either dying, missing, in trouble, or shaking her down. Plus, she needed the money.

This was one effed-up world. Where rich people complained about stupid shit, and poor people withered away between the cracks and died of cancer with no hope. Where gorgeous, privileged girls got the best boyfriends and good jobs, and the Jennas of the world were being pimped out by derelict boyfriends and the Honeys could be getting arrested anytime soon for doing nothing. She didn't want to get salty. She knew that in order for her heart to heal she'd need to stay positive. But she was only human. And she needed to take five from her positivity perch today.

Honey blew her nose. She was feeling like a failure for so much. She couldn't fail the cop.

At the cop's side, Honey examined her fancy black pants. They were messed up now, torn and bloodstained. At least they were wide-legged, making it easy for Honey to hike them up so the fabric didn't stick to the open wound. It wasn't a sight for wusses. Honey wrapped it in a hand towel so neither one of them had to see how gross it was.

Honey's phone pinged with a text from the Craigslist guy to confirm the TV pickup tomorrow. She totally forgot about him. She couldn't have him walk into her DIY triage, which is what Mr. Moretti's living room turned into overnight. Honey would need to shuffle some things around. Seeing a barely conscious cop could be alarming for anyone.

She couldn't think about any of that now. Her mind was mush.

The diner was open on New Year's Day, and Honey was scheduled to work. It was impossible to imagine herself working today. She was numb. Empty. How could she leave Momma? Well, she could leave Momma now. There was nothing she could do for her anymore. Honey should call 911. But that would mean she'd need to say her goodbyes. She couldn't bear that yet.

Was it okay to leave the cop? She couldn't stay home for the cop. If she called out on New Year's Day, Enrique would fire her. She needed this job. And there was nothing more she could do for the cop in the next few hours that she hadn't done already. Honey left her some Advil, a bowl of dry cereal and a glass of water.

Going to work would give Honey some distance. Maybe she'd see a clearer plan of action. The word *action* was too aggressive for her current state of mind. But strong, wise and resourceful would need to kick in soon, regardless of whether she was past grief-stricken and paralyzed.

She couldn't even move Jenna to the back burner. Honey wondered if Jimmy had taken Jenna's phone away. She hadn't returned a call or text in days. None of the explanations for that were attractive. Honey sat in her car in front of her house shaking like a leaf visualizing her pile of troubles. She didn't have the luxury of spreading things out. Things were barreling down on her all at once.

Honey jumped out of the car and returned to the house. On her way to the diner, she was stopping at Sweet Dreams, the motel where Jenna had been staying with Jimmy, and she needed her wig. She didn't want to walk up the parking lot stairs to their room on the third floor in broad daylight, when the back stairs were more secluded and hardly used by anyone. But the last time she was there she noticed that someone busted the security cameras on the parking lot stairs. So it was the better option as long as no one was hanging out in the lot.

She'd worn her wig more in the last week than she had in years. Maybe she was kidding herself, but she hoped her Demi Lovato hair would be enough to throw off someone who'd otherwise recognize her. Like Jimmy. Over the years, it had given her some kind of superpower when she needed it.

She had history with that wig. It wasn't always Demi hair.

When Honey was young, the girl next door was having a moving sale in her front yard. Out of curiosity, Honey went to check it out. Not that she had money to buy anything, she wanted to see what other people owned. What she saw was a big pile of sad, wrinkled clothes lumped on the ground. It was the strands of a wig that caught her attention. The black hair was long and straight, with gray mixed in, part of a zombie costume. Nobody was around, so Honey pulled the wig from the pile. It was surprisingly silky. She imagined what she'd look like in it. She wanted that wig so bad. Even with the gray—she could color over it. Honey wasn't allowed to wear her hair long because Denise didn't want to be combing lice out of Honey's hair every time some dumb kid at school got it. So Denise cropped Honey's hair short. And kept it that way. Honey looked like a boy and hated it. She never complained about not having a nice place to live, or nice clothes, or nice shoes, or a nice backpack, or nice things. Or even a nice mother. Her hair was the only nice thing she had. It cost Denise nothing, but she wouldn't let Honey have it. She never did get lice, not once. The last day Honey remembers having hair long enough to wear in a ponytail was the day Denise's boyfriend said, "Honey sure is pretty. Where'd she get that hair? Not from you, Denise."

She longed to feel her hair tickle her shoulders. That wig would be the only way. At least for Halloween. That nice girl ended up hiding the costume under Honey's front steps before she moved away. The next Halloween, Honey put on the black, bloody shredded zombie robe, and Denise approved.

When Honey put the wig on and smiled like a beauty queen, Denise shook her head.

"You know what your problem is?" Denise said. "You smile too much. All day long, that *smile*. What do you have to smile about? I'll tell you what—*nothing*. Your smile's as dumb as you are."

Denise couldn't ever let Honey be glad about anything. She wanted all the happiness for herself, even though her happy tank was always empty.

Momma told Honey all people have kindness somewhere inside even if they don't show it on the outside. Honey didn't know what kind of flashlight, magnifying glass, x-ray machine, or K9 dog would be able to find Denise's, but Honey sure as hell couldn't. Except Denise's boyfriends could. For them she oozed her special brand of Southern nectar. All pink in the middle like a Venus flytrap.

As she turned to leave something caught her eye. The gun she kept under a glass bowl on the hall table like some kind of museum artifact. She snatched that, too. It dropped like a brick to the bottom of her bag. Well, not *her* bag, exactly—the cop's bag. Honey convinced herself it was okay to borrow it. Now there was another mouth to feed, and she'd need to bring home more leftovers from the diner.

Everyone knew assorted unfortunates lived at the motel on Esplanade. It was one step above homeless. Momma and Honey could've ended up there if the church hadn't given them a place to stay. That thought made her shake more.

Jimmy's car wasn't in the lot or anywhere in sight. Honey put herself in some kind of trance to get out of the car and walk up the stairs with the spotlight of the sun on her, wearing her wig like it was armor. If only the staircase wasn't in full view of the lot. Anyone could see her taking those stairs to his room. She knocked softly but kept her eye on the stairs and any cars coming or going. Usually there was a lot of commotion around here, but it was quiet as church on Monday. She knocked again, real light. The last time she "visited," she gave it a regular knock, and the guy next door came out.

No answer.

Honey's body was humming. She swore she'd never come back here. So what the hell was she doing? This was a bad idea ten miles away. She ignored her fear, and her sweaty hand tried the knob. No MF pimp junkie was going to take her girl and scare the crap out of her. No MFing way to that. Her other hand was in her bag, fingers on the pistol. She prayed she wouldn't need to use it.

Honey had a bad feeling all of a sudden that Jimmy was in there. Just because his car wasn't around didn't mean anything. She could open the door, and he could be standing right there with that cocky grin on his face. Honey curled her fingers around the barrel of the gun, ready to clock him in the head.

She twisted the knob. And pushed. The door swung open like the cover of *Us Weekly*. It was too dark. She couldn't see anything. In the time it took to adjust her eyes, Jimmy could've jumped her.

No sign of anyone. Honey kept squinting to avoid seeing the specifics. As she snuck into the room, she knew she was pussy-footing into a movie she'd never watch in a million years. She left the door ajar for a fast exit. Her heart was beating hard, like someone was punching her chest from the inside. What a hellhole. The smell of vomit hit her hard in the face. Honey lived in a palace compared to this.

No Jenna.

She was about to leave when she spotted a truckload of pill bottles on the nightstand. Could be Jimmy's stuff. But Jenna's name was on the labels. Sweet Jesus, she had more pills than Tijuana. Honey recognized a couple: amoxicillin, clindamycin. Jenna wouldn't notice a few missing. Honey could use them for the cop.

God helped those who help themselves. Hopefully.

Later that day, after her shift at the diner, Honey realized things were no less grim at home. Not a twitch from the cop, lying there with her mouth open. It reminded Honey of Denise after a bender. Except the cop had blood in her beauty-pageant hair instead of vomit. One of her fake eyelashes was stuck to her cheek. Maybe it was a good thing the cop was sleeping, but Honey needed to get her to drink something and take some antibiotics.

There was something else she had to do that she wasn't looking forward to, but Honey didn't see an alternative. She searched around the house for a pair of scissors and found them downstairs in the dresser. Back at the cop's side, she considered the best way to do what she was about to do.

First, she'd need to take off the cop's pants.

CHAPTER 17

Shae

Friday, January, 1, 2016, 5:30 p.m.

S HARP flicks jabbed at Shae's mouth. Her lips were forced apart
and fingers shoved their way past her teeth. Fingers writhed
on her tongue. She wanted to pull her head back, to bite, to spit.
But her reflexes didn't work.

A hand grabbed her chin and held her head still. Something
bitter lay on her tongue. She gagged. Her head flung forward.
A sharp mass jutted into the side of her throat. She coughed vi-
olently, gagging. Fingers returned. Nails flicked the back of her
mouth. She convulsed, hurling everything.

"Jesus, girl! I don't have time for this! You need to take these."

The girl.

"You wanna die?"

Die? Maybe. Shae didn't know. She had no thoughts. At least
none were accessible. She couldn't hold onto a single one.

"Rose, I need your help!"

Someone else was here. Rose. What did they want with Shae?

As voices crept into her consciousness, Shae's sleep coma slowly dissolved. She needed to be alert. She struggled to be attentive. But her body and mind weren't listening to instructions.

Then an idea emerged. Maybe she could persuade Rose to help her.

A light went on overhead. The glow warmed her eyelids.

A hand at the back of Shae's head forced it up. Her neck strained. Something pried her lips apart and smacked against her teeth.

Shae peeked through slits. The girl stood over her. She held a cup at Shae's chin. The smooth plastic of a straw touched her lips. Without thinking, Shae sucked at the drink. What was it? Where was Rose? Her eyeballs were hot. The girl's lips moved. Over and over. Words upon words upon words.

Then everything went dark.

Voices hovered over Shae. She slowly opened her eyes and peered through a gauzy blur. It was difficult to focus. Shae found her hand wedged into the crevice between two cushions, hard and musty smelling. Like the couch was eating her. Her other hand grazed the floor.

Voices drifted. In and out of Shae's consciousness.

Bleeding... Fever... Yank the clot... Dead... Jenna's pills...

A phone chimed in the distance.

A *phone*. It sounded like a rescue.

The girl appeared with the phone to her ear. "Hello?"

Shae sent a message to her brain: *Stay awake, keep your eyes open.* Every small act challenged her. If Shae could get her hands on that phone, she could call someone. If only she could speak to the person on the phone right now.

Shae told her brain to speak. *Words, Shae.*

Nothing.

"Yes, she's still here." The girl sank heavily into a chair.

Help me! Shae screamed in her head. Words piled up in her mouth. They tried to get out. *Open your mouth, Shae!*

"Yeah, I spoke to him." The girl turned away. "He's gonna dig the hole. She's small but still needs a big hole."

Shae's mouth finally opened.

But the words were gone.

CHAPTER 18

Shae

Saturday, January 2, 2016, 9:05 a.m.

SHAE felt fingers on her stomach. They curled around the waist of her pants and tugged. Shae jerked and reached for her pants.

"Shit!" someone blurted.

Shae's heart gonged. She struggled to emerge from a fog.

The light in the room stung her eyes. She blinked and squinted to adjust to the brightness. She couldn't remember where she was or what day it was. Her head pounded—the blood throbbed through her ears. She was desperate for water. Her tongue stuck to her teeth.

The girl burst from a door in the corner, talking on the phone. She looked crazed. What was this place? Nothing looked familiar. A patchwork of cardboard squares, drawings of people, lined the walls. The air was cool. There was a musty smell. Her heart raced like it knew something that hadn't arrived at her brain yet. It was strange, this place. It wasn't the girl's living room. No turquoise couch. No radio. No plant. No dog.

Could it be Rose's house?

The girl lowered her voice. "I still have her…no, I didn't call 911." She spoke fast. Shae struggled to keep up. "Know what a casket goes for? How can people afford to die anymore?"

Was Shae dead?

"I'm not whispering." The girl slammed a drawer. "You have to help me. I don't know what to do…I had to shuffle things around —I didn't want to—the guy came early—wasn't supposed to be till later—" She walked in circles. "I'm *not* going to keep her here!"

Shae forced herself to think. But as soon as she had a thought, it disappeared like the trail of a plane in the sky. Separating into tiny specks until it was gone.

"I don't know what I'm talking about—stop yelling at me!"

Shae's heavy-lidded half-opened eyes peered through black bars. *Bars?* Where was she?

"The weasel who bought the TV swindled me out of five bucks. I let him have it. I don't have time for negotiations and sob stories. I needed the $25. Couch goes tomorrow."

Shae pressed her eyes closed and opened again. This time the bars were crooked. She rubbed her eye with a fist, and her lashes stuck to it.

The ones Figgy glued on.

Figgy.

Shae rolled Figgy's name around her mind. It was strange to think about her. How long had it been? Where was Figgy now? Was she looking for Shae?

"Wait, somebody's calling." The girl looked at her phone. "It's the diner. Pray it's not Enrique. Call you later."

The girl noticed Shae looking at her. She fumbled with her phone and put it back to her ear. "Hello—oh, Enrique. Every-thing okay?"

Shae stared down at her body like it wasn't hers. She gasped. She wasn't wearing her pants.

A pair of track shorts cut across her legs mid-thigh. Shae's hands moved to tug the shorts up. She pulled, but every move was clumsy and labored. She had no strength. The shorts were stuck—on *a diaper*.

Shae gasped again without sound.

"I don't know where Jenna is...I wouldn't call her a dope head ...I wouldn't call her *that*, either, where'd you hear that? Okay —it's none of my business...I haven't heard from her." The girl paced frantically. "I know you're not running a charity halfway house for no effed-up junkie losers in your restaurant." She rolled her eyes. "Stealing?" She stopped pacing. "Nobody I know. Like what, straws—or something bigger?"

The girl retrieved her handbag from the top of a red dresser. It looked like Shae's handbag. Then, as if windshield wipers turned on in Shae's mind, things slowly came into focus. It *was* Shae's handbag. Shae's chest fluttered. It was like seeing an old friend. If only Shae could have it next to her, to touch it, to smell it, to have her things...to call someone.

The girl rifled through Shae's bag. What was she looking for? Shae's ankle throbbed with pain. She squeezed the sides of the stiff canvas cushion underneath her.

The girl pulled something from the bag wrapped in white paper.

Shae didn't recognize it. The girl skittered around the room. The phone pressed to her ear with her shoulder. Her hands obscured the small white package. She walked to a bookcase under a tiny window that was near the ceiling. This must be the girl's basement. She threw the crumbled white bag on top of the bookcase and wiped her hands on her pants.

"I don't know if anybody's stealing. For the record, though, people could be taking leftovers home—I'm just saying." She chewed her nails.

"Yes, I know what time it is…I *won't* be late!" She poked the phone screen. "Yuck! What a sleazebag. I need a shower!"

She flitted around stuffing things into Shae's purse. Fixing her hair. Powdering her face. Lipstick. She was a blur. It made Shae dizzy.

"I don't know how much of Enrique I can take today," the girl mumbled to herself. "Thinking about his angry spittle on my face as he gets going about Jenna missing three days in a row makes me want to cry! Even though it's not me who's the no-show, it won't stop him from screaming at me." Was she talking to Shae? "I'm the one covering for that girl!"

The girl swung the bag over her shoulder and ran to the stairs. She smacked her head with her palm and came back. At the dresser, she rummaged through the top drawer, twirled around, and before Shae realized what was happening, something flew through the air and landed on her lap. She flinched.

"I cut the sides so it slides under your bottom."

A pull-up.

Shae struggled to keep her eyes open. She was so drowsy. *Stay alert.*

The girl rambled on. She snapped her fingers, and Shae's eyes popped open.

"Listen."

Talking and talking. Words flew through the air like diapers.

"Keep drinking…lost blood…can't be late."

Her hand disappeared into the bag. "Pretty sure these are antibiotics." She shook a pack of Tic Tacs above her head. "Pink ones

…blue ones…three times a day, or all together for extra help…eat some food…hurt your stomach…means you're alive."

Did Shae see Capucine in the room? Ask Capucine what to do.

"Didn't touch the sandwich…don't waste…egg salad's no good, eat the bread…more later."

She dragged a small table within reach. She left the Tic Tacs, water, and sandwich. She wanted to drug Shae. Give her rancid eggs.

"Going to work…your ankle…don't look…the pus…getting better." She waved. "It's nothing."

How could Shae go to *work*? In these clothes? A diaper?

Shae's handbag hung from the girl's shoulder.

The girl pulled it close. "Just borrowing…hide food…not getting *fired*."

Shae would definitely be fired if she showed up to work in a diaper. Shae was pulling away now, taking off. Floating high above on a magic carpet.

"Depends." She pointed. "Bed pan." She pointed closer. "Toilet." She pointed far. "When you have get-up-and-go." She climbed the stairs.

Get up and go. That's *it*.

"Jijee ma ma ffff."

The girl whipped around. "What?"

Shae said something. *That's right, Shae. Speak up for yourself!*

"Jijee ma ma ffff."

But the girl was gone. The basement door bolted. The front door clicked shut. A jingle from the wobbly metal doorknob. Shae felt it in her hand. She was holding it tight. Time was a thief. And a liar.

Shae's stomach lurched. The smell of rotten fish filled her nose. A warm, putrid, fishy smell. A pungent awful fish guts stench. It repulsed her. It roused her stomach with grief. She noticed a metallic chalkiness laced her tongue. She was desperate for water. Did the girl drug her water? She'd dump the water. And flush the pills.

Then *get up and go.*

Finally. A plan.

CHAPTER 19

Lawrence

Saturday, January 2, 2016, 9:15 a.m.

L AWRENCE tore open the bedroom door. "Rita! What did you do with my ring?"

He hated when Rita closed the bedroom door. She always woke first. Then she'd close the door and slink downstairs. What was she hiding?

"Rita!"

She bolted up the stairs, panting. "I'm coming!"

He hated waiting for her. But with his sour mood mounting steadily, everything she did this weekend poked his patience. Stoked his snit. Frankly speaking, he couldn't deny that the source of his petulance was not actually Rita.

He shouldn't have brought Shae's file home this weekend. Not because it was against protocol and could potentially cost him his job—Shae's well-being and safety were worth the risk, and his actions were absolutely defensible—but spending the weekend pouring over the horrific details of her stalking, albeit in the past

—thank *God*—not only preoccupied him for the last two days but exacerbated his bad mood.

Add to that, coincidentally, not a word from Shae in thirty-six hours. Certainly, she deserved a day or two off, but it wasn't like her to abandon her social pages, especially on New Year's Eve. Not a single pic of a party? A glamour shot in an alluring dress, clinking champagne glasses? Highly unusual.

And now—his missing ring!

Rita bounded through the bedroom door and made a beeline to the bed, tucking the sheets in the corners and smoothing the comforter.

"Your ring? I didn't do anything with your ring."

"Well, somebody did something with it. I left it right there," Lawrence flung his hand—pointer finger taut—toward his night-stand, "where I always leave it. This isn't good. It's a bad sign when my ring is lost."

She dropped to her knees to look under the bed.

"Don't get ahead of yourself, Lawrence. We'll find it," she yelled into the dark cavern.

Half of her disappeared under the bed, leaving her ass in the air. She had a pretty nice ass, actually. It wasn't the first time Lawrence noticed, but he had a new appreciation from this angle.

Lawrence touched the smooth skin of his ring finger, where his Delta State 2000 Football Championship college ring would typi-cally be. The skin was soft and silky, like the inside cup of a rose petal. Skin protected from the harsh realities of life.

"This is bad luck, Rita." He paced the foot of the bed. "I've never not worn that ring. Not since my senior year of college. It's not a good omen."

"It's right *here*! Here it is! Lawrence, I told you." She jumped up from the floor, blowing on the ring. "Oh, it's a beauty."

"Okay, all right, you don't have to breathe on it like that."

She rubbed it on her shirt.

"I never noticed how stunning it is." She examined both sides, then weighed it in her hand. "It's heavy! And *sparkly*. I'll wash it if you want."

"No. That's enough. Just give it to me."

She smiled as she handed it over. "You must've been quite the football star. I wish I could've seen you play, Lawrence." She squeezed his bicep and oozed Rita-gush. "You must've looked hot in those pants!"

He shrugged while rubbing the ring on his shirt before returning it to his finger.

She opened the blinds and cracked a window.

"Did you press my khakis? Or my shirt? No one will take me seriously in a wrinkled shirt."

Her shoulders slumped forward. "Not yet."

"What are you waiting for? You want me to go out in my boxers?"

"It's your day off, Lawrence. Put on some jeans. You'd look hot in jeans. You haven't worn the ones I gave you for Christmas." She knelt at his dresser and pulled open the bottom drawer. She stood up and offered them to Lawrence.

"I told you to return them. I'm not a jeans guy. Jeans are for slouches. I'm a khakis guy. Why are you trying to change me? There are plenty of women out there who'd appreciate me for who I am."

She walked back to the dresser. "Yeah, I'm sure they'd appreciate being the ironing girl, too." She mumbled and shut the drawer.

"What was that?"

"Nothing." She walked into the hall. Hopefully, for her sake, to heat up the iron.

"I don't want to be an asshole, Rita, but—"

Rita sighed dramatically. "I've got news for you," she called back. "Someone who says that as often as you do is not very convincing."

Lawrence followed her to the laundry room.

"I worked the late shift last night," she added. As if that was an excuse to shirk one's responsibilities. She took the ironing board from the laundry and opened it in Lawrence's office.

"You need to find a new place to do the ironing. This is my office. Things happen here that shouldn't mingle with domesticity."

Rita sprayed starch on the pants. "I don't even know what that means." She turned around, looking for something.

Lawrence pointed to the iron on the floor, which *someone* left under his desk. It wasn't him.

"After I iron these clothes of yours, I'm going to the grocery. And a quick stop for a chai latte, so if you want anything from Starbucks, text me. I won't be long. It's better if we leave on the early side for the Botanical Gardens."

"Botanical Gardens? I can't go to the Botanical Gardens. I've got work to do. Sorry I can't smell the roses with you, Rita. Not everyone is free as a bird like you."

She plugged in the iron, then faced him. "But Lawrence, you've been working so hard. It's making you irritable. You've practically moved into the Ironing Room."

"It's my *office*," he said, clenching his teeth.

She threw her hands up, then flipped the pants over. "You can take a few hours off."

"I don't think you understand. I'm working on something that could save someone's life. Someone in peril! What if something happened to her? What would I tell her loved ones? 'Sorry, I wanted to go to the Botanical Gardens.'"

She sprayed more starch. "Your favorite horticulturist is doing a talk at eleven. I thought you'd like to catch that."

"Okay, all right," Lawrence put up a hand, "you don't have to say that. I don't have a favorite horticulturist. That makes me sound gay. You mean the rose guy?"

"The lily guy."

"Oh. I like that guy." Lawrence looked out the window. "He might have something new. He better be working on a hybrid. The daylilies I planted are not thriving."

It was nice of Rita to suggest they go see his favorite horticulturist.

"Listen...I've worked hard to get where I am today. I'm still proving myself. It's important work I do, okay? Not like—" He stopped himself. Nursing was probably important, too.

She kept her head down the whole time. Attentively listening and not interrupting.

Rita's head popped up. "Sorry, did you ask me something?"

"Were you even listening to me!"

"Of course I was." She pulled the plug from the wall. "I agree."

"With what?"

She smoothed her hand over the pressed pants. "Everything."

Lawrence huffed. "Maybe I can be productive while you're at the grocery. If you'd stop distracting me, I could get something done."

Rita kissed him on the cheek and handed him his khakis. "Oh, good! It'll be fun. The butterfly habitat is there too this weekend!

You watch, all your crabbiness will disappear with some fresh air, butterflies, and flowers!" She smiled.

For all her obvious flaws, Rita was pretty solid. Still, there was a reason she was forty and unmarried. Before Lawrence came along, Rita was still living with her mother. Yes, it was the right thing for a daughter to do, especially a nurse, when her mother's Alzheimer's advanced. It's not like Rita's brother could do it—he had an important job. But six years? Rita told Lawrence it was impossible to maintain a job at the hospital and a social life while caring for her mother. Maybe it became a crutch for Rita.

It's not like Lawrence considered himself a hero, but he did swoop in to save Rita from a doomed life of lonely decrepitness. But he knew better than to be the sucker who gave in with a ring. People undoubtedly questioned why he was with someone so average. Truthfully, the hot ones weren't worth the trouble. They were always rubbing your nose in their hotness, threatening to leave you if you didn't buy them this or tell them that. The hotties always moved on. Rita, she'd stick around. How could she do better than Lawrence?

Once Rita's car pulled out and the garage door chugged closed, he withdrew a ziplock bag from the back of his pants.

When not at headquarters, Lawrence kept evidence in a plastic ziplock bag tucked into his pants. Of course, he could use a brief-case, but he wasn't a briefcase guy. When you carried a briefcase, people speculate what's in it. No need to rouse suspicion that he'd removed files from the Evidence Room. A violation that would get him fired. *If* he got caught. It was clear to Lawrence risks needed to be taken if an investigation as complicated and sensitive as this were to be solved. He'd be rewarded handsomely. Hence, his covert transport of evidence. Necessary even at home, with Rita the snooper.

He wriggled his large pale hands into the snug quarters of a new pair of gloves, snapped the cuff out of habit, and laid the contents of the file onto his desk. With undue difficulty, he squeezed into the chair, now pinned within inches of the desk because the damn ironing board was left out.

Looking at the interior photos of Shae's home—of her nightstand, the inside of closets, her medicine cabinet—reminded him of how strangely conflicted he was when Shae posted photos on Facebook of herself in her kitchen, cooking breakfast on a day off. Of course, he wanted to see her in the privacy of her natural habitat, but he didn't want everyone else to. He wanted that for himself. It took every ounce of strength not to take off his gloves and really touch the pictures, but he was a pro, if nothing else. He wasn't going to throw away everything he'd worked so hard for to indulge his urges.

When he first saw her real kitchen, he discovered those Facebook photos weren't taken in her kitchen after all. It was another IShop set. It surprised him, he had to admit. Her interaction with the coffee maker and the skillets were so natural. Even the open refrigerator was convincing. All her favorite things. Greek yogurt and Bibb lettuce, French mustard and almond milk.

Before seeing her home for the first time, Lawrence fantasized every detail. Part of it was a game; he wanted to see how well he knew her, how spot-on he was. There'd be some surprises, of course. How well can you ever know someone?

He gingerly removed the letters from the ziplock protective bag. Shae's stalker sent four letters. Three arrived at the studio in September—when Lawrence was working at his former precinct. A suspect was held for questioning back then but later released.

Someone was questioned two weeks ago for a separate incident. An alarming note and box of cookies were left in Shae's car. That person was released as well. It was determined she was a fan of Shae's, visiting the studio for a tour and innocently left Shae a Christmas gift. She saw Shae jump out of her car and tossed the package through an open window. Apparently, she was too starstruck to hand them to Shae. As far as Lawrence was concerned, this idiot remained a person of interest. It's textbook for stalkers to claim they're "fans" and, therefore, "harmless."

The disturbing news this week was that Shae received a new —fourth—letter, which resembled the ones she received in September. However, she hadn't yet been told about it. After the last "innocent" cookie farce, IShop management sent the new letter directly to headquarters to investigate so as not to cause Shae undue concern. Lawrence had already left for the day when it arrived, so even he hadn't read it yet. The only thing he knew was that the letter was postmarked September 30, 2015, yet it arrived on December 30.

He was told part of the address was missing from the envelope, which explained how it was delivered to the wrong address and meandered through the postal system for months. A truncated version of the address appeared on a small clear label, printed, strangely, on the diagonal. There was evidence of a missing second label. A small rectangular patch of chafed envelope—the same size of the label still stuck to the envelope—juxtaposed it. As if two were placed side by side, each bearing part of the address. Why would someone address an envelope that way? Astonishing it ever got to IShop.

He was crawling out of his skin, waiting for an email from Forensics with the report, which would include the letter itself.

For the last thirty-six hours, he'd refreshed his email inbox every few minutes.

Holiday weekends always slowed things down. As if that was an excuse to put up the "gone fishing" sign! He'd never condone the slightest lag in an investigation, but since he was the new guy, he wasn't about to crack the whip yet.

The sick bastard responsible for sending the letters would pay. Lawrence would see to that himself. To think of Shae living in terror, every day wondering if this psycho was across the country watching her on television or standing next to her at the dry cleaner—enraged him. Whoever this scumbag was, Lawrence would hunt him down, humiliate and punish him to the full extent of the law.

Lawrence placed the first three letters on the desktop in chronological order according to the postmarks. The envelopes were identical 9x12 brown Kraft. He opened the first with restrained rage and smelled the inside flap. His glove stuck to the tacky residue, which meant it was a glue-based adhesive, not the lickable kind which would furnish DNA.

He carefully tweezed out the stationary.

> *Dearest Shae,*
>
> *You're so pretty. Apart from your huge pores. I wouldn't have known, except I saw them close up. So close, I could touch you.*
>
> *Until next time.*
>
> *Forever yours.*

The second letter came in an identical envelope with an identical small clear rectangular label—one inch by two and a half inches. Identical typeface.

Dearest Shae,

Just kidding. You're not pretty at all. But nothing I can't fix with manicure scissors and a glue gun. You'll thank me.

Until next time.

Forever yours.

Lawrence shoved his back against the chair, causing it to screech wildly against the floor, pinning the ironing board against the opposite wall. He bolted from the chair. He didn't know what to do with himself. He was livid. He ripped his gloves off, threw them against the window and flipped the ironing board over.

In a rush so fast Lawrence couldn't defend himself, the gangly legs of the ironing board—with their enormous rolling pin feet—swung upwards like a croquet mallet and struck him in the balls.

"For fuck's sake!" He winced in pain, clutching himself. "How am I supposed to work in here!" He saw stars. "Assaulted in my own house!"

Rita knew that a man his size needed more room to roam than the average man. How did she expect him to function in his office with the ironing board left out! Jesus, she was kicking him in the balls even when she wasn't around.

Lawrence gathered himself. He'd make no progress if he let his emotions get in the way. *Man up, Lawrence.* He placed the ironing board upside down with the board on the floor. He'd fold it up and put it away. Even if it wasn't his job. Even if *he* wasn't the one who left it out. It wasn't even his ironing board!

He couldn't get the legs to fold. He grasped the feet and tried thrusting them together like a hedge clipper. They didn't budge.

"Jesus!" He was spending too much time on this, and Rita would be home soon, and he hadn't finished reading the letters.

Out of frustration and without thinking, he slammed his bare foot down on the mechanism. He yelped in pain. Electric-like tremors shot up his shin. Why the hell were there no directions? No buttons. No arrows. You needed to be an engineer to figure out this asshole contraption.

He wasn't going to ask Rita how to do it. She wouldn't show him up, closing an ironing board.

He righted the board again with its feet squarely on the ground, placed his palms on the flat surface, and pushed with all his might.

Nothing.

"Damn it!"

He shoved the board over again and instantly cupped his balls.

Lawrence roared in frustration. Thanks to Rita, it was highly improbable he'd be able to check his anger by the time they'd leave for the gardens to catch the lily guy.

He flared his nostrils and got a grip on himself. He stepped over the splayed legs of the ironing board to sit back down at the desk. From the top drawer, Lawrence plucked two fresh gloves and rammed his hands in.

The rumble of the garage door broke his seething. Damn it. He hadn't finished. He quickly returned the first two letters to their respective envelopes. It would take Rita *at least* sixty seconds to get out of the car, remove the packages, walk to the kitchen, put the packages down, and yell to Lawrence. When he didn't answer, she would walk down the hall to his office, at which time she'd knock. She wouldn't dare open the door without knocking. Rita was a shuffler, thankfully for Lawrence. God help her hospital patients breathing their last breath!

The third letter. Identical envelope, identical label, identical typeface, identical paper stock. He hated cheap printer paper.

Dingy color, texture, weight. Clearly, this guy knew nothing of such things. No class. Not an iota of pedigree, obviously. If he cared, he'd have used good stationery.

> *Dearest Shae,*
>
> *All those dairy items in your refrigerator. Fresh mozzarella and Dove Bars? You should know better than that. Aren't you lactose intolerant? Looking out for you.*
>
> *Forever yours.*

Lawrence could feel the rage in his chest. It coursed through every limb. He could barely contain himself. He had read this letter before, but the anger felt as raw as the first time.

The jingle of keys and the kitchen door opened.

How in God's name did this madman get into her kitchen to see the inside of her refrigerator? Lawrence had assumed the stalker was some garden-variety creep. The kind of middle-aged lowlife who lived in his mother's basement in the forgotten backroads of Arkansas and binge-watched Shae on IShop while he wrote these vile letters. It didn't look like that now. It appeared this degenerate was too close for comfort.

Rita's handbag whooshed across the kitchen table. "Lawrence!"

He hurried to stack the photos and returned them to the ziplock bag.

Rita's shuffle was getting closer.

Lawrence quickly refreshed his screen, and there it was. An email from Forensics!

A knock at the office door. Lawrence dove over the papers on his desk, using his broad shoulders to conceal his computer screen with the classified details of the email, in case Rita felt extra bold.

"Hold on!"

He clicked open the email. Lawrence bypassed the report and opened the attachment with photos of the newest letter.

"Lawrence?"

It was short. One line. No salutation. No closing. Rather hurried.

The police have the wrong suspect. I'm still here.

CHAPTER 20

Shae

Saturday, January 2, 2016, 10:35 am

THE cats wouldn't stop crying. Their eerie pleas crept under Shae's skin. Capucine said it was strange when strays came to this neighborhood. There was no loose garbage for them to rummage through on a nice street like this. They must be in heat. If you were unlucky enough to have a cat in heat under your window, it meant one thing, Capucine warned. "Trouble is coming."

Behind the wheel of her car, Shae was back in Paris. She turned up the radio to drown out the cats' cries. She wouldn't let them ruin her giddy mood. She was going home. She hadn't been there in so long, and her body tingled with joy. She was nearly there.

Shae sang a tune and couldn't remember being this happy. She whistled, driving faster, eager to get there. The neighborhood was exactly the same, like an old friend. Her favorite cafe with the best coffee. The place with amazing moules frites. She could practically smell the mussels.

The full moon with a subtle, wry smile across its face made her laugh out loud. She could see her apartment in the distance!

In front of her car, something appeared in the road. A cat. Shae slammed on the brakes. It pranced with high, exaggerated steps as if taunting her. It didn't even flinch from nearly being hit.

Shae's foot remained pressed on the brake until the cat was safely out of the way. Even then, she couldn't drive away, now that she realized it was a black cat. Capucine once cautioned that it was bad luck when a black cat crossed in front of your car. To erase the curse, another car would need to drive past Shae. She'd wait for another car, but her rearview mirror revealed a gray ribbon of open road. She'd pull over and wait. Shae surveyed the road ahead and gasped. Cats poured into the street. Hundreds of them. Every color and size.

There was no room for them all. They crawled on top of one another, piling high in order to fit. Shae shoved the gearshift into reverse and turned in her seat to look out through the back.

More cats. Thousands of them.

They cried their haunting yowl. Shae covered her ears and hummed to drown them out. Outside the driver's window, cats climbed on each other's backs to reach the roof of her car. They crawled on the hood and pressed against the windshield. Completely obscuring her view.

She'd run home. That's what she'd do. She was so close. She didn't need her car. She'd abandon it. And run. She grabbed the door handle and pushed. It wouldn't budge. The flood of cats rose quickly. Inch by inch, layers of cat bodies blocked her escape.

She couldn't get home.

She *wouldn't* get home.

The meows grew louder. Shae whipped her head from side to side; she felt something soft on her cheek. A pillow.

Her eyes fluttered open. *She'd been dreaming.*

She uncurled her grip of the stiff couch cushion. Her other hand had snuck through the back of the couch, through bars of the bamboo frame, her fingers curled tightly around one. Her left leg, too long for the length of the couch, teetered off the edge.

The dream shook her. The smell of rancid fish poked sharp bristles at Shae's nose. A framed picture of Jesus, Joseph, and Mary hung on the wall opposite her. Huddled around this picture were dozens of sketches—portraits—on torn pieces of cardboard, like a homemade patchwork wallpaper stuck to a cinderblock wall.

This was not Shae's house, indeed. The picture of Jesus, Joseph, and Mary made her uncomfortable. It pecked at the memory of her own family portrait, one she had drawn in grade school. Her classmates' taunts were inextricably entwined in that memory. It was odd when memories from a week ago were elusive, but those from childhood couldn't be buried deep enough to ever be free of.

In Shae's rudimentary drawing, she made a childish mistake of including their cleaning lady. She couldn't draw only herself and her father—two people didn't make a family. Plus, Capucine was the most interesting thing about Shae. If only Shae's portrait wasn't hung next to the classmate with a mom, dad, grandmother, two sisters, and a hamster. Some five-year-olds were very mean. Humiliation was a tattoo etched on the soul.

Shae hated art. Her pictures never resembled the thing they were supposed to. She much preferred writing stories. But the only kids who got to read their stories aloud on Storytelling Night were those whose family came. Shae never read hers. In the end, the activity that never let her down was reading. It didn't require a companion or audience.

She didn't stay long at that school. Her father's job changed often and took them from Florida to Dallas to Zurich, and back to Paris. In her next school, there was no artwork in the hall. No comparisons. No measuring up. No assignments that made kids reveal family matters or private things. Shae liked it there.

It seemed ridiculous now, after all these years and distance, that she never questioned her father about her mother. Shae was appalled at herself. Certainly, she thought about it all the time as a young girl. It was like a wound on her heart. Or a hole. Or a defect of her chromosomes. Half of her DNA was unaccounted for. She only knew of her father's half. Who did the other half of her DNA belong to? Why wasn't there any mention of her? Shae never felt like a whole person. Even to this day.

But she never asked. Did the opportunity never present itself? Actually, the discussion was effectively forbidden. Like a restricted area with taped off boundaries: "Caution. Do Not Enter."

Did it bring her father too much pain to think about? Was her mother a terrible person? Too awful to discuss with a young child?

When Shae was very young, she just thought she came without a mother. But the children at school told her differently. "Everyone has a mother," they said. "Where's yours?"

She didn't know.

"Who's yours?" they asked.

She didn't know that either.

Shae didn't realize until she was in college, maybe even early in her career, that's what kept her from making friends. In the second high school she attended (and sixth school in all), she was very close to having a new friend. Shae visited the girl's house several times, and it was time for Shae to reciprocate. But she didn't. It would ruin everything. The subject would eventually come up. The girl would want to know. "Where's your mom?" "Why doesn't she live here?" "Is she dead?"

Some combination of those questions would be asked. It made Shae sick in her stomach. It gave her a headache that would last days.

It became easier and less painful, to be by herself. To avoid making friends.

Shae got used to it. She didn't get lonely. Books kept her company.

A beam of sun shot through an open window, exposing a strip of window screen. Sun soaked a crumbled white bag at the top of the bookcase. Shae now recalled the girl tossed it there. Was there fish in it, soaking in the heat? The smell was sickening.

Shae craved the sun. She was desperate to feel it on her skin.

The beam of light reached all the way to the tiny table beside her and licked the water pitcher that sat on the table. Shae extended her arm to touch the sun, but her fingers wouldn't reach. She stretched her longest finger to peck at the pitcher's handle. If only she could curl her finger around it, she could pull the sun closer. Finally, her finger wrapped around the handle, and she inched it toward her. But the sun stayed behind, painting the tabletop instead. Her finger cramped. The pitcher teetered at the table's edge and crashed hard to the concrete floor—fireworks of brown pottery flashed everywhere. The water streaked in wispy streams. One lone drop of water remained on the table. It shimmered and shimmied though there wasn't so much as a tired breeze in the still room. How could it move? It gave Shae some kind of perverse hope.

A meow leaked through the window. Then another. And another. A chorus of cats. Was her mind playing tricks on her? Was she dreaming? She squeezed her eyes shut.

When her eyes flicked open, something moved outside the window. The sweep of a tail. The grass flattened under a paw. It was a cat. More paws, several legs.

Go away! She hated cats. More crowded into Shae's tiny rectangle of the world. She bit her lip and pinched her cheek. Was she awake or asleep?

A sliver of the girl's diatribe from New Year's Eve flashed across Shae's mind. *Big Marty*, the neighbor. The *nosy busybody* with tons of cats.

Another glance at the window, now they were gone.

"Hey!"

Shae craned her neck in hopes of seeing them again.

"Hey!" Shae heard her own voice; she was speaking aloud!

She tried to prop herself up with her fingertips against the couch cushions. The most dramatic movement she'd had in days. All her weight on ten skinny fingers elevated her butt an inch off the couch; her arms shook. Soaring pain shot down both legs. She didn't care.

"Hey!" she yelled with more effort. Where did they go? If she could only get them back, maybe Marty would come. The house next door was so close. Bars lined the basement window a few inches from the screen, but the window was open. Someone could hear her.

Her left leg slid off the couch, unintentionally. Like it was trying to escape. Shae wailed. What was wrong with this leg? It was her good one. She couldn't think about that now. She braced herself against the pain and arched her back.

Her body took over without conscious effort. Shae ignored the cold stabs of steel through the knee. Digging into bone. In and out like a screaming saw. She tried to lean on the ball of her foot. But instead, she collapsed to the floor, taking the table down with her.

Cries poured out of her. Pain ricocheted up and down both legs. Even the groans hurt. The sandwich plate shattered against the floor.

She ignored a sharp pull in her neck and the stabbing in her knee and the knife jabs in her ankle. The muscles in her fingers quivered as they tried to hold her body off the floor. She collapsed again. It was futile.

Shae massaged her neck. Sharp flashes of heat traveled up her neck behind her ear. Her right leg was swollen; an angry red ring circled the wound. A patchwork of gauze squares stuck to her ankle. They were shaded red and pink and yellow and gray, from various flesh conditions and stages of infection. Pus oozed through the crosshatch of the gauze. A bulge the size of a grapefruit obscured the knee of her "good" leg.

"Hey!" Shae called with a vestige of faux vigor.

A noise came in response. A rustling in the grass. A crunching of the weeds.

Oh my God, someone!

A long snout poked through the bars. Shae's head jerked back and hit the tabletop. She grabbed her head and winced in pain. She saw stars. She pressed her eyes shut and cradled her head.

The dog couldn't get in, but her body trembled regardless. The snout sniffed at the window and slipped through the bars, sticking its head as far as it could go. Then pressed its nose against the screen. Slowly, it opened its mouth and panted. Matted hair, saliva, and teeth. The dog retrieved its nose and twirled in a circle. Its long mangy tail teased at the window.

"Help!" Shae cried in a feeble voice. Her cheeks were wet from fear. The dog's head returned. It barked one crisp alarm. Upstairs, the girl's dog responded. They argued angrily.

The dog disappeared. Just like that.

Shae kept her eye on the barred rectangle. Her only access to the outside world.

She prayed for the cats to return. She clasped her hands and prayed.

This was a first. Formal prayer was not her thing. The picture of Jesus was looking at her. A cross hung on a tiny strip of wall between two doors across from the couch. Underneath it was a picture of the Virgin Mary holding Baby Jesus. Rosary beads dangled off the corner of the wood frame.

Hello, God?—Shae paused to consider what to say—then, like a miracle, outside the window—a shoe appeared! *My God.* And pants! Marty!

Her heart fluttered, and she pressed her hand against her chest to calm down so she could think. Her eyes leaked tears.

Nosy people loved to help people. She'd tell him about the girl and the gun. How she tried to shoot Shae. That the dog attacked her, that she was badly injured. That the girl tried to drug her. And stole her bag. She'd tell him about the old man who was missing or dead. She lifted her butt off the ground and tried to get closer. So he could see her.

Shae combed through her hair with her fingers—it was heavy and oily. She wet her fingertips with saliva and wiped under her eyes. She felt fake lashes stuck to her cheek and pulled them off her face. Her right arm stretched as far as it could toward the window. The sun! Across her arm, like a warm caress of hope. Then disappeared.

Because of Marty!

He cast a deep shadow into the room.

"Hey!" Shae cried.

Now knees poked through the bars!

"Hello?" A disembodied voice asked into the window. Shae couldn't see his face. Only his knees and the tips of his shoes.

"Hello!" Shae said. "Help!"

The knees parted, and a face appeared.

Shae gasped.

"What's going on?"

Shae jerked back and whacked her head hard on the table leg. It was the girl.

The girl shaded her eyes with her hand and peered into the basement. Pink fingertips curled around the iron bars. With her face squeezed between them, her nose touched the screen.

"What's happening down there!" The girl's face bobbed in and out of view. "It's so dark. *Jesus!*" Her face disappeared. "You're on the floor?"

She pulled on the bars and dipped in for another look.

"I can't deal with this right now! For God's sake—Enrique's gonna kill me if I'm late!"

Her knees disappeared. "I'm coming!" The girl ranted on her way around the house. The front door swooshed open and snapped shut. "Rose!" she called into the house.

Rose was here! Thank God. Now that Shae was caught yelling for help, what would the girl do to her?

The girl ran through the living room. Her footfall vibrated the ceiling. "First the Craigslist guy, now this!"

Shae struggled to lift herself off the floor. She couldn't.

The girl unbolted the basement door. It swung open, hit the wall, and shook the house. "Rose!" the girl yelled again.

The dog howled.

Shae prayed Rose would come downstairs this time.

The girl turned on the light and descended the stairs. A phone rang. She stopped midway. Only her shoes were in view.

"Marianne? I can't talk, the other Craigslist guy is coming *now*, not *tomorrow* like he was supposed to, and…" The girl was breathless. "What? Yes, yes, I promise. Okay, Sass Master. I wasn't going to keep her forever! I was emotional…do you know how hard this is for me? I know it's the right thing to do. Today. I promise."

Shae's head pounded as she struggled to catch every word. *Not keeping her forever. I'll let her go today. I promise.* Thank God! She rested her head on the floor for relief. Under the couch, she spotted a pen nestled in the dust bunnies. She snatched it and concealed it. She gripped a couch leg to steady the room from spinning.

The girl bolted down the remaining stairs and slammed the phone on the dresser.

"Jesus, Mary, and Joseph! What the hell is going on? I don't have time for this!"

Where was Rose?

A glint of metal glimmered from the girl's hand. Something caught the light of the single bulb hanging from the ceiling and twinkled. Something silver. She focused on the girl's hand. It twinkled again and winked at Shae.

Shae's keys! Her Tiffany silver keyring with little silver balls at each end. The "Return to Tiffany" tag, which the rep from Luminesence had engraved on the other side to say: #1.

The girl sailed by her. Shae's handbag hung from her shoulder like a third arm. She slid the keychain up and down the front of her shirt, wiping it clean, while darting around the tiny room—passing Shae twice, on the floor.

The girl blew hot breath on the keychain charm and rubbed some more while pinching the edges of it with her shirt like she didn't want to leave fingerprints. She worked quickly and placed it on the dresser.

Shae didn't need to worry, after all. Or scheme. Or plot. She didn't need Marty. She let go of the pen in her hand. She didn't need Rose. The girl had come to her senses. She was giving Shae her keys. And letting her go.

Shae felt ridiculous, now, lying on the floor. Attempting to get Marty's attention so he could save her? From what? The girl wasn't going to *harm* her.

"Sweet Jesus, how did you get down there? What's all this on the floor! Momma would be horrified!" She stopped short. "Wait. Is that Mr. Moretti's pitcher?" She paused her frantic pacing and examined the mess. "In all this time, we've never disrespected anything of his. His stuff was old, but he took care of it. He was proud of his stuff. I guess when you're privileged, you can break other people's stuff without caring." She threw her arms in the air.

She tiptoed but couldn't avoid stepping on the shards of ceramic crunching underfoot. At the side of the bed, she crouched and brushed the cracked pieces away, then knelt on the floor. She peered underneath the bed and shouted, "All you've done is destroy stuff! Blood on the couch, the rug, a smashed pitcher, bloody cushions! We're gonna have nothing left by the time you're gone!"

This time you're gone. Shae heard it straight from the girl's mouth. Shae was leaving!

Shae's thoughts became fuzzy, blurry. She forced herself to stay lucid. Holding onto images of home—luxurious things. Sleeping in her bed. The smell of clean sheets from the dryer. A hot bath. Thick tufts of soap lathering her skin. Her toilet. Her books.

The girl disappeared through a door in the corner of the room.

"Where the heck—" she mumbled as she swept in and out of view like a mosquito.

Visions of the dog flickered through Shae's thoughts. Could she get past the dog? In her mind, she practiced kicking the dog in the throat.

The girl dropped to the floor again and disappeared under the bed. She tugged and pushed things and sneezed.

"There it is!"

She pulled out a crutch. She blew away dust clusters with aggressive blasts.

Butterflies flitted around Shae's heart. All she cared about was going home.

The girl stood next to Shae. "Wake up. Come on." The girl winced at the sight of Shae's ankle. "Ooh, Jesus." Shae looked down at her leg, which, up until now, she had deliberately avoided. If she wasn't getting out of this place, seeing the curdling white pus and the angry red orbit on the tree stump of a mauled leg would've scared her. But she put it out of her mind. She was going home. She had the best doctors; they would take care of her.

The girl shook her head. "Come on. Let's do this. We need to hurry, I forgot all about the Craigslist guy coming, and I told Enrique I'd be on time!"

She bent over and grabbed Shae under the arm.

"Let's go." She pulled her from the floor.

They both wobbled; Shae was clumsy and awkward. Unable to stand.

"Can you put any weight on that leg? Try. Come on. You're doing good."

Shae pressed down on the heel of her left leg. Being vertical overwhelmed her with joy and gave her strength. Her eyes misted. Sharp, stabbing pain shot through her leg and settled in her knee. She buckled. She wouldn't let that defeat her. She exhaled deeply and tucked the crutch under her armpit. The pain in her leg was excruciating, but she didn't utter a sound. She leaned on a steel pole that supported the ceiling. The pole was cold and sweaty. A patch of peeling paint came off in her palm, leaving a splotch of rust behind. Shae paused with her hand resting on the pole to catch her breath before she tried again, while the girl quickly plucked the cushions from the couch. Shae's breath was rapid and raspy. How would she make it up the stairs? Her knee buckled, and she collapsed to the floor like a tower of toothpicks.

"Oh, Jesus!" The girl dropped the cushions. "You can't put weight on either leg." In one quick motion, the girl picked Shae up, cradled her, and brought her to the bed—in the opposite direction of the stairs.

She let go too high above the bed, and when Shae's body met it, her limbs bounced and rattled against the mattress. "Used to be Momma's—during better times." She choked up. "I'll take care of you next, Momma," the girl mumbled.

Who was she talking to? Shae was the only one there.

The girl quickly plucked four cushions from the floor where she dropped them. "Guess I'll take Moretti's bed—" she muttered. "I'll clean this mess up later. I don't have time now."

What was happening?

"You better eat up; you're as light as a rag doll." She threw the cushions up the stairs like she was playing ring toss. "Wish I was carrying you instead of this couch."

What?

Shae tried to process what the girl said. She didn't understand. Her keys remained on the dresser. The crutch lay on the floor among the broken pottery. She reviewed in her mind the progression of events. Shae was transfixed on the girl's every move and clung to every muttered syllable, hoping it would drive a stake through her crippling confusion. Which slowly morphed into rage.

Shae shouted at the girl. *What the hell's going on? What are you doing?*

The girl didn't flinch.

Shae shouted again, *Hey! Get me out of here!*

No reaction from the girl. She didn't pay Shae a sliver of attention.

Because Shae was shouting in her *mind*—not out loud!

The words were stuck in Shae's throat. She couldn't get them out. What was the matter with her? She was good at speaking. She was paid a lot of money to speak!

Shae shouted at the top of her lungs. But made no sound.

Shae started to cough wildly, but the girl was deliberate and worked quickly, folding the rattan frame of the couch. It snapped shut like a mousetrap on a tail. She tried to lift it but dragged it instead toward the stairs.

What do you want from me? Let me go! The girl was oblivious to Shae's tirade.

Jim's coming back. He's coming to arrest you.

How pathetic. Shae was threatening the girl *in her mind* with a guy who was no closer to being a cop than Shae was a caterpillar. Jim was a cameraman. Who needlessly carried a clipboard with a string tied to a pen, its cap smothered with teeth mark indentations. The clipboard had a single sheet of paper with doodles and tic-tac-toe games. By all accounts, Jim was a loser. How ironic that Shae was masquerading him as some modern-day Horatio Caine. In her *mind*, no less! Jim wasn't going to find her. It was rare that he could find his own car in the studio parking lot. Threatening this girl with Jim was absurd, even in fantasy.

A heavy knock at the front door startled both of them.

"Flygirl!" The sound of a man's voice stopped the girl in her tracks. Her eyes popped.

"Flygirl?" She bit her lip. "My user name!" She ran to her phone. "What time is it? My God, *Enrique's gonna kill me!*" She tucked the phone into her apron. At the steps, she shouted, "I'm coming!"

She picked up the end of the couch and dragged it against the concrete floor, sparking high-pitched shrieks. She struggled with the bulk of the couch frame, standing in the back of it while heaving the front half up in the air and shoving it onto the first step. She did this four more times. The handbag on her shoulder kept swinging into the couch, counteracting her efforts. She put it around her neck instead.

"Flygirl!" More pounding. "You coming or what!"

"Jesus—I hate being rushed," she muttered under her breath. "I'm coming! You were supposed to pick up tomorrow, *buddy!*" The girl squeezed her way between the couch and the wall to the other end and tried pulling instead.

If Shae screamed, the guy at the door would hear her. She opened her mouth, tightened her stomach muscles, and *screamed.* But nothing came. Not a word.

Don't worry, Shae. Rose will help. Rose was in the house. She would help Shae get out.

Shae quietly stewed and silently plotted. She was leaving today, one way or another, that was certain. She glanced at her keys on the dresser.

The couch barreled down the steps. "Jesus, Mary, and Joseph!" the girl screamed. Its bulky arms slammed the wall so hard the frame sprang open. "Goddammit!" She scrambled after it to wrestle it closed and yanked it back up the stairs. With every slam against the wall, Shae prayed the couch would burst into a million pieces.

The girl's body disappeared up the stairs, body part by body part.

Head, gone.

Elbows, gone.

Waist, gone.

When only her knees were visible, she bent down and stuck her head low enough for Shae to see her face. Her eyes searched the basement. Shae prayed she wasn't looking for the keys. She held her breath.

"After I unload this couch, I'm going to work." Her head disappeared.

She wasn't coming back for the keys.

The girl's hand grasped the railing, and her head shot back down again.

"By the way, I mailed your phone bill. It had a stamp. No point in getting a late fee."

What?

"That's how I knew your name was Rose."

Shae's breath stopped.

Figgy's phone bill.

Fire shot up her leg...it reached her heart and strangled it... squeezed it so hard the pounding pulsed through its grasp...or was that pounding at the door?

"I would've never guessed Rose. I've got a talent for guessing people's names. I would've said Sheila."

There was *no* Rose. Shae couldn't catch her breath. Her chest tightened. She couldn't see the girl anymore through the spots in her eyes.

Shae grabbed the side of the bed. She pinched a slender bit of skin on her stomach, making sure her nails dug deep, then repeated this around her waistline. Her thoughts became slippery. *Hold on, Shae.* She wouldn't let herself succumb. She pinched herself again, harder. *Stay alert.*

Anger and confusion rose like floodwater inch by inch until it reached Shae's brain.

Her keys were still there, next to a small pillow. That's all that mattered. Nothing else. She didn't need her phone charger. Or her phone. Or Rose. Only her keys.

Oh, I can use my leg. No matter what. If I had only one leg, I'd use it. If I screamed in pain the entire way, I'd use it. If I had to crawl on my knees, if I was delirious with fever. Nothing would stop me.

"Should've charged more than thirty bucks for this! This is no crap couch." The girl called from the top of the stairs.

Shae eyeballed the crutch on the floor and her keys on the dresser.

There was a commotion at the door, which Shae blocked out in deference to her own fading mental capacity. She needed to parse her energy and strength and presence of mind. While Shae funneled all her focus on a plan, she didn't notice the girl. She was back in the room, mumbling about a throw pillow.

"I should've never had it in the photo, all this for $30! What am I, crazy?" She ran straight to the dresser, picked up the pillow, and swirled around. Her eyes met Shae's.

"I left your keys there with your stuff. I don't know if anything I say gets through. Most of the time, you look like you're asleep." She jogged to the steps and ran halfway up. She leaned on the railing. "I notice you don't keep your driver's license in your bag. Maybe when you're a cop, you don't have to worry about that—like normal people."

Shae blocked her out. She wouldn't allow that deranged psycho to defeat her. She couldn't risk losing courage or stamina for her escape. She wasn't asleep now! She dug deep into her own thoughts. Bolstering her resolve, repeating her plan to herself.

"I couldn't find your badge, either. I hope they're not in your glove compartment—"

Shae's heart beat wildly, her eyes were so heavy. They were closing. What? What about the glove compartment?

"Because your car's gone."

What did she say?

"You can't leave a nice car like that around here."

Shae looked at her keys, then at the girl. No. *No.*

The girl grimaced. "Gonzo Alonzo." She saluted.

No!

And just like that—so was she.

CHAPTER 21

Lawrence

Saturday, January 2, 2016, 12:30 p.m.

"Yes, sir." Lawrence swallowed hard as he ducked out of the conservatory where the lily guy was presenting: Water Lilies and Lotuses, Plants of Myth and Magic. Not what Lawrence anticipated, but fascinating just the same. A flash of bright light caught him in the eye as a cloud drifted away. He teetered for a second. This call from headquarters was highly unusual, causing him to feel off balance. "Got it," he said crisply.

The call ended. He stared into the distance at the enclosed butterfly garden. Numb. Incredulous. A butterfly broke his gaze as it flew right in front of his nose. Shockingly, it was a Blue Morpho. They were a rain forest butterfly from South America. Stunning with their blue iridescent wings. Lawrence had never seen one in real life. It must have escaped. He had once studied the Morpho. Intrigued by their glamour; their exotic metallic beauty. The fact that they were undoubtedly the most alluring species, but lived a solitary life, alone, had irritated and confused him. All that beauty wasted. It landed on a milkweed flower, the exact species he had planted in his own garden for precisely this reason. To lure butterflies, albeit monarchs. A creature which he typically marveled at. But even to this dazzling specimen he paid scant attention. Slowly, he slipped his phone into his khakis and closed his eyes.

He never imagined this call. Or had he? The conversation was brief. He feigned composure, confidence, courage. Because he had none. The news shook him. Perhaps there were other words spoken. Theories. Protocol. Next steps. But he didn't hear them. One sentence tilted his entire world.

"Shae Wilmont, the TV celebrity, is missing."

CHAPTER 22

Honey

Saturday, January 2, 2016, 6:20 p.m.

H ONEY was given a break between her double shifts. She went home to check on the cop.

She peered across the basement from the steps. Honey's heart hurt looking over at Momma's old bed, when she and Momma shared the basement. With Momma gone. And someone else in it.

She had never felt more like an adult than she did calling 911 and watching the ambulance take Momma away. She grew up pretty fast in that moment. But at the same time, she felt like a kid all on her own. There was so much she wished she had asked Momma. All that learning she missed out on; there was so much she didn't know about life.

She thought back on her last conversation with Momma. What had they talked about? Or the last time they laughed together. Or the last time they ate together. All the last times. But Honey didn't know it then.

Honey had a heavy lump of despair in her chest. It most likely wasn't going anywhere anytime soon. Maybe Momma was praying to go. If that was true, was it wrong to grieve? Was grieving feeling sorry for herself?

She didn't have the time or energy or strength to indulge herself in nostalgia now. She had precious minutes to check the cop for fever, change her bandage, give her antibiotics and something to drink. Maybe she could even get her to eat.

The cop was still as stone, her cheeks had taken on a flushed red. Honey quickly felt her forehead. The heat was troubling.

"I'm not fishing those pills out of your throat again." Honey knew she was talking mostly to herself. With the flat side of a butter knife, she crushed the pills—a couple of Jenna's and a couple Tylenol—and swept the powder into the cop's water, then used the straw to stir. She touched the straw to the cop's mouth, and she miraculously drank without opening her eyes. "You've got to keep hydrated. Don't let the fever spike."

Who knew if the cop heard anything, but she kept talking anyway. She had eaten some of her food. Now Honey needed to get her to drink more. Honey's phone vibrated in her pocket.

"Nice of you to call, Marianne. Did you listen to my messages?" Honey drummed her fingers on her hip.

"Yeah, sorry. Did you decide on Momma's funeral?"

Honey sighed. "Not exactly."

"Well, what are you waiting for? You don't have all the time in the world!"

"I know, Marianne! I've got—it's not—back off!"

"I'm sorry." Marianne huffed. "Listen, I don't mean to get on you. I'm a little frazzled right now." She started whimpering, then full-out crying a sloppy sandwich. "My girl's missing, and I'm a wreck!"

"I'm freaking, too! I've been searching like crazy—I even went to the Boulevard! I didn't tell you because…well, it's a long story. Some guy thought I was working! I almost got arrested! I'm not cut out for this. I even went back to Sweet Dreams looking for her. And now Jimmy's taking her to Texas! They might've left already!"

Nothing from Marianne.

"Who are you talking about?" Marianne finally said. *"Jenna?* What do you mean *missing*? I'm not talking about her. I'm talking about my girl from IShop."

Marianne blew her nose in B flat.

"Your girl from IShop? Jesus, Marianne. Are you serious? Stop crying over fake people. I have no time for that." Honey filled a glass with fresh water from the laundry sink and put it on the side table for the cop.

"She's not fake, Honey. She posted a video cooking breakfast on Thursday morning. Egg white omelet with red peppers, red and white for the holidays. She's creative like that. She even had a couple of shows that day. No one's seen her since! Who'll do *So Chic with Shae* now!"

How in God's name did people call Marianne the sensible one?

"You're working my last nerve! I got big-ass problems! Real ones! Are you listening?"

Wet whimpering from Marianne.

"I hate to tell you this, Marianne, but this IShop girl—you did not just *see* her. And she is *not* your friend. So stop calling her that. I don't have time or energy to talk you off a cliff over a fake friend."

"Well, we're friends on Facebook." Marianne exhaled. "I'm sorry, Honey, really I am. Especially about Momma. I know she was your everything. Life sucks. You know I'm here for you. Sorry I couldn't get you the money. My brother's so cheap. But I'll think of something. I promise." She blew her nose. "I don't know what to say about Jenna. I know you're worried. But let's face it, she's messed up. She could be a million places. But my IShop girl, how does a celebrity disappear? Everybody knows her!"

Jesus, Mary, and Joseph. Talk about gone.

"I'm sure you know every little short-hair about Shae or whatever her name is, but I have news for you—she doesn't know a goddamn thing about you. Because if she *did*, she'd know your best friend Honey is in a shitload of trouble!"

Right then, the cop let out a groan that sounded like a whale. Honey quickly pressed her phone against her chest and waited for the cop to finish.

"What the hell was that?" Marianne said.

"The TV."

"Thought you sold it."

"I mean...Mooch. He's farting like crazy!"

"You better get rid of that dog, Honey. Seriously, you can't even feed yourself. He's better off on the street."

That stung. "That's low, Marianne. That's real offensive—after everything I've done for Mooch. Listen to yourself. You're crying for a make-believe friend while I'm losing real people left and right and looking after a dog I took mercy on!"

Honey rolled her eyes. At Mission Hills Community College, Honey was the one who got straight A's, but Marianne was the one with common sense, the street smarts. She was the problem solver. She could get you out of a mess in the flash. It was almost a sport for her. But there were times that girl was some kind of stupid.

The cop hadn't moved a hair since the whale cry. It was probably time to take the hand towel off her leg and let it air out. Honey searched the room for the peroxide.

"Marianne, I gotta get back to work. I'll talk to you later. I'm multi-tasking up my ass while you're checking *Us Weekly* Insta posts."

The patchwork of gauze squares under the towel was reddish-brown in the middle and yellow around the edges. They clung to the cop's ankle in a way that the bloody, swollen, skinless tissue beaded through the flimsy cheesecloth. Honey grabbed the side of the bed to keep herself from passing out from the sight of the bloody Jell-O, though it looked a little better. She hoped it wasn't her imagination. She tried not to focus too closely as she cleaned the wound and applied clean gauze. This sight reminded her why she chose to be a hygienist instead of a dental assistant: less blood, more money.

Honey couldn't deal with Marianne right now.

"Maybe you can put your phone down for five minutes and help me find Jenna. Let me know." Honey snapped the phone shut before she said anything else she'd regret.

CHAPTER 23

Shae

Saturday, January 2, 2016, 11:45 p.m.

L IKE a headlight through fog, the girl's voice emerged in the basement. Shae drifted in and out of awareness. She had lost grasp of her condition, whereabouts, day, or time.

"Thanks for stopping by tonight. And for the tip. You didn't have to do that. You only ordered pie. It's not your fault you got a cold-hearted brother."

The girl was sitting on the basement stairs. Her feet, legs, lap, and one hand were visible.

"Yeah? What kind of ideas? ... Geez, why didn't I think of that? Father Joseph loved Momma. He would do anything for her. I'll ask him about the funeral. And the burial ... Cremation? Really? I'll call him tomorrow ... Yes, Marianne, you always come through." She stood up.

"What other idea? ... The handbag I brought to the diner last night? What about it?"

She sat back down.

"You've never seen that handbag before because it's new." She dipped her head down to peek between the spindles at Shae. "I didn't *buy* it. Seriously? I'm broke! You think I'm buying hand-bags?" She caressed the handbag on her lap. "It was a gift," she said softly.

"Tory Burch?" She held it in front of her face. "Never heard of her." She examined it closely, then lowered her voice. "No, she doesn't want it back…"

The girl stood and continued down the stairs with the hand-bag hung from her shoulder. "Really?" At the bedside table, she flicked open the Tic Tac box and tapped out two capsules. Twisted them open and poured the contents into Shae's water. Mixed it with a spoon. She walked toward the dresser.

"You sure?" With her pinkies erect, she daintily opened the handbag. "Yeah, I see it." She stuck her head inside. Then pulled her head out sharply. "Whoa—tuna. I better air it out." She waved her hand inside.

She turned her back to Shae, who had her eyes open a sliver. "On eBay? What can we get for it?" She gasped and held her hand over her mouth. "Jesus." She side-glanced Shae.

"Yes, I promise, she doesn't need it—*want it*—whatever! She gave it to me—as a thank-you gift." The girl became agitated. "You don't know *all* my friends! … Seven *days*? No way." She paced the room in short snaps. "I could be dead by then. Can't you sell stuff without an auction? … How *much* more?" The girl made eyes like the moon. "Okay, fine. Do the auction. Three days —that's it. And pray for a bidding war. I'll bring it in the morn-ing."

CHAPTER 24

Shae

Sunday, January 3, 2016, 1:10 a.m.

WHEN Shae woke up, she was shaking and sweating from a nightmare. She ran her fingertips across her mouth. No tape. And across her wrists. No chains. It wasn't real; it was a dream. She tried to reassure herself. The only problem was, being awake wasn't any better.

There was no sound of activity upstairs. The house was eerily calm.

Darkness filled the room except for the meek glow of a nightlight next to the dresser.

The sound of a key in the front door, metal dovetailing metal, rushed goosebumps across Shae's arms. The flimsy doorknob rattled and wobbled like a loose tooth. Shae could feel the phantom doorknob in her own grip—when her fate was still in her hands. How close she was to being free.

The front door swished open against the floor and slammed against the wall. The house trembled. The dog's tail thumped. Upstairs was only eight feet above but a million miles away.

Shae promised herself today would be the day she'd get out. She had promised herself that yesterday too.

Words were power in Shae's world. Shae knew how to use them. So where had they gone? Had she none left? Had she used them all up? Unspoken words piled up inside her. Creating a bunker she hid behind.

There was a struggle at the basement door. The muscles in Shae's stomach tensed. When the girl was home, Shae's fitful heart flip-flopped between panic and hope.

"Mooch—no! Get away!" the girl snapped. "Go!"

A door closed, and the dog's barks became muffled.

Something scraped along the ceiling. A thud hit the floor.

The front door slapped closed. The swish of the bolt. Footsteps. Running water in the kitchen. Muffled yelps.

"Shut up, Mooch! You're giving me a headache!"

Someone pounded on the front door. Shae jerked. She inhaled and held it.

The water turned off.

Silence.

Stillness.

More pounding. "Honey! You better open this fucking door! It's Jimmy. I know you're in there!"

Jim? Shae's heart leaped into her throat. *Oh my God!* He's here? Wait. He knows the girl? Shae tried to sew together fragments of memories, snippets of conversations. No. This was another Jim. This was Jimmy, the scumbag.

The slow creak of the basement door bolt slid back. Barely a squeak from the knob. The door whispered open. Then, an urgent swoosh. Something came barreling down the steps. Shae grabbed the sides of the mattress.

"I'm sorry," the girl whispered aggressively. "I'm so sorry."

A large green—something—a garment bag—hurtled down the stairs like a sled on ice. Halfway down, it slowed. Lumps and bulges got stuck in the bend. Then it shifted and wormed its way down, slowing almost to a complete stop on the last step when it thumped to the floor.

Shae gasped. Something happened she was sure was a delusion. It couldn't be real. Shae was in a pain haze, after all. She couldn't trust what she saw.

She rubbed her eyes with her fist. It was still there. She stared in horror. From the hole at the top of the bag, where the hanger should be, leaked a long tuft of straight brown hair and the tips of three fingers. Shae examined the rest of the bag. Lumps and bulges. More like elbows and knees. There was a body in that bag.

The basement door clicked softly closed. It wasn't clear what side of it the girl was on. Then she ran down after the bag. Shae shut her mouth and closed her eyes tight. *Please make all this go away. Please make this girl go away. And the bag with brown hair and fingers go away. Please let Jimmy go away.* Shae pretended she was sleeping. She pretended she was dead. Shae didn't want to be aware, awake, alive.

More pounding.

The dog howled an eerie call.

"Jimmy?" the girl whispered. "How does he know where I live?" she mumbled urgently. "How?" She paced. "He knows! He knows I have Jenna. *He* killed her! *He* did this! That lowlife sleazebag bastard! He's a criminal!"

Shae peeked through barely opened lids.

The girl bent over the garment bag and grabbed a corner. "Don't worry, Jenna. I won't let him take you," she said and pulled the bag across the floor to where the couch used to be.

The girl ran through a door in the corner and closed it softly behind her.

More pounding. *"Honey! I'm gonna bust this fucking door! I want my money now!"*

The door swung open in a whir, and the girl appeared with her eyes stretched open.

"Money? This can't be happening. Jesus, help me!"

She clasped her hands together and bowed her head. "Dear Heavenly Father," she whispered, "forgive me for getting in touch so last minute. But I don't have eight hundred dollars…don't ask me how *that* was calculated! I need your help!" She bolted to the red dresser. She yanked and slammed drawers, pulling things out with great flourish, like a magician.

Shae saw something familiar on top of the dresser. Her silver makeup bag. Right there. The girl pulled more from the drawer. Shae's things. *Her hairbrush. Her sunglass case.* A pang of longing thrummed in her chest. These were her things—it seemed from another lifetime. It was incredible to see them, like she hadn't seen them in years. The girl picked through Shae's belongings, half of them dropped to the floor.

"Who doesn't carry a wallet, *who!*"

The girl's cyclone came to an abrupt stop. "The gun." She chewed her bottom lip. "I missed Mooch, for God's sake! If I missed the goddamn dog ten feet away, how could I…" She shook her head. She was vomiting words Shae didn't want to hear. "He'll use it on *me!*"

She missed the *dog?* But...Shae was a knot of confusion. Her thoughts were colliding with one another and racing on a freeway in her mind. *The girl tried to shoot the dog?*

Why did Jimmy want money? To dig the hole? Yes. No. That was Angel. Shae was slipping into darkness. Who was Jim again? The cameraman? Yes, the pimp cameraman.

Shae was floating over the bed now, hovering in the air. But she could still feel the mattress beneath her. How could that be? She saw the brown-haired garment bag. With bumps and bulges. And elbows and knees. Jenna. With the tips of three fingers waving hello.

The dog's yelps were synchronized with the girl's panic and Shae's heartbeat. The girl darted around the room, swirling in circles like a Roomba. She stopped at the foot of the bed, yanked up the corner of the mattress, and stuck her head down there. "Where did I put those earrings?" she chastised herself. Her attention shifted back to the door in the corner. She shoved it open with such force it slammed the wall and swung back, hitting her. *"Jesus!"* She opened it again, slower, and disappeared from view.

"Here they are!" The girl was breathless. "Oh, Momma, please forgive me," she whispered. "But I need these." She emerged from the room, looking into a tiny box.

"Honey! I know you're in there!" He rapped hard against a window.

Shae felt woozy and blurry. Her thoughts were forming outside her body, not in her head. She could see sentences in the air.

A massive shove hit the house. "I'm gonna bust this fucking door!"

The girl's eyes darted everywhere. She looked scared, possessed, distraught. Her body flicked to a frenzy. She tinkered with something in her apron pocket while making a beeline toward Shae, who pressed her eyes shut, promising never to open them again.

Another eruption came from the front door.

"I need that bracelet. Is it real silver? Can I borrow that?" the girl asked Shae softly but urgently. "Maybe when you wake up, you won't remember you had it on, but if you do, I'm sorry. This is not stealing, because I'm asking for it. Plus, you're asleep, and if you're ever gonna wake up, this is protecting both of us, because, to be honest, our lives are at stake right now, trust me. If this guy says, 'I'm gonna kill you,' he's not over-promising."

The girl unfastened Shae's bracelet.

"If he kills me, where do you think that leaves you? Maybe with this bracelet, we'll both live another day. And honestly, it would've been nice for you to be awake right now. You could arrest that piece of shit."

CHAPTER 25

Honey

Sunday, January 3, 2016, 11:20 a.m.

It was later than Honey thought. She was moving like slow motion tree sap. She'd need to leave now if she wanted to drop the bag at Marianne's on her way to work.

When Marianne answered her door, she was talking on the phone as usual. She waved Honey inside, but Honey shook her head. She wanted to tell Marianne about Jenna, but she couldn't risk unraveling, and there'd be no avoiding it. A lot of effed up stuff was happening. Her emotions were bubbling close to the surface. She needed to keep herself pulled together. Honey would tell her later. She passed Marianne the handbag and left.

Driving to work, Honey felt herself sliding into despair despite every effort not to. It wasn't easy losing a loved one and a friend all in a weekend. It made her consider how she wanted to live her life, which seemed precious all of a sudden.

To Honey's surprise and relief, there was a parking spot on the side street adjacent to the diner. She never got one there. Now she could cut through the back alley and maybe still be on time. It might've been childish, but Honey always thought that getting a good parking spot meant it was a sign it would be a good day.

She grabbed her old handbag from the passenger seat, jumped out, and locked the car. She was about to silence her phone when she saw a new text from the financial aid lady at Mission Hills Community College. "We're reviewing your scholarship application." That couldn't be bad news, could it? It had to be good news, right?

It felt like she was getting angel love. There was an angel in heaven right now rooting for her. She found herself feeling something she hadn't felt in a long time: hopeful.

She put her phone in her apron and, out of habit, looked over her shoulder before walking into the alley like she did at night. But since it was the middle of the day, she had nothing to worry about.

People didn't ordinarily cut through the alley unless they worked at the diner or one of the shops next to it because there was no outlet on the other side. And because the alley was disgusting. The smell of garbage was repulsive. Rats shuffled around the dumpsters during the day like they owned the place. Plus, the shady owner of the bodega smoked cigarettes back there and yelled lewd stuff at Honey. Cutting through the alley was often the difference between being on time or bawled out by Enrique, so she held her breath and hustled through.

As she turned into the alley, she sensed someone walking behind her. More than one set of feet, actually. Their steps were faster than hers, which was unsettling. Despite the good vibes, Honey couldn't shake a creeping sense that something didn't feel right. Her positivity perch was getting shaken all of a sudden. Her legs quivered for no reason at all. She gave herself a pep talk and quickened her pace toward the diner.

She pulled her handbag close, though she didn't have any money. And picked up her pace. Fear was a real buzz kill.

"Hey, Honey," somebody called out. It was hard to tell if he was using a capital H or lowercase. She ignored him. She was nearly there.

As she arrived at the kitchen door and reached for the handle, someone from behind grabbed her handbag. She tried frantically to open the bulky door, but someone blocked her and shoved it closed. She opened her mouth to scream when a heavy blow across her back folded her in two.

CHAPTER 26

Lawrence

Monday, January 4, 2016, 7:45 a.m.

L AWRENCE listened from the upstairs hall to discern whether Rita was in the kitchen. He couldn't recall if she had the early shift. He hoped she'd left already. It was becoming exceedingly difficult to be charming in light of Shae's disappearance.

New information had recently come in. Shae's car had been re-covered fifty miles south of Vista Verde. Surprisingly, her wallet was in the car, under the passenger seat. Studying the latest information that the last time Shae was seen was at IShop studios on December 31 at approximately 9:30 p.m., leaving for a party she never showed up to, it was ludicrous that she wasn't reported missing until the morning of January 2, when she was due at the studio. Why had it taken so long? Precious time was lost. It made no sense. More confounding still was the arrival of a note, three months late, from a stalker who had been silent for months.

He tucked the plastic bag into the back waist of his pants and left his shirttails untucked. He didn't subscribe to this slovenly look, but he'd need to adopt it temporarily.

Rita was in the kitchen opening mail, eating oatmeal. "Good morning," he said.

She looked startled as she scrutinized Lawrence.

"You're not tucked in, Lawrence." She put down her spoon. "Where are your garters?"

"Jesus, Rita." She knew he hated that word. "You know what they're called. How difficult is it to say Tidy Tucks?"

"Tidy Tucks." She bounced her head from side to side. "You're right—and fun to say!" She waved her hand in the air like a white flag. "Sorry. You're so sensitive. Did you forget your Tidy Tucks?"

"No. I didn't forget them. I'm at home. A guy doesn't need to stay tucked at home." Lawrence tugged on the hem of his button-down.

"Oh." Her eyebrows bounced. "That's new." She eyed him up and down, smiling. "Very nice. I like the casual look on you, Lawrence. It shows a whole different side."

"Thanks." In the window of the kitchen door, he caught his reflection and fixed a tuft of hair that swept across his forehead while doing that thing with his eyes when he liked what he saw. Maybe it wasn't such a bad idea to adopt the casual look for the long run. He considered all the things he could hide in his pants and grabbed a mug from the cabinet.

The ziplock bag was stuck to his skin, his sweat sealing the deal. Exactly the way he liked it. Sweat drops trickled down his ass crack right there in the kitchen. Bodily fluids resulting from Shae as he chatted with suspicious Rita. He couldn't have planned for the excitement of this combination. The wild abandon of uncontrolled fluids felt pleasurable beyond expectation.

Even so, he was anxious for Rita to leave. A pointy plastic corner of the ziplock dug into the sensitive skin of his ass crack, and he badly needed to scratch. He tightened and relaxed his ass muscles repeatedly to try and shift things.

"Aren't you late?"

"No." Her eyes shifted to the clock on the stove. "You know I go in later. Let's have breakfast together."

"I can't." He sighed. "I'm late."

Rita squinted. "No, you're not."

"Well, I'm late if I want to be early." He returned the mug and grabbed his travel cup.

"Oh." She flipped through the mail before looking at his shirt. He grabbed the milk from the fridge and faced Rita so she wouldn't focus on his back. "This casual look suits you, Lawrence. It's nice to see you lightening up a bit."

He stopped pouring milk. "I'm not lightening up. I'm as serious as ever, tucked or untucked."

"I'm just saying, when you're smart and ambitious, no one cares about how you dress."

"And good-looking!"

"Of course!" she said with her mouth full of oatmeal.

"That's where you're wrong, Rita. If I'm going to be a triple threat, I need to look the part. You wouldn't understand. You don't have to worry about how you look when you're a nurse. You wear the same dreary uniform every day. Your brown hair is in a ponytail like everybody else's.

"It doesn't matter how I look! I'm an excellent nurse!"

Lawrence decided to keep his mouth shut.

She pulled her hair from her ponytail and took a sip of her latte.

In the car, he quickly peeled away the ziplock bag stuck to his back. He placed it on his lap and rested his hand on top while he drove. His eyebrow spasmed. Gently, he tugged a few strands of hair to settle it down.

Shae's disappearance was being investigated as an abduction, thus making it impossible to be excited about the access to her private life—newly available to Lawrence in his new position. Including information dating back to September. Lawrence wasn't completely surprised, because of his suspicions back then, that on September 17, Shae filed an official stalking complaint. It was about mid-September that Lawrence—well, all her fans—lost access to Shae. That's when he started the "Where's Shae?" Facebook campaign. His instincts were validated. He was spot-on. It enraged Lawrence to envision the fear that must've wracked her. A madman was out there, somewhere. Harassing Shae, sending her threatening letters. Who was it? Where was he now?

Isn't it funny how life works? Rewards, like the privileges of his new job, resulted from tenacity and perseverance. Putting one's nose to the grindstone. Keeping one's nose clean. There was a magical serendipity happening, but one he couldn't fully celebrate under the circumstances.

The universe was bellowing a succinct message to Lawrence: find Shae. He could and *would* be the hero.

His left eye twitched. It had a mind of its own, that eye. It wasn't actually his eye, but his brow. The eyebrow jerked so aggressively that his lid flicked upwards. A gentle tug of the brow was often all it took to soothe things, but not today.

A new text alerted him to a time change for the phone interview with Rose Figueroa, Shae's makeup artist at IShop. *Damn.* There'd be no chance of getting to headquarters by then. He'd pull over for the call so he could take notes. Lawrence took the next exit and parked at a Target. Another eyebrow spasm. It was driving him crazy today. Lawrence pressed his palm into his brow.

As a college freshman, Lawrence got the nickname Twitch because of that damn eyebrow. Courtesy of his roommate—the loser —Charlie. By all accounts, Charlie was a zero. He had pretty much nothing going for him. Except for fancy clothes, laundry service, and his father's credit card. Lawrence didn't need Charlie pointing out to him that his clothes were old-fashioned and worn out compared to Charlie's. It was strikingly obvious. Lawrence didn't know anyone who dressed like Charlie. Even Lawrence's own father didn't dress like Charlie, and he had somewhere to go.

"Did your grandpa loan you some clothes?" Charlie would smirk. Or "Salvation Army having a sale?"

The other guys on campus treated Charlie with a certain reverence because of the way he dressed. The guy was an absolute hamburger but garnered a disproportionate amount of respect courtesy of his pullover sweater, button-down shirt, and khakis pressed with a sharp crease running down the front. Pants that Lawrence didn't own. Actually, he owned none of it. Lawrence was a dumb kid, after all. He'd never met anyone like Charlie.

"You don't say too much, do you, Lawrence?" Charlie noted.

Why would that have bothered his roommate? Weren't quiet roommates favored?

"My father says to be careful of the quiet ones." Charlie loved to hear himself speak. "They're the ones who were watching instead of talking. Do I have to be worried about you watching me, Lawrence?" He shoved his hands in his khakis and straddled his feet. "I notice stuff too. Like when your eyebrow does that spastic thing, it twitches like it's doing right now." Lawrence reached up to touch his eyebrow to settle it. "Usually means you're up to something. Like that time you took that sweater from the lost and found before Christmas break. That wasn't your sweater, Twitch. Everybody knew your mother didn't buy you that. You were stupid enough to get caught. Dumb idea to wear it in front of the guy who lost it. Then you got accused of stealing. At least you're not a slacker. Everyone knows slackers are never crowned hero. If you're going to advance your cause by cutting corners, you can't get caught. You better learn to control that twitch, Twitch. It's an advertisement that you're up to something unsavory."

Unsavory? Who talked like that? None of the eighteen-year-olds Lawrence knew. Why couldn't Charlie use words everyone did? He was a loser all the same. Charlie cheated on tests and talked his way out of assignments. Lawrence heard he paid somebody to write his papers. A lot of good his fancy vocabulary did him. Talk about cutting corners to advance your cause. Charlie didn't think any of the rules applied to him. Guys like Charlie pissed Lawrence off. Charlie was right about one thing: Lawrence did his fair share of watching.

That summer, Lawrence got a job bagging groceries and saved his money to buy a pair of khakis, a V-neck sweater, and a dress shirt at the Salvation Army store in the wealthy town adjacent to Northbend. Rich people always gave away new clothes. Lawrence didn't dare ask his parents to buy them. They already thought college was a waste of money. He didn't want his parents changing their minds about college.

Back at school, he wore his new clothes every day. Even on the weekends. He jerry-rigged a technique to create the Charlie-crease for his khakis. He'd lay the heaviest textbooks on the legs of his pants overnight while they were slightly damp. By morning, they were pressed to perfection—with a rather sharp crease down the middle of each leg.

One day, he saw the girls upstairs using an iron. Who knew that asking to borrow it would score him residual points with the ladies? The new wardrobe stepped up Lawrence's social game. People took notice. They made certain assumptions they hadn't before. Appearances were everything, he learned. It was important to create a persona for oneself. Because if you didn't control your persona, someone else would. People started to see him for who he truly was. The real Lawrence.

Lawrence checked his phone. He punched in the phone number. Then entered his PIN.

"Hello?"

"Ms. Figueroa?"

"Yes."

"This is Detective Tramball from Vista Verde Police Department. I'm calling regarding the Shae Wilmont missing person's case."

"Yes. Hello, detective."

"Thank you for speaking with me today. Could you please state your name and spell your last name for the transcript? We are recording this call."

Rose Figueroa: My name is Rose Figueroa, F-I-G-U-E-R-O-A. My friends and people at work call me Figgy, my family calls me Rose.

Detective Tramball: Thank you, Ms. Figueroa. Could you tell me how you know Shae Wilmont and your relationship to her?

R. Figueroa: We work together at IShop. I do her makeup and hair. We're family. I'd do anything for her. So whatever you need from me, just ask.

L. Tramball: To clarify, when you say "family," you mean you're good friends or related?

R. Figueroa: She's like a sister to me. It doesn't matter that we're not blood-related.

L. Tramball: Do you know her family?

R. Figueroa: Her family? Uh, not really. Shae's always been vague about family. Something's going on there, but I don't pry. She hasn't talked to her father in years. No siblings. She doesn't know her mother. Never met her. Her father raised her with a bunch of nannies. All kinds of families out there. I'm not going to judge anyone for anything they have or don't have.

L. Tramball: When was the last time you saw Shae?

R. Figueroa: On New Year's Eve at the studio. Right before she left for the party. I was supposed to go with her, but the other makeup artist called in sick, so I stayed a few more hours to cover. I told Shae to wait for me so we'd go together. Shae didn't really want to go by herself, but she didn't want to wait, and she didn't want to jump in with somebody else, either. So that was that. I can't feel guilty. She made her own grown-up decisions. Even if they were the wrong ones. It was like she had something to prove, going. So look what happened. That girl—you don't always know what she's thinking.

L. Tramball: Could you tell me what she was wearing?

R. Figueroa: Oh, yeah, she looked good. Gray iridescent top, sleeveless Michael Kors, and black pants. Beautiful Tory Burch handbag that Tory made for her. Even autographed the inside! She made it special for Shae, the only one in the world in gold.

L. Tramball: Did she say anything that night that made you think she wasn't going to the party?

R. Figueroa: Not exactly. But you know, it wouldn't be the first time she said she was going somewhere and didn't show up. She's done that before. Even when I got to the party hours later, nobody thought something happened to her. We thought she never planned on coming. A few of us called her, but no answer. It still took too long to report her missing. I knew something was up when she didn't call back. They waited until she didn't come in to do her show on Saturday.

L. Tramball: What did Ms. Wilmont do at IShop?

R. Figueroa: What do you mean? She's a host! The biggest host we have. She's a celebrity. Look at her Instagram. She has more people following her than Beyonce, practically. Her fans are everything to her. She never wants to disappoint them. Maybe she cares too much what people think of her. She's always second-guessing everything she does. She might look like Homecoming Queen to the rest of the world, but I can tell you, she's never at ease. She must like to torture herself. Some people are like that. Nothing easy breezy about them.

L. Tramball: How do you mean, tortures herself?

R. Figueroa: You know, one day she's worried they'll give her shows to another host. She's worried they'll find someone new to replace her. She's afraid she won't sell anything, won't make her numbers. That girl could sell hair to a grizzly. You know she's #1 in sales—every month! She's obviously doing something right.

L. Tramball: Do you think she can't take the pressure of her job or the stalkers and that she might've checked out? Maybe she's not missing. Maybe she left and didn't tell anyone?

R. Figueroa: I thought about that. We're close, you know. If she wanted to do that, wouldn't she tell me? So I wouldn't worry. Who'd blame her? You think you know people, right? I hope she's on a beach somewhere. But that's not what my hunch is telling me. I have a bad feeling.

L. Tramball: Do people harass her on social media?

R. Figueroa: Well, IShop blocks the weirdos on her Facebook page. Can't blame Shae if she had enough of that. Never knowing if one of them is coming after her. Maybe one did this time.

You know, there was a guy who called the testimonial line recently, making strange comments. A real wacko. He wanted to see Shae wearing ham slices. You know—the spiral ham Shae sells? He wanted to smell her in them.

L. Tramball: Really?

R. Figueroa: Yeah, they blocked that guy. If I was in charge of this investigation, I'd start with him. And what about the package left in her car? From a fan? Hell, no! I never believed that. And those crazy letters she got in September. Whoever sent them said he wanted to cut her face up and glue it back together. Honestly, if it were me, I'd want out.

L. Tramball: Did Ms. Wilmont ever suspect anyone for sending the letters?

R. Figueroa: You mean Bryan? Is that what she told you? I'm not getting in the middle of that. But did you talk to Theo, the security guard? I'm not accusing him, but something's weird about him. He never talks to anyone but Shae. And not that this means anything, but get a good look at his eyes. You can learn a lot about somebody from their eyes. He's got a lot of white and just a little brown. Take a look. You're a detective, so you know what I'm talking about.

L. Tramball: Is Ms. Wilmont in a relationship with anyone?

R. Figueroa: Good question. We're always asking ourselves the same thing, why doesn't she have a boyfriend? Or maybe a girlfriend—who knows? A pretty girl. Successful. Nice to everyone.

Making all that money. And treating her friends to everything she has. Everyone's always trying to set her up, you know. She has plenty of interested guys. She tells people she's "taken." I can tell you, I've never seen her with anyone.

Sometimes you might hear her talking about her nephews, but the kids she's talking about are no relation to her. They're *my* little brothers. She came to my mother's funeral, you know. Didn't tell me she was coming. Just showed up in my tiny hometown outside of Toronto. She took off three days for the travel and everything. That really touched me.

L. Tramball: That's very nice.

R. Figueroa: She has a lot of people looking for her. Even her fans. People are playing detective—posting clues on social. People are claiming they've seen her. We're depending on you to find her.

L. Tramball: Are there any physical traits that would identify her—moles, tattoos, colored contacts, et cetera?

R. Figueroa: Oh yeah, she has a butterfly tattoo on the back of her neck. Same color as her hair. We had a strange conversation about that once, come to think of it. I always remember it when I see a butterfly flying around. She told me butterflies have the best of both worlds. People like looking at them because they're beautiful, but they can disguise themselves whenever they want. They camouflage themselves to hide from predators. That stuck with me. Made me sad. She seemed jealous of a butterfly. All because it could disappear in plain sight.

L. Tramball: Are you saying—

R. Figueroa: I'm not saying anything. I just remembered that story, that's all.

CHAPTER 27

Shae

Monday, January 4, 2016, 11:00 a.m.

THE pain came on a steady, unrelenting loop. It corroded Shae's capacity to think, shifting her mind's mechanism. Her cognitive wheels had become unnotched, spinning out of orbit, lost in the universe. Shae's delusions were real and her reality absurd. It was no longer possible to tell them apart.

Shae was alone in the room. It had been a while since she'd seen or heard the girl, though she had no concept of time. The room felt different, forgotten. Like a faded photograph. A bleached window curtain.

All was still and quiet. Dim and blurry. Was she floating? Yes. She was someplace in the middle. She had entered another place. She was leaving. Untethered to reality. Time was a ghost. She existed between the minutes. Between the hours. Nothing marked time or place. Not a wash of sunshine, chirping birds, hunger pains, bathroom urges, the girl, the dog—nothing.

At some point, pieces of sound congealed. Sounds became voices. Talking and laughing. Reels and reels of chatter. Men and women. Circles of words. Swirling and swirling.

"An accident. Critical condition. Looking for the driver. Traffic backup. Right lane closed."

Maybe Shae was driving, though she didn't feel the wheel in her hands. No brake pedal underfoot.

"Leaving on a jet plane...Peter, Paul, and Mary."

The airport. That's where she was. Waiting for a plane. But she didn't pack. No change of clothes.

"Test drive the new Honda. New information about Shae Wilmont...missing...IShop. After this."

Shae's eyelids fluttered. Her hands flew outstretched in front of her to grab the voices. To pull the words back. They slipped through her fingers. Where did they go? They were sold out. No more words. She could hear their faint trail. She could taste them. They were in her mouth. Lots and lots of them. Stuffed into her cheeks for safekeeping.

Not the slightest whisper of voices remained. Instead, thumping. Slow, intermittent thumping. A long, pained groan followed. Human? Animal? Thumps morphed into footfall. On the stairs? Nudging Shae's memory. Breaking into her consciousness. She was vaguely aware of stairs. At random, Shae grasped snatches of the world around her. Slipping in, sliding out.

Thump. *Groan*.

Quiet.

Thump. *Groan*.

Quiet.

Louder. Closer. Someone with one leg. Careful plodding. Shae's heart changed its patter.

"If he kills me, you're next."

Someone warned Shae. The frightened girl. Where had she gone? Did he kill her? He was coming for Shae.

Thump. *Groan.*

Mr. Moretti.

Who *was* Mr. Moretti? Shae didn't know, but she feared him. *You've destroyed everything of his.*

Maybe it was her imagination. Maybe her eyes were closed. Maybe her mind was closed. Maybe her mind was in her handbag. Maybe her words were in her car. Maybe her phone was in the dog. Maybe she was missing a leg. Maybe someone stole it with her bracelet.

She couldn't feel her feet or her legs. It didn't matter. She'd stand behind the display counter with the lotions. No one could see she was missing a leg behind the counter. She didn't need to talk. Just be pretty. And smile.

Jesus watched Shae. His mother and father were there, too. They all came to see her. Shae hoped they'd buy some lotion. She needed to sell them all. Mary would love VaLavender.

Jesus's voice leaked into the room. He moaned louder. Shae's heartbeat thrummed faster.

Thump. *Moan.*

Jesus was on the stairs. She could see his feet in blue ankle socks.

Shae reached into her mind to find something. First, she'd need to clear away the grime concealing her thoughts. But the chamois cloth and Grime Away were sold out! Three thousand units gone!

A swollen knee appeared. Huge like a melon. A gash sliced through both knees. Bloody bandages. He was coming for her.

A faded blue skirt. Above the swollen bloody knee. Faded blue was the new black. With bloodstains. Shae hoped it was a cotton /poly blend. Machine washable.

It was a wrap dress tied at the waist. So flattering. For any figure. Even Jesus. Or Mr. Moretti. Or Jimmy, the sleazebag. Anyone, really, would look thin and beautiful in a wrap dress.

Hospital gowns were the new wrap dress. Dingy and bloody.

Thump. *Moan. Groan.*

Mr. Moretti was hurt.

A thick white corset cinched tight over the blue gown. The gown
bulged out above and below it. Shae didn't know anyone who'd
wear that.

A hand gripped the railing. An elbow and a shoulder.

Shae's heart raced like a hamster wheel. She needed to look.
Who was it? Shae slid like an eel in and out of lucidity. She pressed
her eyes shut. Squeezing her lids down as far as they'd go.

CHAPTER 28

Honey

Monday, January 4, 2016, 11:05 a.m.

HONEY lumbered like a penguin off the last step into the basement. She stood still a moment to catch her breath. The smell in the room whacked her in the face. It made her queasy. Then a sick kind of dread mixed with heartache when she realized it must've been coming from Jenna.

Thank God, Rose was breathing, although not with exuberance. She made a deal with God on the drive from the hospital: if the cop was alive when she got home, she was ready to change her strategy. She was in over her head, and the cop's only chance of getting better was not going to be by Honey's hand anymore. If ever.

Honey's phone buzzed against her chest. It was tucked into the top of the body brace they gave her at the hospital for her fractured ribs and collarbone. Before she could get to her phone, she fished out two apple juice cups, a bag of mini carrots, and chocolate pudding, along with some bandages and bacitracin packets.

"Hello?" Even her voice felt bruised.

"*Honey!* Where the hell are you? I've been looking everywhere! I called the diner. They told me you were in the hospital. I called the hospital; they told me you were gone. Girl, I thought they meant *gone*—gone! Why weren't you answering? I thought you were dead!"

How long was Marianne going to go on before she let Honey speak?

"No. I'm alive." She could barely inhale without hurting.

"Where are you? What the hell happened?"

"Home. Angel brought me. I couldn't stay there—I had to check on—I needed to—I have too much going on." She sighed, thinking about it all.

"Jimmy's assholes stole my bag with my good makeup. They followed me into the alley behind the diner. Took a swipe at my back, then shoved me against the dumpster so hard it cracked my collarbone and a rib. I hit my head and have a concussion. Bunch of pricks. Angel was bringing out the garbage and found me unconscious. Thank God I had my phone in my apron. The only payback was, there was no money in that bag. I wish I could laugh, but it hurts too much. He should've known. He wrung me dry the day before. I guess a silver bracelet doesn't amount to much. Momma's earrings must've been fake."

"Jesus! Are you fucking kidding me? That motherfucking shit!" She paused. "Wrung you dry? What about Momma's earrings? What are you talking about? Why would Jimmy be after you?"

Honey swallowed hard. She tried to avoid looking at anything in the basement that was still one of those unknown-to-Marianne things. There was a lot she hadn't told her. But her eyeballs kept finding Jenna in the bag and the cop in the bed. She shook her head. Some stuff Honey did could be described as either a stroke of genius or something she'd go straight to hell for. She had too much on her plate and needed help dealing with it.

"Marianne, I gotta tell you something."

"Oh, Lord."

"Remember how the other day the guy came for the TV, and the other guy from Craigslist came for the couch a day early—by mistake, and my head was spinning, and I had to work a double the day after Momma died because money doesn't make itself, and add to that an unexpected predicament and untimely trouble?"

"Uh-huh."

"And Sunday on my way to work I was jumped and left for dead in the alley, then overnight in a hospital—"

"Would you just spit it out!"

"I have some new money problems I can't elaborate on right now, plus I needed Momma's bed—I'll explain that later too. Anyway, I guess what I'm saying is I used Momma's earrings."

"For what?" Marianne sounded exasperated. "Sounds like something else you need to tell me."

That comment was unsettling. "No." It was hard to tell if Marianne was one step ahead or one step behind. Honey never told Marianne about the "Jimmy transactions." She told her she was paying off hospital bills—which was true. But she also told her Momma had chemo bills. This was not the time to tell her those "doctor bills" were "dealer bills." Marianne would come around to understanding, but it'd take energy Honey didn't have at the moment.

"Honey, you sound messed up. You're not making any sense. Did they dope you at the hospital?"

"Probably. I look even worse than I sound. I can barely stand, and I can barely sit because of this brace they put me in for the broken bones. I don't know how I'm gonna drive. I need to get my car before it's towed. It's a miracle it's still at the diner." Honey waddled over to the dresser. With the scissors, she snipped the sides of a pull-up. "Must be my angel in heaven looking after me. Actually, two now. Though I'm not sure if I can count on Jenna for much."

"Jenna?"

Honey teetered across the room to the bag with Jenna in it.

"Jenna's dead." Honey had no energy for emotion. She was in pain everywhere. Including her heart.

Marianne gasped.

"I found her at Sweet Dreams. I can't even talk about *that* scene." She sighed heavily to slow her heartbeat. "When I got there, Jimmy's car was in the lot. So I parked at Denny's until he drove away. Obviously, he didn't leave town yet—so where the hell was Jenna—and why was she freezing me out? I knew something was up—she wasn't at church in *two* weeks—she never misses a Sunday! But I couldn't find her! How many times I told her to get away from him—she could've lived with me—I was too late! Now she's gone!"

Honey broke down and cried. All the grief she was feeling came at her.

"Okay, all right, Honey. I know...sweetie..."

"That scumbag left her there like that! Left her there dead!"

"Fucking scumbag." She was quiet for an entire minute. "Jesus —*Jenna*? I was not prepared for that."

Marianne ran out of stuff to say, and so did Honey.

"That poor, poor girl."

"Yeah, well, that's not all, unfortunately. Later that night, Jimmy came after me." Honey skipped the part about him looking to collect. "I was so scared. I thought it was because...well...I need to tell you something else."

"Dear Lord, Honey, what the hell else! I better sit down."

"Listen, Marianne, I did something very stupid." Honey gulped, sensing the gravity of her stupidity.

"'*Very* stupid'? I'm bracing myself, girl. I'm shaking right now."

"Well. I brought her here. Like I promised. Jenna's in my house. Right now. But not alive like I planned. That was stupid, I realize. But I wasn't thinking."

"Oh, *Jesus*."

A timid ray of sun leaked into the basement. It transfixed Honey. She stared at that measly glow, thinking about how dying was so black and white. There's no gray period to work out mistakes, second chances, or broken promises. It wasn't even black *and* white. Just black.

"That girl had nobody looking after her. Except for God, and He wasn't doing such a great job." Honey stared into space. "When you're a high-school dropout, on your own and mixed up with a loser boyfriend who's selling you out, you're screwed." Honey wiped her cheek. "She was a kid. She never stood a chance." Honey's tears were mixing up with nose drippings into one sad, sorry cocktail.

"Honey, blow your nose. I can't understand anything you're saying."

"I couldn't believe she was dead lying there. Marianne, I freaked! I was *too late*! I know I wasn't thinking. My head's been like a junkyard. Can't find anything worth shit in there. That

MF pimped out that child! She was too high to take control of her life. Now she's dead!"

"I can't believe it, Honey." Marianne's voice trembled. "I can't believe it."

"She had a garment bag hanging on her bathroom door. With a gown in it. Somebody left the dress behind in the last room they lived in. She thought it was a sign. She told me she was going back to school, and she was gonna wear it to prom. She promised!" Honey's whole body shook in tiny tremors. "I stuck her in that bag and brought her here. She's wearing it now. In my basement."

Honey grabbed a tissue from the bookcase and wiped her nose. "I know bringing her here was stupid. It's not like she's coming back to life, like a shriveled cactus with a spritz of water. Now I'm jumpy because I have a dead girl in my house. I need to get her back there. You need to help me."

Marianne yelled at Honey for ten straight minutes.

"Jesus, Honey. Je-*sus*," she finally said, exhausted. "You got two dead ladies in your basement? Girl, that ain't good."

"The cop!" Honey spun around.

"The *cop*?"

"What? No. I said, 'the *mop*.' Mooch's been pissing all over the place." Honey threw her hand up in fake exasperation and winced from the pain. "Like I got time to clean up. Where's the mop?"

Honey needed to get a grip. She needed to pull herself together before she unraveled to nothing. She was hanging by a skimpy cornhusk hair. She couldn't keep track of what she told Marianne and what she didn't.

"I'm talking about Momma. Honey, what's wrong with you?"

"Momma's not here anymore. Didn't I tell you?" Honey opened the dresser drawer and pulled out one of Momma's sweaters and brought it to her nose. "They came for her Saturday. I thought I told you. God, I miss her, Marianne. How am I gonna make it without her?"

They both got quiet, except for the whimpering and nose blowing.

"Honey, remember how we used to spend the day at the movies, sneaking in and out of theaters? Remember how we used to dye each other's hair? We'd go to class and flirt with the cute guys hanging out on the quad. Remember drinking leftover wine from the outside tables at Cinzano's—remember that? We need to get back to that."

Honey tried to keep still; she hurt everywhere. She was so thirsty. Maybe from the drugs they gave her? She put the phone down on the dresser and peeled back the foil on the juice cup. She brought the cup to her puffy lip and took a tiny sip. She opened the bag of carrots, shuffled over to the side table, and dumped a few on the cop's plate. She stuck a tiny straw into the second juice cup and brought it to the cop's mouth, who sucked at it with her eyes closed.

Honey was in a daze, thinking about how much she missed Momma. She waddled over to Momma's portrait hanging on the wall and pressed her palm to it, hoping Momma-sense would seep through.

Marianne was quiet. Sometimes she picked up her call waiting while Honey was talking and didn't even tell her. Then Honey spotted her phone on the dresser. She shuffled to the dresser and snatched up her phone. "Sorry, you still there?"

"Where'd you go?"

"Forgot I put the phone down."

"I don't want to start up on you again, but seeing as I'm part of the reverse-recovery mission...what the hell were you thinking! I know this is tragic. But what did you expect? You need a dose of reality. I don't want to be cold, but that girl was working for Jimmy while he fed her drugs like potato chips. Yes, he *stole* that girl. Her *soul*. Her *life*. I know you wanted to save her, but you can't save everybody!

"You took care of Mr. Moretti when Momma couldn't. Then you took care of Momma. And I guess we should throw the dog in there, too. You gave Mooch a home—though I don't really get that, if I'm being honest. You're an angel. You *got* your wings, Honey. Yes, it's a fucked up, unjust world. But you don't need to be the one saving everybody.

"You need to focus on saving yourself. Read the writing, Honey. Jenna was in too deep. You were never getting her away from Jimmy. Never. Not without putting a target on your own back. And now you've got trouble. People do crazy things when they're in trouble. I'm worried about you. If Jimmy comes for you again, he won't mess around. Now I need to worry about whether you end up dead or kidnapped like my girl Shae."

"*Shae?*" Just then, the cop thrust her head to the side and moaned.

"I already told you. From IShop."

Honey huffed. "Sorry if I've been distracted by getting assaulted and having loved ones die." Honey bit into a carrot. "Jimmy's gonna get his."

"What did you say? What's wrong with you? Let karma get that boy's ass. Did you learn anything? Next time, forget the alley—you'll end up where no one will find you. You think they found

Shae yet? And she's a celebrity. She's worth something. People are looking."

"Oh, thanks."

"You know what I mean. She's high profile. People are on the case. Nobody would be on our case. Don't be stupid."

"Believe me, I'm trying to undo my stupid right now." She let out a heavy sigh. "I should never have gotten Jenna a job. I feel bad saying that, but it brought me trouble." Honey glanced at the garment bag on the floor. "Who knows when I'll be able to go back to work. How long do I have before Enrique lets me go? You think he's gonna wait for my bones to heal?"

"If he doesn't, he's the lowest form of human. And he's pretty close to that already."

"I work hard! I might not have blue eyes and double D's in full view, but I sell my share of full entrees and specials. It's not like it's my dream job. When you're a waitress, that's how people identify you. They don't see everything else you are. Everything you're gonna be. No one includes a waitress in the ambitious, clever and talented club. Just the opposite. When people don't expect you to dazzle the world, you forget that you can. But I need this job until I get my dental hygiene license. And how am I going to do that if I can't pay the tuition?"

"Don't give up on that scholarship, Honey. I'm still praying."

"Well, I'm praying I don't lose my job. Because I'm on my own right now—in case I need to remind you." Honey tried to keep her body still, but it was impossible.

"If he has half a brain—which I understand is up for debate—he'll never fire you. You're the best waitress he's got. He'd be a damn fool! People request you, Honey. Who else draws portraits of customers!"

"One guy gave me a $20 tip for the sketch I drew of him on his check. I never got a $20 tip in my life. They call me the Artist." Honey looked at the wall of portraits she'd drawn.

"You're a survivor, and you do what it takes to survive. So if that means…that means you do what it takes. Let's not talk about it now. It hasn't even happened. You've got to heal yourself."

"I can't work for anyone in this condition." Honey shook her head. "I don't know what I'm gonna do. I was broke *with* a job."

"Oh my God, the bag! I almost forgot!"

Honey forgot, too.

"It's really Tory Burch's signature! I didn't know until one of the bidders sent me a question. She asked if the writing on the lining was her autograph. It was a weird question. I didn't take a photo of the lining, so how'd she know? Then I did a little googling and found out. The bag is gold, right? Tory Burch doesn't make that bag in gold. Your bag is custom. One of a kind. She makes special edition bags for special people. Your bag is one of them!"

Special people? Rose didn't look special to Honey. She was pretty, and she had nice clothes, but under all that, she was clueless.

Honey gave Rose another sip of juice, then a spoonful of pudding.

"I have to ask you this, Honey. Don't get mad at me. I need to know if this bag is hot. I mean, you have to admit it's a little strange how you came upon an expensive handbag this week."

"Are you accusing—*what the hell*?"

"I'm not accusing you. I'm just saying. You got it from a friend? This is no ordinary bag. It's one of a kind, limited edition. With an autograph. *The* Tory Burch signed it. Like the actual person. With a pen. She must be pretty special, that friend of yours. Why would she give it away? Why would she give it to *you*? No disrespect, but the whole thing sounds…"

Marianne got quiet, waiting for Honey to say something. But Honey had nothing.

"Maybe I should unload it, the bids are getting crazy. It's already double what I expected."

Honey was lost in her head. "Maybe it's a sign God is finally helping me out," she said quietly while running her fingers over Momma's rosary beads hanging from a lampshade. "If I can pay our bills and get Momma buried, take Jenna back and settle a few other tight spots I'm in…" Like next steps with the cop. It was looking like she might need to trust Marianne with this, too. "Maybe there's a fresh start for me on the other side." Honey was scratching and clawing her way back up to her positivity perch, but it wasn't easy getting there. She let out a sigh. "How much longer on the auction?"

"One more day. I guess we'll wait it out. But I'm telling you. This bag better not be shady shit."

CHAPTER 29

Honey

Monday, January 4, 2016, 1:20 p.m.

WHEN Honey woke from a nap an hour later, her body was in full-blown assault hangover. She slept sitting upright in the basement chair because hoisting herself from a horizontal position was painful to even think about. Plus, she couldn't deal with an extra trip up the stairs. She twirled her ankles in circles to get blood flowing and was grateful to have two body parts that worked without complaining.

The sun had already passed by the window, leaving a watered-down lemonade glow to the room. Honey never noticed how gloomy the basement was in this dismal light. She tried to make it cheery by hanging all her drawings on the wall—the ones she drew of Momma were her favorites. Momma sure did have an expressive face. All those years of worry settled into deep folds of skin on her forehead and cheeks. She had a habit of pressing her lips together when she had an opinion that she kept to herself. That woman had a hundred different expressions.

Honey shuffled across the room to pick up Momma's rosary beads. She wrapped them around her wrist like a bracelet so she could feel them against her skin. Maybe she'd absorb some kind of blessing.

The water level in the pitcher didn't move as fast as Honey'd like, and the cop hadn't eaten much, either. What did Honey expect? She'd pour herself a drink and fix an omelet while Honey was at the hospital?

A sour-tasting dread crept up Honey's throat and filled the back of her mouth. Walls were closing in. Honey doubted she had the wherewithal to deal with the mounting disasters. How could so much go wrong in such a short time? Momma hadn't been gone but a few days and Honey was unglued.

She held the straw against Rose's lips.

"You and I aren't looking so good, Rose. Drink up."

Honey redressed Rose's leg and noticed, thankfully, it hadn't gotten worse. Still, it was time for a decisive change in plans, but what exactly felt a million miles away.

The trill of the phone made Honey jump. The phone was crosstown on the dresser.

"I'm coming!" Honey called out.

The call went to voicemail as she reached it. When Honey looked at the phone, there were seven texts and four voicemails from Marianne.

The texts were a variety of "Call me right now," "Where the hell are you?", "We need to talk." And "HONEY!!!" She skipped the voicemails and called instead.

"What took you so long?" Marianne's voice was like vinegar on a hangnail.

"Hello to you, too."

"We might have an issue on our hands with your friend, the handbag whisperer."

"What do you mean?" Honey tucked her hand into the top of the body brace to press down her chest and quiet the jitters starting up.

"You know how I livestream IShop, right?"

"Yeah." Honey rolled her eyes. "More like your money's 'livestreaming' its way to IShop."

Honey lumbered back to the bed to give the cop some water. She brought the straw to Rose's mouth. Just then, Rose whipped her head to the side, startling Honey. Her head thrashed back and forth. Marianne's voice buzzed on, but Honey couldn't focus.

"*Rose!*" Honey yelled.

"*Rose?* It's *Marianne*," Marianne barked. "Who the hell is Rose?"

"What? Nobody." Damn, Marianne didn't miss a trick. She could talk and listen simultaneously. She was probably streaming IShop and liking Insta pics while she was having a conversation with Honey.

Rose stopped her head whipping, and her hair now covered her face.

"I'm reading a magazine," Honey stammered. "One of those quizzes, if you were a flower, which would you be. Turns out I'm a rose. What flower you think you'd be?"

"Jesus, Honey. I'm talking about your situation, and you're reading a magazine!"

The cop's hair was parted in a zigzag down the back of her head, revealing her scalp—and, to Honey's shock—a large bald spot of skin. Round, as big as a cucumber slice. Right above her hairline. The bald skin was smooth and shiny. It gave Honey the creeps— like Honey was looking at a secret.

She also had a tattoo right below her hairline on her neck. Honey always wondered why people put tattoos in places they couldn't see themselves. When was she ever going to get a look at the back of her neck? What was the sense of that? Unless she had short hair or wore it up, how would anyone else see it either? All that trouble and money and pain—all for a butterfly nobody's going to see. The butterfly was brown—light and dark and everything in between—like tree bark. Or actually, the same colors as her hair and her highlights. It camouflaged right in.

Without thinking, Honey touched the cop's bald spot. It was slippery smooth. She snatched her hand back. Why'd she do that? It felt like she touched the cop's private parts. Jesus, she wished she could un-feel it. She wished she could unsee it, too. And that tattoo, she wished she never saw that either. It brought up all kinds of memory-lane pain. Like someone busted down the rickety door to Honey's yesteryear, all with the sight of a lousy butterfly wanting to fly away.

The tattoo made her think of Carl, Denise's worst, always wasted, monster boyfriend. She was so scared of him. She was scared of a few of Denise's boyfriends, but at least Carl never tried to touch her. Just the same, he was mean. He was known for starting fist fights and getting thrown out of bars. He picked on animals, too. Shot squirrels and chipmunks for sport with a BB gun. But how could someone be mean to a butterfly? He'd catch butterflies to rip their wings apart. Never outright killed them, just took away their freedom and purpose. Their very essence. Leaving them to starve and die.

"Are you listening to me? I'm not selling your shit for my health! Who's your friend?"

Marianne's voice was a hacksaw cutting through Honey's mental ramblings.

"You are," Honey singsonged. Marianne needed more petting than a puppy. *"You're* my friend, Marianne."

"No, Honey. I know I'm your friend! Stop playing with me. Your friend who gave you the Tory Burch!" she snapped.

Honey's eyes shifted back to the cop. *Friend* was a bit of an exaggeration. To say the least. "Oh, her?"

"Yeah. Who is she?"

"Why do you want to know?"

"Remember that girl I told you about, Shae Wilmont? The kidnapped girl from IShop?"

"Shae Wilmont? No."

Marianne huffed. "Well, why should that surprise me? Miss *Lilac.* You never listen! I told you. *Yesterday.* I told you the kidnapper sent a letter. Ring a bell?"

Maybe it was a good sign the cop was thrashing her head. Maybe she was breaking her fever.

"Because I got worried you were kidnapped by the same guy. Remember?"

"Just go on."

Honey felt bad for not remembering, but Marianne could talk and talk. It was hard to tell what was important.

"Well, it wasn't a ransom letter, after all. It was a letter that got lost in the mail. It was sent back in September. After all these months, it showed up this week at the IShop studios. Three months later! Somebody posted a pic of the envelope on Facebook asking Shae's fans for help, but they took the post down already because it's evidence. Luckily I saw it."

"Uh-huh." Honey's head was spinning, and Marianne talking like she was four coffees into her day wasn't helping. Honey's heart banged in her chest, trying to alarm her, but her head was lagging behind.

Honey tried to shove her anxiety aside to focus on what Marianne was saying but didn't see how it had anything to do with the cop. All the same, Honey started to shake. She tried to talk herself out of it, hug herself out of it. It sure was silly to be shaking over nothing. She grabbed a pen and nervous-doodled on the back of some junk mail. Marianne was gearing up in the way she did when she's about to dump something heavy. Like when Marianne told her Jenna was working for Jimmy on the Boulevard. She didn't say, "Jimmy's pimping Jenna." No. She babbled through ten minutes of buildup first. Drove Honey crazy.

Honey comforted herself by remembering Marianne lived in a universe where *People Magazine* Instagram meets *E!* Snapchat. She got off on this stuff. Marianne thought she was friends with the girls from *Bachelor in Paradise*. Fifty percent of the time, Marianne and Honey didn't live in the same world. This—whatever Marianne was talking about—had nothing to do with Honey. This had nothing to do with the cop.

Honey waddled across the basement floor from wall to wall, touching the picture of Baby Jesus at one end and the Virgin Mary at the other, even though it was hurting just to breathe. This pilgrimage expended nervous energy. She fingered the rosary beads hanging from her wrist. This story of Marianne's, most likely, would lead nowhere. But a tragic little seed burrowed in the back of Honey's mind, and Marianne was spritzing it with her own special fertilizer.

"So instead of it going to 1807 Fiesta Boulevard, Vista Verde, which is IShop's address, the envelope had 807 Fiesta Boulevard because the number one fell off! God knows where the envelope went all this time—months!—or how it made its way back to the right place, but it finally did. Got it now?"

"I guess…" Was she actually quizzing Honey?

"It was missing the one, Honey. That stalker letter finally showed up four months later. You know why it was missing the one?"

Help me, Jesus. "Marianne, if you don't tell me now, I'm hanging up."

"Because the address got printed across two labels. Half the address on one, half on the other. Got it? The envelope had just one label with 807 Fiesta Boulevard. There must've been another label on the envelope with the one, but it fell off."

Panic was building like a hurricane in Honey's chest.

"Marianne. I can't play *Law & Order* with you. Sell the goddamn bag. Okay. I know you want to be Olivia Benson, but I don't. You're giving me a heart attack."

Marianne let out a huge sigh. She was losing patience, too.

"Don't get short with me, Marianne. I'm listening. There were two labels on the envelope. The letter got lost in the mail. Finally it got to IShop. One label was missing. Half the address. Missing the one. Blah, blah, blah. That's it? I'm about to throw up you're making me so nervous. Over that?! I can't listen to this anymore. I got big-ass problems of my own."

"Well, Honey, you better add this to your list of problems. Because I found something in your friend's bag."

"*What?* What did you find in the bag?"

"The label that should've been on that envelope. With the missing one."

CHAPTER 30

Honey

Monday, January 4, 2016, 1:35 p.m.

Honey stepped back from the bed. The rosary slid off her wrist and fell to the floor. She held onto the back of a chair to steady herself. Her thoughts swirled. She switched the phone to her other ear. Maybe she'd understand better through that one.

"The missing label?" Honey kept repeating that to herself. Now she wished she had paid attention to everything else Marianne had said. Jesus. If only Marianne's monologues came with an alert to indicate when the important stuff was coming. Like a "listen-up" speed bump.

The person who owned the bag was somehow involved in a ransom letter for the kidnapped celebrity? Was that it? Honey should've taken notes.

Honey's rationale of late was not dazzling in any way. Grief, worry, stress, fear, assault, fractures, pain, and debt had stymied things. She didn't have the strength to keep up with Marianne.

Honey cupped her hand to the side of her mouth, turned her back on Rose, and whispered to Marianne, "Well, she's a cop."

"Who?"

"My friend. The one who gave me the bag."

"*A cop?*" Marianne clucked. "A *girl* cop?" Then nothing. It was pretty scary when Marianne was quiet. "You're saying you want me to believe *you* are *friends* with a *cop*?"

Honey could picture Marianne's arms waving around to punctuate her barbs.

"Why are you whispering?" Marianne said.

"Uh, yeah." Honey cleared her throat. "Yup."

"Yup what? You're friends with a cop? You are. Friends with a cop." She kept saying it, each time a little differently, emphasizing another word, like the rhythm would unlock some kind of truth.

Then she laughed that clown-in-a-horror-movie laugh, which Honey didn't appreciate.

"Now what's wrong with this picture, Honey? Something smells bad to me. First, you have a friend who owns a five-hundred-dollar custom Tory Burch bag with a real Tory Burch signature. Currently getting bids over $900. All right. That's okay. Why not, right? You have a fancy friend who I never heard about. That's okay. Maybe I don't know all your friends. Maybe you don't know all mine. Now, you tell me this friend's a cop. You expect me to believe that? You're scared to death of cops! Why don't you get your cop friend to bust Jimmy? Tell me that."

"Well, right now, I owe the cop a favor. Not the other way around." Honey was impressed by how quickly that came to her.

"Girl, you know what this smells like to me? It smells like trouble. What do you say about that?"

Honey had nothing to say because her mind was presently vacant.

230

"Nothing, huh? Honey, you've been doing some crazy brainless shit lately, and I don't like where this conversation is heading."

This wasn't the right time, if there would ever be, to let Marianne in on the Rose situation. Honey couldn't see how telling Marianne that, when she was looking for Jenna, a cop followed her home and broke into her house to arrest her for nothing, then her shit-for-brains dog jumped the cop while Honey tried to shoot the dog but missed with a gun she never told Marianne she found in Mr. Moretti's cookie jar, and Honey's plan to resuscitate the cop in hopes of keeping her scared ass out of jail wasn't going as planned in Honey's basement right now, was going to help things.

Marianne currently lacked the sensitivity and empathy and extra dollop of kindness and forgiveness necessary to fully process things in the way Honey needed her to.

"I don't appreciate your tone. I haven't done anything illegal. And one of those brainless things happened out of grief and panic, which we're gonna fix tonight. What time are you coming?"

"Well, let's see. Since I'm not super stoked about carrying a dead girl into a monthly motel for junkies and pimps in broad daylight alongside a girl wearing a body brace and bruises—which means I'll be carrying the dead girl—let's say eleven. Could we get back to the handbag?"

Honey didn't want to go back to the handbag. She didn't like where it was heading, though she wasn't as clear as Marianne about where that was.

"If that envelope ended up at the wrong address, that means it was missing the one by the time it got to the post office. I mean, it could have fallen off *at* the post office, or *en route* from the post office to the address, but then how would it end up in your friend's handbag? Nope. My guess is that the one fell off before someone

231

mailed it. The person who mailed it stuck it in her handbag, and when she took it out of her handbag to mail it, the label with the one fell off and was left behind *in her bag. Stuck to the inside pocket.* Even I missed it the first few times I went through the bag. It's a clear sticker. It looks like a Made in China sticker you find at the bottom of your shoe. When I swooshed my hand in the pocket today, it stuck to my hand. It's mostly blank. Except it's got an 'I' for IShop, a '1' for 1807 Fiesta Boulevard, and a 'V' for Vista Verde. I'm telling you, if you put it on the envelope I saw on Facebook, it would line up to create the IShop address. If this was in a cop's bag, the cop sent the letter. Now, what's a cop doing stalking a girl on TV?"

Honey had no answer for that.

"They said it matched three other notes Shae received. No fingerprints on any of them. Makes sense now that a cop sent them. A cop would know not to leave fingerprints."

"The cop sent letters to stalk the IShop girl?" Honey asked out loud while turning to look at the cop, whose eyes blinked.

"I always figured it was a guy stalking her. No way I would've predicted it was a girl."

Marianne stopped talking for a second.

"Imagine that, Honey. Only you and me right now at this very moment know more about this case than anyone. We know even more than the detectives!"

Honey wasn't as excited as Marianne.

Why would a cop stalk a celebrity? Honey should've been more concerned about who Rose was from the beginning. She should've known people would've been looking for her. Not everybody was like Honey or Jenna, flying solo. This cop was in some kind of trouble. Other than the state of her health.

Honey carefully picked through the pile of the cop's belongings. If only Honey could show Marianne. She'd find something important there.

"Marianne," Honey said in the soberest tone. "I gotta tell you something."

"Oh, Lord. The six scariest words in the English language."

While she weighed exactly what to tell Marianne, Honey counted on her fingers.

"Unfortunately," Marianne said, "that phrase is never followed by, 'Victoria's Secret is having a bra sale,' or 'I won a trip to Mexico and I'm taking you with me.' No. It's more like, 'I brought Jenna home in a duffle bag,' or 'I was jumped and left for dead in an alley.'" She huffed. "Okay, what is it?"

"Never mind."

Something told Honey not to share the rest of her troubles. No sense weaving Marianne in any more than she had already. This was Honey's mess to clean up, and telling Marianne might get her in trouble, too. Honey couldn't let that happen. Marianne was family. One of the only people Honey could trust. She couldn't live with herself if she got Marianne in trouble.

Honey picked up the fancy mirrored compact. Advil. Tissues. The good kind of dental floss that tasted like peppermint. Makeup. Hairbrush. Sunglasses. All regular things. But she was finding out this cop was anything but regular.

"What are you going to do, Honey? Now that you know your girl's involved? How do you explain that?"

"*Me?*"

"She's *your* friend!"

"Yeah, you're my friend, too. There's a lot of shit you do I can't explain!"

"Like what?"

"Well, for one, you wouldn't know anything about all this if you didn't live in la-la land thinking you're friends with famous TV people who you buy stuff from! Spending money on things you don't need and can't afford. You're probably as broke as me, only you pretend you're rich because you have a credit card!"

"Really? Should I remind you who's currently selling an expensive handbag for you on eBay right now, so you have money for your shit!"

"*My* shit? If I didn't owe Jimmy eight hundred dollars, I wouldn't need to pawn everything I own—"

Honey froze, eyes bulging. She pressed her lips together, but it was too late. It was out there like a torpedo you want to grab back. But everyone knows you can't change the direction of a torpedo mid-strike. Contact was as sure as sorrow. She braced herself.

The air got real chilly. Not a peep from Marianne.

That made Honey nervous. The silence elongated between them.

"What'd you...*what*?" Marianne finally said. "Wait. You told me you needed money for Momma's hospital bill. And chemo. And to bury her. Why do you owe Jimmy...*wait*. Wait—wait—wait—wait—wait."

Honey could hear Marianne's lightbulb going off, and the harsh white light of accusation cast a spotlight on Honey through the phone.

"Girl. Seriously? I know you've been a little off in the decision-making department, but if you're doing business with Jimmy, there's only one thing *that* means. Please tell me I'm not selling your shit so you can get high! Say something, Honey. And don't consider anything but the straight-up truth."

CHAPTER 31

Honey

Monday, January 4, 2016, 1:55 p.m.

Honey swallowed a big lump of shame before she spit it out. "I was giving Momma morphine, okay?" Honey pressed her palms together and closed her eyes. She mouthed, "Forgive me, Jesus."

"*Momma?*"

"She wasn't getting chemo. *Morphine* was her chemo. That's what we called it. That's what I told her when I gave it to her. She didn't know—well, maybe she did. You know that woman was smart. But she didn't ask questions once she got relief. I couldn't afford morphine, but at least I could get my hands on it. You think I wanted to get mixed up with him? I dropped out of school—ran away from home—left my family—became *homeless*—to avoid people like Jimmy! It took a lot for me to go there. I was desperate."

Honey dropped her face in her hands. A ripple of grief and guilt flitted through her body. At the same time, her heart filled with loneliness for Momma. The pain in her body was coming from everywhere now. She let the tears come.

"That's why I asked you for money. I have more than emergency room bills. I have to pay off Jimmy. He knows I can't come up with it. He's got his guys scaring me so I'll give up and work for him. I'm not doing it!" Honey lowered herself into the wooden chair, but the brace hit the chair before her butt and shot up and stabbed her armpits. "Ow!"

Honey couldn't remember being so low. Her world was caving in like a sand hole.

"How could you think I was doing drugs?" she pleaded with Marianne. "That hurts so bad. I didn't want to tell you I was giving it to Momma. I didn't want you to think, I—it—"

Honey was surprised how badly Marianne's accusation stung. It was like trying all your life to do the right thing, and sometimes knowing it wasn't going to make you Homecoming Queen, but you did it anyway. Then somebody accuses you of the very thing you were working hard not to do—after all that goddamn work!

"Oh jeez, I'm sorry, Honey. Really, I am. Of course I didn't *think so*. It's that…you have to admit, you're not thinking straight lately. So maybe you said, 'Screw it.' I don't know, sometimes it seems like you're living in some fairy tale. With rainbows, butterflies, flat tummies, and good hair days. I mean, I love that about you. And I pray you get your happy ending, I do. But you can't blame me. All your optimism when things were falling apart around you made me think maybe you *were* getting high. But no, that's just you."

Honey pulled the last carrot out of the tiny bag she took from the hospital, aged to a white patina. Still had a nice crunch, though.

"Don't lose it now, Honey. You've had some bad things thrown your way before, and you always find a way to be positive. We'll get the money for Jimmy. Let's figure out this handbag thing. What should we do with this evidence? Turn your girl in with this sticker? Or sell the bag to the highest bidder so you can pay off Jimmy? And get that scumbag out of your life for good?"

"Honestly, if you met this cop, you wouldn't think she could tie her shoelaces."

Honey opened the Tic Tac box and tapped out an Advil. Maybe it would help take the edge off. She dropped it on her tongue and tried to collect enough saliva on her tongue so she wouldn't have to get up from the chair for water.

"Let's think this through. Say we call the cops on our way to returning a dead juvie addict sex worker to her shithole motel and tell them we 'came upon evidence' that would implicate one of their own. What do you think they'll do, Honey?"

"They'll lock us up. I've narrowly escaped that a few times already this week." Honey forced the pill down her dry throat. "You can leave me out of that."

"Jesus, I hope Shae Wilmont will forgive me. It's killing me to do this to her. I mean, honestly, I could be a hero right now. She might invite me to IShop to formally thank me. Maybe she'd give me a gift card or a shopping spree! Imagine that! I could meet her! *And* be on TV, get free stuff, and we'd be *real* friends!"

Honey prayed it was the right decision. It sure felt better having someone to make it with. A partner in crime, so to speak.

"I guess I'll flush the sticker and unload the bag. This situation is getting too exciting for us. We have enough bids, Honey. Honestly, it's higher than I ever dreamed. Let's not get greedy."

CHAPTER 32

Lawrence

Monday, January 4, 2016, 5:47 p.m.

RITA was hosting her book club tonight, and Lawrence had promised to prepare his Hot Spinach and Artichoke Dip In Bread Bowl. Her friends always cooed over his confidence in the kitchen. Unfortunately, that plan was made before he was balls-deep in evidence, interviews, and forensic reports from Shae's investigation. He wasn't in the mood for entertaining, and he'd have no time to be charming, or engage in stimulating conversation and niceties. Rita would need to explain that Lawrence had a new job now. One that required him to work around the clock.

His watch read 5:47 p.m. His last and highly anticipated meeting of the day was about to begin: a phone interview for Shae's case with Thibault Arnie. All Lawrence knew about this guy was that he lived in L.A. and that Shae designated him her emergency contact. The significance of their relationship was unclear. Obviously, they were close. He dreaded hearing *how* close. Heading down the hall toward his desk, he spotted someone hunched over, rummaging through his wastepaper basket.

Lawrence cleared his throat. "Can I help?"

She turned to face him. *Late Again.* She held a fistful of used latex gloves in one hand, printouts in the other.

She was unfazed, not at all rattled by being caught red-handed. Not a single face muscle pinged. What the hell was she doing?

"Quite an accumulation of gloves. I guess you can never be too careful." She smirked.

Lawrence was beside her in a flash. He tore the basket from the floor. Perhaps too aggressively, but he didn't care.

"What exactly are you looking for? Lost your virginity in there?" He coughed out a snide chuckle while he wrapped his arm around the pail, tucking it close to his chest. Was that sexual harassment? It seemed everything was these days.

Her mouth twisted, and she shook her head slowly. As if to say Lawrence was some kind of a loser. Lawrence stared at the papers in her hand. He considered grabbing them, too. How would that come off?

"I'm in a meeting with Lamar. He's looking for an interview and couldn't find it anywhere. He told me to look on your desk."

Lawrence's eyebrow flinched. What interview? Why wouldn't Lamar have asked Lawrence? Why was he asking Late Again? Lawrence rehashed what was in the wastebasket. And what he'd placed in a baggie, already in the back of his pants for a quick get-away after the interview.

"You could've asked me. I'm right here." Lawrence really wanted to know why *he* wasn't in the meeting. But he didn't dare give Late Again the satisfaction.

"You weren't a few minutes ago."

"What's he working on? If it's something—I could pop in—what case?" Lawrence checked his watch again. Would the interview need to be pushed back? Not to mention, the artichoke dip?

Lawrence strained to think of what might be in the trash. Nothing. Nothing was in there. He tried to look casual. Why wouldn't he be casual? This lame pencil-pusher wasn't going to ruffle his feathers. Lawrence straddled his feet. Flexed his shoulders. A trickle of sweat dripped down his ass crack.

"Joanne!" Fruity Tums yelled from down the hall. She rarely ventured into the Detective Bureau. What was going on? "Never mind!" she called out in a hurried tone. "Lamar said he'd take care of it."

Late Again studied Lawrence as she dropped the gloves—with a braggadocious gesture—into the trash can he still held and walked away with papers in hand.

"Looks like you're off the hook, for now." She headed toward the conference room, as smug as ever.

"I was never on the hook!" His words chased her down the hall. He wished he hadn't said that. It gave the impression he cared. Which he didn't. He couldn't wait for the opportunity to squash that paper-shuffler.

"Don't worry. I got what I need." She called out, holding the fistful of papers above her head without turning around.

That sent a shiver he wasn't expecting down his spine.

He was sweating like a fire hose. He wished he hadn't put the evidence in his pants so early. Lawrence felt jittery. He didn't like it. It wasn't something he typically felt. Damn Late Again! She was getting under his skin. Time Lawrence zeroed in on her. He needed to be ready with something uncompromising if, God forbid, she turned out to be an enemy. Undoubtedly, she had secrets of her own. Everyone did. And Lawrence would sniff them out if anyone could.

Lamar emerged from the meeting and nodded at Lawrence. A minute later, Lawrence picked up his phone and tapped in the number for the interview. He entered the PIN.

"Hello, Mr. Arnie?"

"Yes…"

"One moment, please."

"Hello. This is Detective Tramball, from the Vista Verde Police Department. I'm calling to ask you a few questions about Shae Wilmont. Unfortunately, she is a missing person, and I'm heading the investigation. Do you have a minute?"

"Yes, I…yes. Wow. Shae? That's…terrible. Of course. How can I help?"

"Could you start by stating your name and spell your last name for the transcript? We are recording this call."

Thibault Arnie: My name is Thibault Arnie. A-R-N-I-E. Some people call me T. Or Teebo. It doesn't matter. People don't know how to pronounce Thibault. Too many silent letters. It's pronounced Tee-Bo. You can call me Tee if you want. Sorry if I sound nervous. I never talked to a detective before.

Detective Tramball: Please don't be nervous. We're going to have a casual conversation. There's nothing to be nervous about.

T. Arnie: How did you get my number?

L. Tramball: You're Shae Wilmont's emergency contact. On her employment form at IShop. Did you know that?

T. Arnie: That's strange. She never told me. I haven't heard from her in years. Since we worked together on *Secrets and Lies*. I'm glad there hasn't been an emergency!

L. Tramball: Well, this is an emergency, of course.

T. Arnie: Oh, yes. Of course. This is definitely an emergency. Right. Sorry. I'm shocked. It's alarming. We were pretty good friends when we worked together. What do you want to know, exactly?

L. Tramball: Could you tell me how you know her, when you met, where?

T. Arnie: We met on *Secrets and Lies*—you know, the show? I did —do—the hair and makeup, and she played Heather Bartell, the spicy neighbor who has an affair with Zach. Do you ever watch? It's a great show. Some people call it a nighttime soap, but the acting is amazing, and there's great writing—lots of shockers. Shae played Heather for almost a year.

L. Tramball: So Shae is an actress?

T. Arnie: It was her first acting role. She was very shy when she started. Not super friendly. People thought she was a snob. I think she was just insecure. Listen, she was inexperienced. I'd be insecure, too! Some of the veterans are mean. A lot of actresses wanted that role. They resented it going to someone basically found in Starbucks. I always felt like I should protect her. It's hard to explain.

L. Tramball: Was she unsuccessful? Why did she leave?

T. Arnie: Well, Shae came into her own, so to speak. It didn't take long. It was odd, actually. Well, I'll tell you, but...I wouldn't want it getting back to her, you know?

L. Tramball: We don't share these interviews with the subject of investigations. There's no need to worry.

T. Arnie: Well, I was going to say, the more she played Heather, the more she became Heather. She talked like her, dressed like her, *off*-camera. Strange, right? Especially because she was nothing like Heather. Heather was trash! Shae would use Heather's expressions, F-bombs and everything. The trashy outfits. Cuckoo.

I guess it's lucky that Heather Bartell wasn't a psychopath, right? Oh, she did poison Zach's wife, now that I think about it.

Tons of actors are shy, but they don't *become* their characters. Well, I know the method actors do, like Heath Ledger becoming the Joker, or De Niro or what's-his-name—Daniel Day Lewis. I don't mean to be mean, but Shae was no Hilary Swank. And for God's sake, who'd want to become Heather?!

L. Tramball: When did you see or talk with her last?

T. Arnie: We had lunch a few weeks after she left the show. That was the last time I saw her. I don't know why we lost touch. I guess we were just work friends. That's why I'm surprised you want to talk to me.

L. Tramball: We assumed you were close since you're her emergency contact.

T. Arnie: Weird. Would've never seen that coming. Strange she didn't pick a boyfriend? Or family? I hope she's got a better friend than me.

L. Tramball: Is there someone she's close to that you think we should speak with?

T. Arnie: Can't help you there. There was a weird family thing I remember the Christmas she was on the show. She was supposedly hosting Christmas, and family from out of town were staying with her, yada yada. She said she was busy decorating and baking and shopping. I was glad for her. She never mentioned any of them, so I was glad they were visiting. Even though we spent a lot of time together—you know, she was in my chair every day—

there were certain things we never talked about. Sometimes you know when *not* to ask certain questions, right?

On Christmas, I stopped by her house on the way to my brother's —unannounced, so bad on me—to drop off Christmas cookies I made. She answered the door in pajamas. She was shocked to see me, *very* uncomfortable. It was totally awkward. I felt bad for showing up like that. She didn't invite me in. As far as I could see, there were no visitors, no chatter, no smells of roasts, no sight of a Christmas tree. It was dark inside. She took the platter quickly and said she was running late so she couldn't chat. We never spoke of it.

L. Tramball: Why did she leave the show?

T. Arnie: Someone at IShop saw her on *Secrets and Lies* and asked if she'd be interested in interviewing for a host job. Funny, that's how she got the *Secrets* job, too. The casting director saw her at Starbucks, literally, and asked her to come in for an audition. He thought she'd be perfect for Heather. She's like a stray dog following the scraps—only prettier and better smelling! Some boats have a sailor, and some travel with the current. I bet she's never written a resume in her life.

L. Tramball: Do you know if she was a drug user?

T. Arnie: Not when I knew her.

L. Tramball: How about her emotional state? Do you know if she had depression or ever contemplated suicide?

T. Arnie: I don't think so. Who knows for sure, right? Hmm... now that you ask. I forgot all about this. I always thought this was strange. You know I did her hair? Well, she's got a bald spot on the back of her head. You can't see it because it's under her hair, close to her neck. I don't know why I'm telling you that, but it always gave me the creeps. Small, at the beginning, when she started the show. And it was totally manageable to do her hair because it was in the back, and I never had to put it up for Heather, thank God. That would've been awkward. But over time, it got bigger. When she left it was bigger than a quarter. We never talked about it. I just worked around it. But I'm pretty sure she was pulling her hair out. I'd sometimes see her in the dressing room on a break and she'd be reading a book, and she'd twirl a few strands of hair around her finger, in the back of her head right where the spot was. Why would anyone want to do that? I guess, now that I think about it, after all that time we spent together at work, I didn't really know her very well.

L. Tramball: Anything else you want to share?

T. Arnie: Not really. I was glad to see she found success after *Secrets*. It seems like she's more popular than ever. She's really found her thing. Good for her. I tuned in a few times—just because I was curious—back when she first started at IShop. I need to say …I don't want to diss her…but I was shocked. I mean, she wasn't Heather anymore. (He laughs.) She was someone new. It was very strange. She was friendly and funny, blowing kisses and winking at the camera. Not anything like the Shae I knew. I had no idea who that person was.

As soon as the call ended, Lawrence bolted from his chair to head to the Evidence Locker. Then he stopped, stepped back toward his desk, and bent over his chair to tap "Thibault Arnie" into the Google search box. Lawrence didn't like this guy. Didn't like him at all.

The guy played with lipstick all day. He clicked "images." He wanted to know what a joker with that kind of name and good fortune looked like. Still, Lawrence couldn't help being envious of a guy who touched Shae every day—and got paid for it.

Torn jeans and black t-shirt with cuffed sleeves. A big grin planted on his tanned face. In practically every photo. Cheek-bones. White teeth. Highlights. Biceps. Tattoos. Not her type. How the hell was he her emergency contact? He pushed the ab-surdity of them being former lovers from his mind.

He resumed his sprint to the Evidence Room and tore open the file cabinet, looking for the photo of Shae's bedroom. The one of the vanity table.

He found it. The table had three mirrors. A large center one and two smaller, skinnier ones flanking it on hinges so one could, presumably, see the different angles of one's face and head. The table's surface was a green pebbly shagreen leather. A coincidence that Shagreen was Shae's given name? Not likely. On it was a black lacquered tray with a collection of beautiful perfume bottles in all shapes and sizes. He wished he had time to be aroused by the fantasy of those scents on Shae's skin. But he was too preoccupied.

It was the table's center drawer, slender like a box of chocolates with a smooth white drawer pull, that he was curious about. In the photo, the drawer was open. It contained a bulging nest of silky, golden-brown hair. A soft puffy pillow of twining strands. Lawrence could practically feel it.

CHAPTER 33

Honey

Monday, January 4, 2016, 11:22 p.m.

WHEN Marianne arrived at Honey's house to pick up Jenna, she let loose on her, calling her all kinds of things, but Honey knew deep down they were still cool. It was just Marianne being nervous. Honey being nervous took the form of puking into a half-empty coffee cup Marianne had in her cup holder. Marianne didn't even get mad. She did have some choice words about the smell of her car and that it would be Honey's job to turn that around if the dead person smell didn't go away.

At the motel parking lot, Marianne pulled into a spot next to the stairs.

"I'm coming with you," Honey said.

"No, you're not." Marianne turned off the car. "Wake up, Honey. You look like somebody ran you over with a lawnmower, then strapped you into a tragic corset from two centuries ago. I can do without that attention while I sneak Jenna back and unbag her. Honestly, I wonder who'll end up looking better. You or her.

And she's been dead in a bag for three days." Marianne was on her second Mike's. She sucked down the last sip while waving air under her armpits.

"Leave the car on," Honey said.

"Good idea." Marianne started the car, then grabbed a lipstick from the coin holder and slicked some on.

"What do you need that for?"

"If I get my mug shot taken tonight, I wanna look half decent."

"Please don't say that." Honey gulped.

Marianne's makeup looked like she worked on it, Honey suddenly noticed. It was the first time she'd ever seen her wear sweatpants or sneakers, but from the waist up, she was typical Marianne. New top, straightened hair, earrings, eyelashes.

Marianne opened the back door to get Jenna. "Pray that room is unlocked and that Jimmy left for Texas."

"I'm praying." Honey felt her eyes get glossy.

"Come on, Jenna," Marianne whispered as she pulled the bag out. Honey jerked when it thumped on the ground. She was brave, that Marianne. People could be fooled by her. She talked a good game, but she was as sensitive as anyone Honey knew. This was not easy for her even though she acted pretty casual. Honey would owe her for a long, long time. She didn't know what she could ever do to make up for this.

Marianne moved as fast as she could, struggling with the bag up twenty-eight steps. Honey looked out the side windows instead, to see if anyone was coming or going, glad the surveillance took her eyes off her friends.

Marianne disappeared once she got to the third floor. Honey clasped her hands tight and prayed fiercely. The corners of her eyes leaked.

Before she knew it, Marianne came running down the stairs. She popped in the car, reversed, and blasted out of there like *Charlie's Angels*.

"How was she?"

"Let's not talk about it," was all Marianne said for what seemed like forever.

Marianne hit the gas pedal hard, and the two of them stared out the window, silently promising each other to leave it all back there with Jenna. Honey just then realized the real reason Marianne didn't want Honey up in the room with her. She wanted to spare Honey from seeing Jenna in whatever condition that was.

Honey reached out for Marianne's hand, and neither one of them could hold back the tears anymore.

A few minutes later, Marianne turned the radio way up. She and Honey sang so loud the air freshener swayed. They were giddy as schoolgirls. All that bottled-up anxiety came loose into little girl giggles. It felt strange for Honey's mouth to be laughing while her heart was breaking. It had been a long time since Honey laughed about anything, even if it was a cover-up for everything else she was feeling.

Marianne opened the glove box and took out her self-named Eau de Hottie and spritzed herself while she told Honey some good news. The Tory Burch bag was on its way to the highest bidder.

"I should've looked up the address before I got to the post office," Marianne said. "Crazy4Bags is in San Clemente. What are the chances of that? I could've driven it there and saved the postage!" She raised one of her eyebrows. "But you never know what kind of crazy people are buying stuff on eBay." That made them both laugh.

When Marianne told Honey the bag sold for $989, she thought Marianne was kidding. What kind of stupid girl pays $1000 for a bag when the knockoff was $25? In the car they played a silly game, naming things they'd buy if they had an extra $1000 hanging around and didn't have to pay off a drug dealer who was coming for them.

"I'd buy a casket for Momma and pay Angel and his friend to dig the hole and sneak her into the cemetery she wanted to be buried in." Then pay off some of Momma's medical bills. She didn't even dare dream about going back to college. There was so much she needed money for, even necessities felt like a pipe dream.

Marianne slapped the steering wheel. "Honey, I thought you were having Momma cremated? You can't have Angel dig a hole at the cemetery—for real? What if he's caught? And get that sweet guy in trouble? If she's cremated, you can *sprinkle* her in the cemetery!"

That girl was even smarter when she was happy. She must've been high on Honey's promise of a twenty-five percent cut from whatever the handbag brought in.

"Things are looking up, Honey! Hey, I forgot to tell you. You remember that girl Zoe we met last year in chemistry? You drew her portrait when we did that group project? I ran into her on campus the other day. She posted the drawing on Insta and tagged you. Your Flygirl page is blowing up! Did you see how many new followers you have?"

"Really?"

Honey hadn't posted anything for a week. Maybe more. Flygirl was her username. It's where she posted her drawings. More followers meant more people were looking at her art. Real people she didn't even know.

Sometimes it felt weird thinking about strangers looking at her portraits on Instagram. That's why she put them there, but still. They were glimpses into her personal life. Selfies people posted were exactly that, too. But somehow drawings were even more personal. Because she made them. Of course, Honey followed her favorite artists. People hovering over each other's lives from afar. Someone hovering over Honey's life, Honey hovering over someone else's. The world was a strange place. It was weird how she didn't know the people who knew something about her.

"Hey, any news on Moretti's house? You ever hear from his family? Does he even have anyone left?" Marianne turned to face Honey.

Honey was paralyzed by that question. She thought about it constantly. Honey had to force herself not to think about it.

"Never mind about that, Honey. Let's think about that another time. By the way," Marianne said, "I'm not taking anything for selling the bag. I don't want my BFF ending up *dead* somewhere. Consider it a donation to your fresh-start fund. You never know when you'll need fallback money. If you really want to pay me something, I'll take my commission in the form of a portrait. What do you think? You've never sketched me before."

Honey shifted in her seat to look at Marianne. She started to ugly cry. She couldn't help it. It was all too much. She didn't have enough tissues to control what was happening. Makeup-tinted teardrops plopped onto her body brace like water balloons.

Later that night when Honey was alone at home—alone with a dog she loved/hated, an injured cop she was responsible for, and no Momma—a wave of panic rushed at her. All her troubles appeared in one big heap. Up until now, she had spread them out, like she used to do as a kid with a plate of lima beans. Looking at them now, lumped together, was scary as hell.

She didn't have a way to provide for herself until her bones healed. Jimmy could show up any minute. Once she handed him the eBay haul, she'd have practically nothing left. Jimmy wasn't the only one who could come knocking. Someday soon, someone would show up looking to claim the house.

If Honey lived in a fairy-tale world, like Marianne accused her of, she'd hate to see the real world.

Honey wasn't equipped to be Florence Nightingale to the cop. Not now, not ever. How did she ever think she could? Waiting on a miracle was not a sound plan.

Before Honey went to sleep, she texted Angel. "I need to ask you a favor. I need to help a friend out and get her a ride to the hospital in the morning, but I can't drive. Are you around?

She wanted to ask Marianne. But something told her not to get Marianne involved.

CHAPTER 34

Honey

Tuesday, January 5, 2016, 9:15 a.m.

Honey woke in a sweat sitting upright in the basement chair. Shaken from a nightmare of a moving van that pulled up in front of Mr. Moretti's to take Honey and her things to her new home. The van was empty, except for Honey's wig. As the van pulled away from the house, Mooch barked in the doorway. She pleaded with the movers to let her bring Mooch, but they said nobody gets to have pets in jail.

Honey carefully hoisted herself from the chair to avoid dislodging any of her bones trying to solder themselves. No one was gonna hire her if she couldn't turn, bend, reach, walk. Everything hurt, but it was her heartache that reminded her she was alive.

When Honey picked up her phone at 9:30 a.m., she already had six texts from Marianne, starting at 2:30 a.m. Did that girl ever sleep?

2:32 a.m.: PayPal didn't clear $ yet.

3:17 a.m.: Honey! We fucked up! There's a $10,000 reward for info on Shae Wilmont!10K fucking $$! I flushed the evidence!

We woulda been set for life! I SOLD THE BAG!! Jesus—$10K! I FLUSHED THE FUCKING STICKER!!!

3:31 a.m.: Damn. When you're cold, you're cold. No way a cop would believe us now. Easy 10K. Poof, gone.

5:30 a.m.: Slimeballs coming out now trying 2 get $$. People. com interviewed hairstylist Shae worked w/ at last job. Says he knows stuff abt her no one does. Like she's got a *bald spot*— AYFKM?! It was his job to hide it. Fuck People for printing that! She has a butterfly tat on her scalp? Never reading People again! All kinds of trash coming 4 their 15 min & 10K!

Honey's eyes grew wide. She read the text again. Maybe she confused something. Her head wasn't right—that was true. She forced herself to read slower. That made her panic more. That speed bump warning she hoped for had come. It nearly stopped her from breathing. The words from that text charged down Honey's throat, smothered her lungs, and knocked the breath right out of her.

Rose's chest had the faintest rise and fall. She was hanging on by a hair.

Honey tried to talk herself out of what was creeping into her brain. Her heart beat so fast it could be back in Louisiana by lunchtime.

Rose isn't a cop, said a voice inside Honey's head. *And her name isn't Rose.*

Honey slid slowly into the chair. She could've sworn the floor shifted under her feet.

She struggled to reach back in her memory, to piece things together.

How didn't she know sooner?

When should it have been obvious?

Honey's heart thumped against the brace. Her whole body lurched. Blood pumped through the veins in her ears, a thick lump swelled in the back of her throat, making it hard to breathe. She rubbed her hands together, but the sweat kept coming. Her fingertips remembered the slippery bald spot; it made Honey shiver. She'd felt ashamed for touching it, like she touched the girl's private area. She realized now, that's exactly what it was.

Honey's mountain of trouble just got steeper.

This pretty girl was the missing TV host.

Ho-*ly* Mother of Jesus.

That explained the shoes. The clothes. The hair. The jewelry. The manicure. No police badge. But not what she was doing in Honey's house—*Mr. Moretti's* house. She didn't follow Honey from the Boulevard to arrest her. Honey stretched her brain muscles to remember anything about that night. New Year's Eve. What did the girl say? She followed the cameraman.

Honey didn't think she looked like a Rose—or a cop. Of all the times to be right. Too bad Honey couldn't brag. That also explained the handbag.

Now Honey knew something Marianne didn't know.

She knew things Marianne would never want to know about this girl. This girl had the address label from the stalker's letter in her handbag. She was mailing that letter to *herself.*

Why?

She was one messed up girl.

People sure were funny like that. You spend all kinds of time with somebody because you work with them, or you serve them a cup of chicken noodle soup every day at 11:30, or you see them on TV cooking omelets in their kitchen, or it's your job to hide their bald spot, but still they're complete strangers to you. What do you know about them, really? Nothing.

At this very moment, Honey knew more than anyone about the missing girl *and* the stalker. She knew where the missing girl was and who her stalker was. One of those things was Honey's secret, and the other was the girl's secret. It seemed they were depending on each other more than ever.

Now that the evidence was gone, would anyone find out the girl was stalking herself? It would shock a lot of people—if they'd ever believe it. It would get her in a lot of trouble.

Honey was in her own zombie state of shock. Numb, but at the same time shaking with disbelief. The phone remained open in her hand. One more unread text from Marianne.

5:47 a.m.: Honey, listen to me. You better keep ur eyes open w/ that friend of urs. Just bc she's a cop means nothing. She's mixed up in this somehow. Don't do anything stupid.

Too late.

CHAPTER 35

Honey

Tuesday, January 5, 2016, 9:20 a.m.

HONEY's arm dropped to her side. The ghost of Marianne's text burned in her eyes, and the silence in the house amplified her sudden sense of solitude. This was no plate of lima beans. The phone burned her hand. It shot fear up her veins. She uncurled her fingers, and the phone fell onto the chair with a thud.

Honey paced from the bed to the stairs and back again, over and over. She didn't know what else to do.

Panic coursed through her, putting her in a spell.

Without looking at the cop—the *TV lady*—Honey put a trembling finger on Rose's—*Shae's* wrist. Did she feel a pulse, or was she imagining it? An imperceptible tap?

She hadn't heard back from Angel yet, but she had to get this girl to the hospital. It was time to tell Marianne. She needed help and badly. She shuffled over to her phone on the chair. A missed call from Marianne and a voicemail message. She checked her volume button and turned it on. Honey dialed Marianne's number. It went straight to voicemail.

"Call me back, Marianne. I gotta tell you something. It's urgent."

Going through the pile of the girl's belongings with fresh perspective didn't reveal anything new. Where was her wallet? Everybody carried a wallet. Honey's head was spinning. She was in no condition to piece together a mystery. On her best days, it wasn't the way her brain worked. Now she had serious questions about whether her brain worked at all.

If this girl died, Honey knew she was heading to jail. Even if they couldn't prove anything against her. What a horrific mistake for Honey not to think people were looking for this girl. She was missing! She had family and friends crazy with concern, searching and praying. People like her—pretty, wealthy, successful, popular—a celebrity!—had tons of friends, all kinds of associations Honey'd never have. She probably needed an assistant to keep them organized. If Marianne was so concerned about her and had never even met her, imagine all the genuine connections who were!

This made Honey feel smaller and smaller. This made Honey feel like the most insignificant living being there ever was. Honey could vanish from the face of the earth, and who'd notice?

At thirty-nine laps across the floor and no text from Marianne, a bad kind of premonition started creeping up to Honey's brain. Marianne's phone grew out of her palm like a sixth finger. She was never without her phone. She'd respond to a text the second she received it. Where the hell was she that she couldn't text right now?

Honey considered the possibilities. There were none. Marianne brought her phone to the bathroom, to bed, to school, to work, driving, she propped it on the towel rack outside her shower so she didn't miss anything while shampooing. She sure as hell wasn't swimming in Puerto Vallarta, though Honey wished she was. There was no place Marianne couldn't text.

Unless she was dead.

Honey flipped her phone over and over a hundred times, like that was going to help. Then she remembered Marianne's message.

She tapped her voicemail.

"Honey!" Marianne shrieked. "I'm in jail! They arrested me! You gotta help me!"

Honey stood very still listening to Marianne's frantic, quivering pleas as the room swirled around her, like she was standing in the eye of a hurricane and somehow, if she didn't move, maybe she wouldn't get hurt.

"The police came to my house." Marianne was gasping for air like somebody was chasing her as she ran for her life. "They tracked me down from that fucking Tory Burch bag. The *police* bought the bag. *They* were 'Crazee4Bags'! They think I kidnapped Shae Wilmont! That fucking bag was hers! I'm scared! You gotta help me!"

CHAPTER 36

Lawrence

Tuesday, January 5, 2016, 9:21 a.m.

L AWRENCE hated admitting it, but he was a mess of nerves. He wasn't expecting to feel such misery, but what should he expect? Shae's father was about to find out she was a missing person. Zurich was nine hours ahead. Lawrence hoped the timing was good.

He sat back at his desk and pulled himself together. When he dialed in, the call had already started.

"Hello. Is this Peter Wilmont?"

"Yes, who's this?"

"My name is Detective Tramball. I'm calling from the Vista Verde, California, Police Department. I'm calling in regard to Shae Wilmont."

"Shae? What's happened? Is she all right?"

"Unfortunately, she's a missing person. I'm sorry to tell you that. I called to ask you some questions. Is this a good time?"

"*Missing?* My God! Missing? When did this happen?"

"Before we begin, could you state your full name and spell your last name for the transcript? This conversation is being recorded."

Peter Wilmont: Yes, my name is Peter D. Wilmont, W-I-L-M-O-N-T.

Detective Tramball: Thank you, Mr. Wilmont. The missing person's report was filed on Saturday. Could you tell me your relationship to Ms. Wilmont?

P. Wilmont: Yes, I'm her…father.

L. Tramball: When did you see her last?

P. Wilmont: Uhh, well, that would be…let me think. In person?

L. Tramball: Yes.

P. Wilmont: Unfortunately, it's been…a long time. I'd say, it's been…I'm embarrassed to say…years.

L. Tramball: When did you last speak to her?

P. Wilmont: Well…let's see…

L. Tramball: Any communication, a text, email, social media?

P. Wilmont: (No response.)

L. Tramball: Were you aware she was a missing person before this phone call?

P. Wilmont: No.

L. Tramball: Are you in contact with Shae's mother? Is it possible she'd know Shae's whereabouts?

P. Wilmont: No, I'm not in contact with her.

L. Tramball: Do you know how I could reach Shae's mother? Her name and phone number would be helpful.

P. Wilmont: No. I don't know if she's alive, to be honest. Her name is Capucine Durand. The last time I saw her was when we lived in Paris; I was with Shae. It was many years ago. Shae was a teenager. Capucine was living on the streets. She was involved with drugs. It was very sad. Actually, Capucine isn't even her real name. She made that up. It was her stage name. Though I doubt she was on a stage of any kind. I don't remember her real name.

I…this—it's…I have to be honest. Hearing this news…I'm devastated. Talking about our relationship is not easy for me. I wasn't expecting to talk about this today, obviously. And much of this, well, Shae doesn't know.

L. Tramball: I understand. I'm sorry. I'm sure this is a very difficult call to receive.

P. Wilmont: There's something I should clarify. Not that this matters—or maybe it does, I don't know. Technically, I'm not Shae's father. I raised her. But my late brother Eric was her father. He died of an overdose when she was born. I don't know for certain if he knew he was a father. I've been told different stories. We—he and I—were not close back then.

L. Tramball: I see.

P. Wilmont: I never got a straight story about their relationship. They weren't married, but Capucine told me they were planning a life together. A friend of Eric's put Capucine in touch with me. As you can imagine, I wasn't prepared for that. I mean, the whole story of the girlfriend, if that's what she was, the baby, it was …shocking. And I was still rattled by his death. He was like a stranger to me.

One of Eric's friends told me Eric had a transactional relationship with Capucine. Another friend told me they were drug buddies—if that's a thing. So I don't know. I heard another story that Eric met her in a club he frequented where she was a dancer. Who knows, maybe they're all true. I don't know if she was using my brother, but, well, that didn't turn out.

Capucine and the baby were living on the streets. She had no money. No one to turn to. I took pity on them, my niece. I hired

Capucine as a live-in housekeeper so she and the baby had a place to stay while I sorted things out. I had to be certain Eric was the father.

L. Tramball: I understand.

P. Wilmont: It was an awful time. I took his death quite hard. Particularly because of our estrangement, and then the additional ripple of the baby and her homeless mother. Capucine was as troubled as a girl could be. I was very conflicted.

Why was this being dumped in my lap? Why was I expected to make good on Eric's mistakes? I got pretty angry about it all. And stayed that way for a long time. I was so angry with Eric, and he wasn't even alive.

Eric had everything going for him. He was smart. He was a successful banker. He was young. But he couldn't get his act together. He made bad decisions. Why am I telling you this?

L. Tramball: It's okay. This information could be useful.

P. Wilmont: Shae's background is complicated. All the more complicated because she doesn't know it. I can't tell you how many times I planned to tell her. I never had the courage. The tremendous guilt I've lived with.

When Shae was about four, Capucine went out for groceries and never came back. She abandoned her own daughter. How could someone do that? To live on the streets. What sense did that make? She had a home, a safe place to live, a place to raise her child. I was stunned. I was disgusted. I was *furious.*

Reflecting back, it's hard for me to see how I went along with this bizarre situation. What I was thinking? These people, Eric and Capucine, they were screw-ups. They didn't care about anyone but themselves. Do you think I feel good saying that about my own brother? But it's true. The problem was, an innocent child was involved. My friends told me to turn Shae in. But how could I? How? I couldn't have that on my conscience.

I made arrangements to keep her. She had a few nannies and even Capucine came back a couple of times. We moved a lot for my job. Twice to the States. I brought Capucine with us to Florida. She never got off the drugs. Honestly, I'm not quite sure how she raised the money to pay for her addiction, apart from stealing from me. I refused to take care of both of them.

L. Tramball: That must have been a very difficult time.

P. Wilmont: I've made my share of bad decisions as well. But there it is. The truth. I could never tell Shae her father died of an overdose and her mother abandoned her to live on the streets and, possibly, work on the streets. How do you tell a girl that?

We were all stunned when Eric died. In the end, I knew very little about my brother.

Shae and I lost touch. It's not surprising. It's my fault. Of course it's my fault. All these secrets wedged between us. She stayed in the States after college. I can't blame her. I was a terrible father. A fake father. There was always distance between us. It must've been awful for her. No mother and a fake father. How terrible. Even when I knew I was falling short, I convinced myself it was okay. I rationalized she would've had it worse if I gave her up or threw them out. I wanted to protect her from the truth, from being hurt, but what did I give her?

L. Tramball: I understand.

P. Wilmont: I tried to tell Shae who her parents were when she was leaving for college. I was such a coward. I told her I wanted to tell her about her mother. I stammered. It was awkward and painful—for both of us. I'll never forget Shae's face, waiting, imploring me to say something. Then she shocked me. She said, "No.

It's okay. I already know. Don't worry." She left me there with my bottled-up admission. She couldn't leave fast enough. I've held on to it ever since.

But how could she know? Maybe she had a hunch about Capucine. But she's always believed I was her father. For that reason, she's likely blamed me for much of her pain. I deserve it. I masqueraded as her father and never took it on.

L. Tramball: Could Capucine have something to do with Shae's disappearance?

P. Wilmont: I can't imagine. It would take a lot of resources for her to get to the States. Maybe it's possible. It's not like she was a stranger to the notion of extortion. I experienced that firsthand. Honestly, I don't think she's alive. The last time I saw her, Shae was a teenager. We were walking through the park. I noticed her before Shae did, and I tried to navigate us so there'd be no interaction. She was singing for coins. She looked homeless. It was terrible. Shae recognized her. She asked me if it was Capucine. She was excited to see her. I lied and said no. And pulled her away.

L. Tramball: Does Shae have any other alias?

P. Wilmont: Her given name is Shagreen, but she's gone by Shae all her life.

L. Tramball: Anyone in her life who would want to do her harm?

P. Wilmont: I can't imagine that. She's a lovely girl. Of course, we've been out of touch for so long it would be foolish for me to speculate. I don't know the people in her life.

L. Tramball: Did she ever try to harm herself or talk about it?

P. Wilmont: Not that I'm aware of.

L. Tramball: Do you have any family in the States that Shae could be in touch with?

P. Wilmont: A few cousins she never met. I haven't been in touch with them.

L. Tramball: Any reason you think she'd disappear on her own?

P. Wilmont: I'm not qualified to answer that. I'm sure there's much about her I don't know. I often wonder about her. How she's doing? I can see her on TV, but that doesn't mean anything. I hope we'll have a chance to reconcile this absence from each other, this distance.

L. Tramball: I hope so, too. Is there anything else you'd like to share?

P. Wilmont: You know, when Shae was young, she used to pretend to be sick so that I'd find Capucine and bring her back home to see her. It was very sad. At school, Shae would go to the nurse, complaining of some ailment. And before the nurse would call me at work, Shae would plead with her to call Capucine. Of course, there was no phone number for her. I didn't go into specifics with the school nurse, but I explained that Capucine was our former housekeeper, and there was no way to get in touch with her. Shae would ask for her repeatedly. It was quite sad and embarrassing.

Shae told people she was going to grow up to be like Capucine. She wanted to be a singer—though we never heard Capucine sing except for that time in the park, if you count that. She would clean the house dressed like she was performing in a cabaret. Shae held her in the highest esteem. What do kids know?

L. Tramball: So are you saying—

P. Wilmont: That maybe her disappearance is a cry for help? I don't know. (Heavy sigh.) I should've married someone so Shae could've had a normal childhood. How hard would that have been? Perhaps I subconsciously blamed Shae for never getting married. Instead, we had a stream of nannies. Surprisingly, Shae never latched on to any of them.

I wanted Shae to hate Capucine. Maybe, in some way, I wanted her to hate me. Maybe that's exactly what she did.

Listen, unless there's something else, I'd like to get on the next flight to California if I can. I'd like to get on a flight today.

L. Tramball: Yes, of course.

P. Wilmont: Please call with any updates. Please...do all you can to find her.

Lawrence pounded his fist against the desk. His jaw was in a knot. He dropped his face into his hands and pressed his eyelids. He tried to breathe. He didn't want to know any more of Shae's secrets. This one, even Shae didn't know.

This investigation was getting to Lawrence.

"What's this, Lawrence?"

Who was that? He couldn't even lift his head. It was Rita, of course. He forgot he was home. Her voice came from the hall and startled him. Thank God she didn't interrupt his call.

She repeated the question. Her interrogating trill ambushed his despair binge. He was not in the mood for Rita right now.

He didn't want Rita to see him in this compromised state. As he sat up, without turning to look, he sensed the door was open. How could that be? Either she opened the door without knocking, or she knocked and he didn't notice.

Through Lawrence's peripheral vision, a figure much larger than Rita's thimble-sized body loomed in the doorway, only a few feet from him. This figure was not only wider and taller than Rita, it was green and fuzzy.

He wanted desperately to ignore her, but he couldn't quell his sudden curiosity or the nagging sense he'd regret looking.

"Look what I found, Lawrence. Are you looking?" Her voice was muted, as if her mouth was covered.

Lawrence slowly turned his head. He was stunned. He clutched the armrests of his chair. "Where'd you get that?"

Blood coursed his veins in hot streams, no doubt coloring his cheeks. He was livid. He wanted to bolt from the chair but there was nowhere to go. Recent IShop deliveries were stacked behind him, including the smoker—a box too big for this tiny room; it should've been left in the garage. The scant available space was inadequate for the Power Pose. Not even the seated one.

"What are you doing with that? Who said you could put it on?" Each word he spit through clenched teeth.

"Why are you getting so upset? I found it in the garage. I was putting away the Christmas decorations in the eaves." Her voice was muted behind the costume's thick fabric. "I wouldn't have found it if you put the decorations away like I asked."

Rita took up the entire width of the doorway; the hallowed green Fighting Okra costume was enormous on her. Her eyes didn't line up with the eye holes, her arms didn't line up with the arm holes. She was so short, the upper half flopped forward in front of her, pathetic and flaccid like a wilted tulip.

"How do I look?" She spun in a circle, whacking things off his desk from the unruly bulk of the parts she couldn't fill. The top half walloped Lawrence in the head. He swatted it.

"You can take it off now. Nobody said you could put it on." He wished he hadn't seen it like this, all floppy and pathetic. He felt deflated. He tried to conjure admonishment. To ratchet up some fire.

"Oh, Lawrence. I'm trying to have some fun with you. What is this, anyway? It's huge! My head can't even reach the top."

"I can hear you, Rita, you don't need to yell."

"Well, my mouth doesn't line up to the mouth hole, so I didn't think you could." She squirmed inside, raising her arms to fill the top of the head. "How can anyone see out this thing?"

Suddenly, her eyeballs appeared in an armhole.

"That's for your arm, Rita, not your head! Don't stick your head through—you'll stretch it!"

The top half flopped forward and dangled lifelessly.

"I wasn't going to." Her eyes disappeared. "What is this, Lawrence?"

"It's an okra, what do you think it is?! Yeah, it's big. That's because I was the biggest Fighting Okra Delta State ever had."

"You mean—" Her squirming stopped. As did her voice. Rita's eyes popped through the armhole again, her fingertips curled around the edges. "What do you mean? At college? You were the mascot?" She stopped for a second, and her eyebrows grew closer to one another. "I thought you were on the football team? You told me you were on the football team. That's what you told me."

"I *was* on the football team, Rita. The mascot is on the team! Everybody knows that."

He rotated his college ring around and around, the smooth green stone gliding against the flesh between his fingers.

"Oh." Her eyes drained of expression. Then they narrowed. "Of course it is." Her eyes vanished. "I thought you were...a player, that's all."

She took a step closer to Lawrence but bumped into the desk. "Ow." Her fingers wriggled out the armholes like she was trying to see with them. "Not that I love you any less." She made contact with the lamp, then rotated to the left. "Think about it, Lawrence. There are dozens of players on a team, but only one mascot!"

Her index finger soared into the air to indicate how many mascots a team had and nearly poked his eye out. Lawrence ducked.

"You must've been an amazing Okra." Her two fists shot threw their respective armholes in unison. "The toughest Okra ever!"

Lawrence couldn't take it anymore. This was not the way he wanted to remember the Fighting Okra.

"I bet all the girls loved your Okra the best. The sexiest Okra in school history!" She held her hands out to touch Lawrence, but he didn't help her. He couldn't bear seeing the head flopped over limp like that, sucking its own knees. Or worse.

"That's enough. Take it off. You're disrespecting the Okra walking around with the top sagging. What if you tear it? It's an important keepsake."

She nodded. "All right, Lawrence." The top half of the Okra bobbed up and down. "I was just having some fun. You're working so hard, getting up before the birds. You could use a break. Have a few laughs. Maybe you'll put it on for me later?" She pulled her hands back in. "You're something else, Lawrence. You know that?" She stepped toward him again, this time to kiss his head. All he could feel was the scratchy fabric against his ear.

"I swear, if I knew you a hundred years, I still wouldn't know everything about you."

CHAPTER 37

Honey

Tuesday, January 5, 2016, 9:22 a.m.

THE phone slipped from Honey's hand and thudded onto the tiny rug remnant at the side of the bed. Marianne's cries echoed in her ears.

It took more fortitude than she had left to connect the dots of this disaster that parked itself at Honey's feet. This much she knew: her best friend in the world was in trouble because of her.

You just got to clean it up. She heard Momma's voice in her head. Momma always made it sound easy, even when it wasn't. That was the only thing that made it seem achievable.

Honey dragged her feet over to the wall with her favorite portrait of Momma and rested her hand against it. Where joy once filled her heart, loneliness replaced it.

"I need your help, Momma," she whispered. "I feel like the worst kind of failure. I'm gonna fix this, but I don't know how. I need to make things right for this injured girl and for Marianne. She's in big trouble because of me. She doesn't deserve any of this. Pray for me, Momma. I need you now more than ever."

Warm tears spilled from her eyes. Fog was looming heavy around Honey. She could barely see through it. More importantly, she had to think through it. And act through it.

Only one idea came to her. She wasn't sure where on the stupid scale it fell, but it didn't matter. She didn't have the luxury of calling a brainstorming meeting with self-starters and go-getters.

This wasn't a good time to think about how hard it would be to leave this peaceful and loving home. Or the warmth and safety she felt here. You can't depend on that kind of stuff lasting forever. Marianne was right—maybe Honey *was* living in a fairy tale.

Happy endings are for princesses.

Honey disappeared into Mr. Moretti's canning room and dug through his old crap. She wondered why it was called "canning" when the food was stored in jars. She forced herself not to think about the jarred peaches Momma used for her pie. All those jars, empty now. The glass vessels covered in dust lined every shelf. They looked like ghosts. It was eerie and sad.

She grabbed a canvas bag and smacked the dust out of it. It was stiff and musty, but it had more dignity than a plastic grocery bag, so she took it.

The last time she packed a bag she was sixteen and running away from home. As much as she was seeking a better life, she couldn't help but wonder at the last minute, if maybe she was already living the high life. She tried to forecast the what-ifs, but there's no doppler for that.

When Honey got to California, she didn't know what she was expecting but it was no Emerald City and no one was waiting to curl her hair. The bus coughed her out like a phlegm ball in El Pueblo, and it dawned on her for the first time, she was a-*lone*. Back home in Louisiana, she was a big-time dreamer. Any courage she had was ignorance with attitude. Foolishness with fringe. In California, she thought the world would lay before her like a yellow brick road to better-than-this. It didn't take long to realize that those bricks were yellow from piss, and the stench from the bus station at the end of the line was smelling salts of a wake-up call. As scary as the beginning was, Honey regretted none of it. Sometimes you have to take a step back to move forward.

Honey took down her portrait of Momma and peeled the tape off the back. It was her favorite drawing. She tore the edges of the cardboard to make it as small as she could without having to fold it to fit in the bag. Wasn't much she could fit in there. She didn't have much to bring. Some clothes, a bar of soap, the last Pop-Tart, her wig—of course, and Momma's apron. Momma was a superhero, and that apron was her cape. Anywhere Honey went, she'd be home as long as she had that apron. Honey grabbed the little plastic Virgin Mary for good measure. *Us girls got to stick together.*

She filled up the TV girl's glass with fresh water one last time, trying to convince herself it wasn't for appearances.

"I'm sorry," Honey choked out. "Maybe it sounds crazy, but I thought you were a cop. I was so terrified of what you'd do to me, I wasn't thinking straight. Guess I'm not the only person who was thinking you're something you're not. I never knew a girl like you could be so messed up. You have so much. What a waste. Guess we both have explaining to do. I thought I could get you on your feet. Turns out I was wrong about a lot. You need to pull through. I'm praying for you. A lot of people are praying for you. You've got to hang on."

Honey never figured a pretty rich girl could be so stupid. Why couldn't she be happy?

"Hold on, girl. Please hold on."

Her racing heart was trying to light a fire under her ass, but she couldn't get her mind and her body to cooperate with each other.

Upstairs, Mooch was sleeping under the kitchen table. With her hands on her hips, Honey let out a sad exhale filled with regret. Was rescuing the dog the right thing to do? Maybe Mooch was just a street dog. How would he survive now after relying on a bowl of food plopped in front of his snout every day and having to do nothing for it?

The day he followed Honey home from the bus stop, he must've known she was a sucker. He sat there on the grass outside the kitchen door all night long. Like a spaghetti sauce stain on your best shirt, he didn't budge. If it wasn't for the moaning, she would have ignored him. Honey couldn't tolerate moaning.

Momma always told Denise, "Stop your moaning, girl. You want people's respect or pity?" It wasn't as motivating as Momma intended. Unfortunately, most of Momma's sage platitudes were wasted on Denise. The first time Honey heard Momma ask that question, Honey stood up a little taller. She knew what her answer would be.

That stupid, sorry mutt stared at Honey from the backyard that day all dopey-eyed with bologna hope.

When Honey thinks of it now, it's obvious that the next thing she did wasn't the smartest strategy for getting rid of a street dog. She threw a piece of bologna over the dog's head like a frisbee, hoping that'd shoo him away. That dog leapt into the sky like a *hallelujah*. He chased down the bologna, and that was the end of that. In that moment, the dog knew more about Honey than she did about the dog. They'd been together ever since.

Honey opened the back door, and Mooch's eyes flicked open. Honey pointed to the back yard.

"Get out of here, Mooch! Go!"

He tilted his head, confused. Honey clapped her hands. "Come on, I don't have all day, get going!" That stupid dog gave her those eyes—same eyes from day one.

He stood up, not knowing what to make of anything, staring at Honey while her heart ached.

"I should've gotten rid of you a long time ago! I wouldn't be in this mess!" She was yelling through misty eyes. She choked on every word. Why was she crying for that animal? All the trouble he caused her. How stupid could Honey be?

"Go! Go find your friends—"

He crept out with his tail dragging behind him. Honey closed the door and left Mooch staring at her. She couldn't bear looking at him.

This was no time for tears. No time for dog-pity or Honey-pity. She never expected this home, so she had to trust she'd have another one someday. Maybe her next home would last forever. She prayed to Momma. To Jesus. Anybody who'd spare a minute for her. She had to keep the faith. She had to believe better days were coming.

Pull yourself together, girl. You need to save the people who need saving most.

And right now, that wasn't Honey.

CHAPTER 38

Shae

FIVE DAYS LATER

Sunday, January 10, 2016, 11:00 a.m.

"You look better today, cookie," Figgy said from the foot of Shae's hospital bed. "You've got more color." Someone with hair the hue of cotton candy piled into a messy bun, a lime-green scoop neck t-shirt, and candy-apple red Chuck Taylor Converse didn't lie about color.

Shae smiled. Just having Figgy around made Shae feel better. "Or maybe I'm reflecting your color?"

"Ha!" She clapped her hands. "Could be!" She pulled her phone out of her tote. "How about a pic for your fans? I'll post it on FB. They're dying to see you!"

"Oh no, Fig." Shae smoothed her hair. "I'm not ready for that."

Figgy put her hand up. "No problem! It's okay. Maybe tomorrow." She looked back at her phone. "I have to show you this." She scrolled through, then held it in front of Shae. "That's what the lobby looks like right now!" The IShop lobby had become a veritable shrine to Shae. Stuffed animals, flowers, balloons. *Get Well Soon!* posters. *Come Back Soon!* posters. *We Miss You!* posters.

Shae didn't say a word. She stared at the photo, then looked up at Figgy sheepishly.

Figgy had wanted to tell Shae everything going on at the studio. Shae thought she wanted to know it all. But oddly, she didn't. A short time ago, it was everything to her. Now it felt almost illegitimate. Like it wasn't even her life.

"What? Don't look so sad, cookie! They love you!"

Shae wished it was that simple. She wished she could indulge herself in the adulation. Isn't that what she always wanted? But the fact that all this would soon come crashing down—very soon —made it more complicated than Figgy knew.

"I'll post this photo instead. We'll get one of you another time. I'll do your hair and makeup if you want." Figgy winked at her. "Maybe you'll go home today? It's been five days."

"I hope so. The doctor said as soon as the infection is under control. It's not the skin infection. It's from the bone surgery. From the metal rod implant."

"Hang in there. The worst is over. We all have to be patient. You'll be back to work before you know it."

The door swung open, and the nurse appeared. "Hi there! How's it going in here?" A new nurse. "I'm subbing for Ronnie today. So you just let me know if you need anything. I'll take the tray if you're finished?" The nurse examined the food tray. Shae hadn't eaten any of it. "You've got to eat, sweetie. If you're going to feel better. Oh, someone brought you the good stuff!" She motioned to the Starbucks bag.

"My friend brought me an egg-white spinach wrap. My favorite. And coffee. No offense."

"No worries! I'm addicted to the chai lattes. I only recommend hospital coffee out of desperation at three in the morning. Glad you're eating. That entire water pitcher should be your goal for the day, if not more. The doctor will be in around lunchtime." She picked up the tray and left.

Shae hoped she'd be going home today. The steady stream of visitors, the chitchat, Shae wasn't up for it. At home no one would stop by unannounced like they did here. As much as she loved seeing Figgy, their visits felt awkward. She didn't know how much Figgy knew about the investigation. Once it was all out in the open, who knew what would be left of their friendship?

"How are the visits with your father going?" Figgy straightened the flimsy blanket that settled into a clump at the end of the bed and covered Shae's left leg, keeping her right leg free.

People from all parts of Shae's life had come to visit in the last five days, but none caught her off guard as much as her father did. Their conversations—the family secrets he revealed—tilted her entire world.

"I don't want to pry," Figgy said when Shae didn't respond.

"No. It's not that, Fig" She exhaled. "I just don't think I can talk about it now. It's been a lot for me to—wrap my mind around."

Peter's concern and the effort it took for him to see Shae was out of the ordinary. But so were the circumstances. There was a period in Shae's youth when she'd pretend to be sick for attention. It rarely worked the way she hoped. It was embarrassing to think of her younger self being so desperate. Even more humiliating to realize she hadn't completely left that behind.

"I know this must sound crazy to you, but I was surprised when he showed up here. It's been a long time since I've seen him. Our relationship has suffered over the years."

"Family is complicated. You know I don't judge." Figgy busied herself picking up the Starbucks wrappers and organizing Shae's table. They both became quiet and lost in thought.

It would be difficult to explain to Figgy the dynamics of her family—if it could even be called that. Compared to Figgy's family—big, boisterous, and benevolent—Shae's was abbreviated, awkward, and adrift. Shae and Peter had done very little to keep in touch. As tiny as their family was—two people—you'd think they'd be close. Shae had convinced herself that her father wasn't interested in hearing from her. When she graduated college, she sensed his relief that she was finally an adult and moving on. Peter was a hard one to get close to. Maybe Shae was, too.

She'd tell Figgy someday. Shae needed time to process Peter's confessions and apologies. Details of her family history she'd obsessed about most of her life, and he'd held onto for just as long. The tragic story of her biological parents. Her father, Eric, dying of an overdose. Her mother, Capucine, with her own demons of addiction. She was stunned. Disoriented. Confused. There it was. What she had wanted to know all her life. Beyond anything she could have predicted. It was difficult to hear she had spent part of her childhood living on the streets with a mother who eventually abandoned her. Even though Capucine had a safe place to live with Peter, and food, she left it behind—left *Shae* behind—to be homeless again. What sense did that make? It was all too confusing. Shocking. Devastating. How did this provenance reflect on Shae? *Did* it? It certainly provided a new lens thru which to view Peter. What did all this say about him? As spare as his parenting was, and for all the reasons he'd fallen short over the years, she obviously had a lot to be grateful for. Without him, would she have followed in her mother's tragic footsteps? Would she have gone to school? College? Had the professional opportunities she'd had? It was time to reflect on the ways she'd squandered these very opportunities, and move forward.

Peter had carried tremendous guilt all these years for the way he raised her. He regretted his distance and his anger. He hoped sharing these truths would bring them closer.

"I'm glad he's here for you. There's no substitute for family." She squeezed Shae's arm. Figgy turned around to fish through her tote bag on the chair. She retrieved a small box from her bag. "The Donna Karan rep dropped this off for you." Figgy extended it to Shae but drew it back when Shae grimaced and quietly groaned. She wished the gifts would stop.

"That's nice, Fig. I'll open it later. Maybe you could help me donate these things?" She pointed to a stack of gifts. "To a women's shelter?"

"A women's shelter." Figgy looked confused. "Sure," she said tentatively.

On the other side of Shae's bed, Figgy placed the box on a pile of unopened gifts.

"I should go, cookie. You need to rest. And I've got to be at the studio." She glanced at her watch and picked up the TV remote. "I'll turn this off if you're going to nap?"

They both looked up at the TV, which was set to the IShop channel. Bryan had just started his Woozu Puffer Coat show. Actually, Shae's Woozu show. Bryan had been stepping in to fill some of Shae's shows. The set was meant to look like the outdoors with the front of a fake house, covered in fake snow. Bryan leaned on a shovel.

"I want to dedicate this show to our girl, Shae," Bryan said looking into the camera.

Figgy turned to look at Shae and said, "Told you."

"Shae, if you're watching, get better and come back soon! This place isn't the same without you!" He blew a kiss.

The Woozu rep stood next to Bryan wearing a bright orange puffer. "We miss Shae so much," she said. "How's she doing?"

"I saw her yesterday, actually," Bryan said. "Even in the hospital, that Shae's as glamorous as ever!"

Shae hid her face in her hands, and Figgy laughed. She hadn't changed her hospital gown or brushed her hair in days.

"He's been dedicating all his shows to you." Figgy clicked off the TV with the remote.

"It's very sweet." Shae sighed heavily. "Who knew he could be so thoughtful."

"Umm, everyone? You're just seeing it now." She patted Shae's hand. "I heard Theo came to see you. Are these from him?" Figgy pointed to an arrangement of yellow daisies.

"How did you know?"

"He told me." Figgy shrugged. "We eat lunch together now."

"Really?" Shae teased.

"He's a good guy, cookie. Once you get to know him."

These colleagues of Shae's were showing her something she hadn't experienced much in her life. Sincerity. Warmth. Concern. Friendship. Shae was ashamed of herself for betraying all that in her misguided attempt to elicit those very things. Through reckless, regrettable behavior. It would all be gone soon. Shae destroyed it.

Figgy filled up Shae's cup from the pitcher. "You need to stay hydrated."

Shae's head snapped in Figgy's direction. The girl from the basement—Shae didn't even know her name—flashed through her mind. Just one of many new triggers Shae would need to get used to. She shuddered as if trying to break free from the thought.

"You okay?"

She looked at Figgy, relieved to see her. "I'm fine."

Figgy pulled a chair up to the side of Shae's bed and sat down.

"Listen, before I go, I want to tell you something. Yesterday when I was leaving, a detective was out in the hall waiting to see you. I told him you were sleeping. He said he'd come back today. I'm sure you have a lot to discuss, but do you remember I texted you on New Year's Eve about the new detective? He wanted to tell you about a new letter that came for you. One that looked like the others you got back in the fall. Val told me they're going through all the mail again that's been sent in the last six months. Some people have come forward with information about the latest one." Figgy patted Shae's hand. "He wants to talk to you about that. I just want you to be prepared."

Shae looked away. It felt like all the blood drained from her face. She knew about that letter arriving at the studio—it was lost for months—but not because anyone told her. She overhead the girl in the basement talking about it on the phone with someone. Someone who was trying to sell Shae's handbag found the address label in it. Shae felt a wave of nausea.

"Oh, I almost forgot." Figgy pulled a bottle of nail polish re-mover and cotton balls from her bag. One by one she rubbed Shae's nails clean.

"Thanks, Fig. I couldn't wait to get that off."

"I showed Val the photo of your nails. Apparently, you're not the only one who had every nail turn red. Some girls even had two colors on one nail!" She laughed. "Wonder what that means? Know what they should do?" She looked at Shae. "Change the name from Intuition to Play Date and market it to five-year-olds! Little girls would love it!"

They both laughed out loud. It felt so good to laugh.

Figgy continued, "Then Val said, 'Shae must have a lot of secrets.'" Figgy winked at Shae. "I guess red was supposed to mean somebody's keeping your secrets safe."

Shae's head jerked back. She subconsciously swallowed hard on a wad of humiliation.

"What? She was kidding!" Figgy insisted.

Shae wasn't convinced Val was kidding. She had no idea how much Val knew at this point. They probably all knew who sent those letters. Everyone at IShop. That would explain the awkward visits. The stilted conversations. Probably why Val hadn't visited. Shae's cheeks felt hot. She didn't want to have secrets anymore. She reached for her water.

Figgy popped out of the seat. "Let me get it for you." She picked up the pitcher and topped off Shae's glass.

"I think I need to sleep," Shae said.

"Of course, cookie. I should go." Figgy grabbed her tote bag from the chair. "Don't worry about anything. Just rest up. Text me later if you're going to leave today."

Figgy was barely out of the room before Shae fell asleep.

Shae hadn't slept deeply in a long time and maybe would never again. On some level, she was aware of sounds or movement outside of her sleep state. She hovered close to the edge of consciousness even while dreaming. It was a sense that someone was in the room with her that nudged her awake. She hesitated to open her eyes—another new habit.

It wasn't unusual for someone to be in the room. Nurses, doctors, cleaning people came in and out all the time.

Whoever was in the room with her now, though, was none of those people. She knew by how unsettled she felt. She knew it because of the prickling of her scalp. And the pang in her stomach. And by the fact that whoever it was, was smelling her.

CHAPTER 39

Shae

Tuesday, January 10, 2016, 12:15 p.m.

SHAE froze, every muscle in her body taut. Her eyes glued shut. Her heart about to burst through her chest.

Three short sniffs. A long inhale. Exhale.

It wasn't a *dog*. Obviously. She knew that. She was in a hospital.

Then again. Three short sniffs. A long inhale. An exhale. Someone's nose was smelling her. Practically touching her. She could feel the heat from their breath. Garlic breath.

Her eyes flew open. Hunched over her, with his nose in her armpit, was a man sniffing her.

"Hey!" Shae shouted and recoiled. "What are you doing?!"

He jumped back. "Oh! Good morning!" He fumbled with his phone. Then dropped to the floor.

Shae wormed her way toward the opposite edge of the bed, though there was no room to distance herself.

"I dropped something down here…" On all fours he looked under the bed. "Hmm, where did it go…" He sprang up. "Nope!

Nothing down there. Not even a dust bunny!" He slid something onto the chair beside the bed, stood up and adjusted the waist of his pants.

He rubbed his nose, flustered. "Oh, here it is!" He held a pen in the air. "Sorry—didn't intend to startle you."

Shae tried to relax. Maybe he wasn't smelling her? That would be absurd. But that's what she heard. That's what she saw.

He had come on official business from the Vista Verde Police Department.

He pulled the hair on his eyebrow.

Shae braced herself for this conversation. But did she need to have it with this guy? She wanted him to leave. She was already flustered. She inhaled deeply to settle down.

Shae always wondered why the last letter never arrived. She mailed it in September. Someone, back then, was held in police custody, suspected of sending them. Falsely accused. Shae was horrified that an innocent person was a suspect for something *she* did. How scared they must have been. What if that person was charged? The only letter sent with urgency took months to arrive. The outcome could've been tragic.

"Finally, my visit is opportune," the detective said while pulling his eyebrow. "The other times I visited, you've been asleep. I almost took it personally." He laughed awkwardly. His breath again. She was repulsed that he stood close enough for her to smell it and that she couldn't move back to dodge it.

Maybe he was right about Shae sleeping subconsciously to avoid him and this discussion. She couldn't sleep forever.

Shae's decision, as difficult as it was, was the right one. She was prepared to live up to her mistakes. She couldn't play the victim anymore. It was time to stand up. Move forward. Take responsibility for her life. Despite the setbacks surely to come.

In Shae's haste to send the last letter quickly, hoping it would convince the police to release the suspect, she was forced to use two labels that each bore part of the name and address. She never intended to use two. The sheet jammed in her printer. And printed diagonally across two labels. It was her last sheet. She obviously couldn't write the address. She had no choice but to use them. En route to mailing it, though, she didn't know one fell off and stuck to the inside pocket of her handbag. Unwittingly, she mailed it with half an address.

When the letter didn't arrive at the studio days later, she grew increasingly panicked. Thank God the suspect was released on other grounds. When it didn't arrive a week later, a month later—she almost forgot about it.

What happened to innocent people who endured someone else's punishment?

Shae would weather this humiliation. Face the punishment. It was sure to include the loss of friends, fans, and her job. An arrest? Two weeks ago, that would've frightened her. Devastated her. But there were far more frightening things one could endure. She'd start over. It wouldn't be the first time. This time, for some odd reason, she felt stronger.

What would her fans think once the truth was out? What shape would the fallout take? When people on a public stage screwed up, it was instant news. Vultures would pick her apart. She was grateful to be alive, and little else mattered. Except for the truth. The truth mattered. Hearing her father's truth these last few days made her realize that. The truth, though humiliating, would strangely free her.

"I won't take much of your time, Ms. Wilmont. You've been through quite an ordeal. You need time to recover. We hope you'll be back soon—to IShop. I'm a huge fan. Your disappearance was quite a scare—four days not knowing where you were and then another five here. IShop has been unwatchable without you!"

She glimpsed the clock to see if her father was due soon. He said he'd visit at two. She wished he was there now. Even at the risk of hearing all this. After what he shared this week, she could swallow some disgrace. How difficult it must've been for him. He didn't want any walls between them anymore. Neither did Shae. Peter wanted a fresh start being Shae's father. And she needed one.

She suddenly thought of the family portrait she drew as a child of Peter, Shae, and their cleaning lady, Capucine. How ironic it was to discover it was a lie for the opposite reason. The person she believed to be her father wasn't, and the person she never imagined to be her mother, was.

Now that she knew the truth, did it matter who her real father was? What did *real* even mean? The person who acts like a father, who acts like a mother, those were the real parents. Maybe in abandoning Shae, Capucine *was* acting like a mother. Maybe Capucine did the noble thing, in the end. Shae'd never know for sure. She knew so little about Capucine. She'd think of her in a new way now.

Though Peter's stories were overwhelming, Shae resisted tucking her emotions away in a box like she had taught herself to do. All these revelations were part of who she was. Maybe she'd get to know herself in the process.

"Need to ask a few questions." He ran a finger up and down the crease of his pants.

Shae didn't like being alone with this detective. Her instincts told her to be wary of him. What a joke that was! How could she ever trust her instincts? Her internal radar had a manufacturer's defect. She glanced at her fingertips. Thank God she was rid of that ridiculous polish. She never took it seriously. Not for a minute. So why did she let it mess with her head? This much she knew: there were places a detective should not stick his nose.

Shae watched the door over his shoulder, hoping the nurse would return. Wasn't the doctor due?

"You were spot-on about the Smokin' Hot! Electric Smoker. My sausages are superb." He blotted his upper lip with a tissue.

Shae didn't respond. What was he talking about?

"I resisted buying it at first, but now, my meats—they're sublime. Ribs practically fall off the bone. Succulent and—" He looked behind him at the door. "Incredibly aromatic." He pulled at his left brow.

She turned to the side to grab her phone. This guy was weird.

He picked up a large ziplock bag and removed a folder from it. Shae let go of her phone. He brought the *letters*? She wasn't prepared to *see* them. Talking about them in the abstract was one thing. Seeing them was quite another. Shae's throat dried up. She tried to gulp, but her tongue stuck to the roof of her mouth.

Her mind sped around like a roulette wheel, spinning and clacking wildly.

"I need some water. I'm very thirsty," she said. Maybe he'd slow down. Maybe he'd defer to her pace.

"Of course, let me pour it for you," he said, then chuckled. "You can probably detect I'm wearing Vetiver. You're so right; it's perfect for men *and* women. Very earthy. And dare I say...*intoxicating*?" He side-glanced Shae while pouring the water.

Shae took the cup from him, avoiding his eyes. Maybe he was just being friendly. Maybe he was trying to put her at ease. However, the opposite was true.

Before opening the folder, he brought it to his face and smelled it.

Jesus. Shae felt queasy. She wished they had sent anyone but this guy.

He looked inside the folder and over at Shae. He gave her a look she couldn't figure out. Shame shot through her body. She couldn't run, and she couldn't hide. Literally and figuratively. Her left ankle throbbed.

Figgy said people came forward with information. There were exactly three people who knew about the missing label. Shae, the girl in the basement, and her friend.

As soon as she was well enough to leave the hospital and face the legal consequences of her actions, she'd go to Zurich and stay with her father. They discussed it. She'd recuperate there. Figure out the future. It was time to plot her own course. Peter offered to help find Capucine, if that's what Shae wanted. They'd go to Paris together. Shae couldn't stay in California, at IShop. She knew that. It would be hard enough to show her face to her colleagues, but her fans? She wasn't ready to tell Figgy. But in time she'd understand.

"We'd like you to review these. Can you do that, Ms. Wilmont? We'd like you to look carefully. Take your time."

Shae glanced at the folder but didn't take it. Should a lawyer be with her?

"I think it's time for my medication; I should call the nurse." She reached for the button, but the detective grabbed her hand.

"This will only take a minute, Ms. Wilmont. It's better if it's just the two of us."

How could he grab her? Where was the medical staff? The endless parade?

She quickly took the folder and put it on her lap. The faster she did this, the faster he'd be gone. If she was obligated to talk to him, there was no point in stalling.

She opened the folder, and her heart stopped. A stack of photos. *Headshots?* She fingered through them. Five or six or seven. No letters.

"What's this?" she asked. Her face hot with humiliation and panic.

"Oh, sorry. Right. It's a photo lineup. We need to make sure the person who tipped us off to your whereabouts is not the abductor. There was a sizable reward. We need to know it wasn't given to the suspect."

Shae stared at the detective. Abductor? That word caught her off guard. She never considered the girl in those terms. Shae walked into her house of her own free will. Then lied and pretended to be a cop. She was probably in trouble for that, too.

"My abductor," she repeated blankly.

"Yes, we need your help. Obviously. We received a tip from someone who led us to you. The reward was $10,000. We make sure the person who comes forward with information isn't the offender. Also, we released a suspect. We can't let the offender take off." He snuck a peek at his phone, then put it away.

The folder started to shake. Someone tipped off the police? Someone came to Shae's rescue. Who?

Only one person knew where she was. The girl. She's the one who went to the police. Told them about finding the address label in Shae's bag. Implicating Shae for not only sending the letters,

EVA LESKO NATIELLO

but for being her own stalker. Then the girl told the police where to find Shae to collect $10,000.

Shae's shame mixed with rage. A fierce, potent cocktail of emotion. The girl denied her medical attention, the ability to go home or call someone for help and made $10,000 in the process. All while throwing Shae under the bus for the stalking.

"Obviously, there's a high likelihood the informant is also responsible for sending the letters."

Shae's head snapped back. "What did you say?"

He sighed and looked uncomfortable. "Unfortunately, that remains unsolved. But the person who abducted you is a suspect for sending the letters, obviously."

They think the *girl* sent the letters. Did they arrest her? Shae started to perspire at the back of her neck. Someone else, a suspect, was released. Jesus, they must've been scared out of their mind.

But the girl *knew* who sent it. She knew about the damn address label. Her friend found it in Shae's handbag! Why didn't she tell the police it was Shae?

She wondered if the girl was in custody. Sweat trickled down between Shae's shoulder blades.

"But I thought there were people—who had evidence—people who came forward—people who knew things about the letters?" Shae's head was reeling. She thought the police knew it was her. And that this was all a formality. She thought everyone knew. She thought her colleagues, Figgy—Val—knew.

He laughed. "I wish I had a dollar for every unstable individual who proclaimed to have 'information.'" He used air quotes and chuckled again. "It's our job to sniff it out before we come to you. I would never waste your time with every Larry, Lars, and Lance who wants to be crowned hero. Lots of crazy people out there who fabricate things to be in the spotlight and live out their fantasies. There was a lady in Pennsylvania, a real scam artist, claimed to have actually sent the letters. We knew she was a fraud instantly. She couldn't confirm what they said or when they were sent."

There was no evidence. No information.

He kept using the term abductor and offender. But no one had asked her a thing about her "abduction." Not even how she ended up in a stranger's house.

Or had they?

Shae'd been in the hospital for five days. She had many visitors. Sometimes she spoke with them, if she was awake and not heavily medicated. She remembered telling someone that a dog attacked her. So they could properly treat the infection. What about the police, the detectives? They'd been here too. Several times. She could have said something to them.

The nurses said a detective stopped by every day. Some days twice. One detective came in the morning and another later in the day. They were discouraged from talking to Shae while she was heavily sedated. Maybe she spoke to them anyway?

"What did you say your name was, Detective? I'm sorry, I—"

"No, no worries, Ms. Wilmont. I'm Lamar Tramball's assistant. Detective Lamar Tramball." He smiled a little too widely.

Shae flipped through the photos quickly. Not focusing on the faces.

"Who are these people?" she asked.

"Well, it's a photo lineup. They're mostly volunteers, college students, homeless—"

Homeless?

"And the like, with the person of interest thrown in. One of them gave us the tip that led to you." He motioned to the photos.

"Hopefully that person is innocent, too." He grinned inappropriately and shifted to look over his shoulder.

Shae adjusted herself in the bed. She exhaled deeply. These people. These anonymous people. Jesus, they were *innocent people*, exposing themselves, "volunteering" for a lineup? So that the "abductor" could be identified? Were they plucked off the street? Why would anyone volunteer for this? She closed her eyes briefly and tilted her head to compose herself. When she opened her eyes, they were fixed on the TV. The IShop channel was on again. She reached for the remote to power off.

The detective cleared his throat. "The hosts filling in for you are rank amateurs. I don't know how anyone tunes in, frankly." He shook his head. "Such bores."

Shae wasn't focused on what he said. She was agitated with this exercise. It felt wrong. Was she kept in the girl's basement beyond her will? It certainly felt that way. Did she ever ask to leave? Ask to call someone or to go to the hospital? She couldn't remember doing any of those things. Why? She walked into a stranger's house and was too fearful of the dog to leave. Too fearful of the girl. She couldn't *speak*. It was a bizarre series of events. Impossible to believe. Nothing went as either of them hoped.

Shae's ankle was on fire.

Shae closed the folder. She squeezed her eyes shut.

"I'm sorry this is upsetting you. I know how awful it must be to face your abductor. Even in a photo. There's no hurry." He inspected the door. "We'll talk more when you're stronger. Once your meds are taken down. I don't need any kind of statement from you today. But I do need you to look at these. The person might be a flight risk."

She didn't want to take her time. She didn't want to look at these faces.

He opened the folder on her lap. "Anyone familiar?"

She shook her head, but it wasn't in response to his question. It was in response to this lunacy. The lunacy of choosing someone in this folder who might not even be "the person." Even if it *was* the person—what did that mean? What was the person guilty of? Taking $10,000? She remembered now how badly the girl needed money. She shook for all these people. Her body shook along with her head. What happens when the wrong person is picked? That must happen. Were mistakes human error? Negligence? Acts of convenience?

"How about number one?" he asked. "What about her?"

"One of these people told you where to find me?"

"That's right." He blotted his forehead with a tissue, and Shae noticed when his shirt sleeve moved up that the skin on his arm was darker than the milky white of his hand. "Let's make sure she's not your kidnapper."

Kidnapper?

It's possible Shae wouldn't recognize anyone. Maybe the person who tipped off the police was someone she'd never met—someone she didn't know.

Relief washed over her. She might not need to point to any of them. She didn't *have* to "pick one." She could pick *none*.

She skimmed the first photo.

It was hard to look at Photo #1. Even with this newfound self-imposed non-pressure. Seeing an honest-to-God human being who couldn't have been twenty years old didn't make this easy. She gulped. Shae didn't want to look at her. Her glassy pink half-closed eyes. Dirty hair. Rumpled shirt. She might've been homeless. Such a young woman. A girl. How long had it been since she was in high school, eating well, living with her parents, and showering regularly? Maybe she was still *in* high school. What happened? Capucine flashed through her mind.

"No. I...no." Shae shook her head. A shot of cold air burst from the air conditioning vent overhead. She pulled the blanket closer.

"What about the next one? Take a good look. Sometimes they change their hair or makeup or something." He dabbed at his temples.

Girl number two was a bit older. Or at least looked older because the whites of her eyes were yellow. All her teeth were in an unruly clump at the front of her mouth like they all tried to escape but got shut down at the gate. She flipped quickly. "No," she said. And that was that.

The detective pressed on. Shae decided to lay the photos out on top of the open folder, across her lap. Maybe that would be quicker. They all stared back at her in unison. Why did the police randomly pick people to face judgment? She felt terribly uneasy. Her head shook again, involuntarily. Her good ankle swirled in circles. It pulled at the blanket, which shifted the photos. They slid to the side and one fell off the bed. The detective bent over to pick it up.

"Sorry," she said. Tears in the back of Shae's eyes multiplied. She didn't know where they were coming from. They piled up back there and were heavy. A storm was brewing.

"Number three?" he repeated.

She stared at the "#3" typed in the top right corner of a white sticker on a headshot. She wanted to act helpful. She wanted to *be* helpful, but in her gut, this didn't seem right.

She tipped her chin down and was concerned that this simple movement would encourage a rush of tears. Gulping down the liquid in her mouth helped to deter them. The headshot was of a woman in her late twenties, maybe. This was absurd, really. Of course she'd never seen these people. Shae remembered hearing a story once about how people who needed money would volunteer for this very thing. To be in a lineup. For cash. How horrible. How do childhood dreams get so trampled?

"Take your time."

One by one they went through them. At each photo, the detective asked the same questions. "Do you recognize her? Do you know her?" Shae didn't. These people were not people she recognized. She didn't know people like this. Except for in the movies. And now, come to think of it, Capucine. Her mother. She recently learned she *did* know someone like these people. The unfortunates. They were lumped together in this awful category. They were *people*, for God's sake. She wanted to say that. To this detective. Had he no empathy? What did he do, throw them a twenty-dollar bill and think he was a sport? How gross. Asking people to risk being chosen—mistakenly. Then what? What if Shae chose one of these people?

She wanted this to be over. She gathered the photos into a pile and placed them back in the folder.

"Not so fast, Ms. Wilmont. Slow down. Did you take a good look at number six?"

Please let this be over. Please. From the bottom of the pile, Shae pulled out the last photo. The sticker said "#6". Thank God it was the last one. Her eyes shifted to her face. She stared at the face—at her eyes.

To her absolute shock, she knew those eyes.

CHAPTER 40

Shae

Tuesday, January 10, 2016, 12:35 p.m.

SHAE's head jerked. She squirmed to adjust herself. Photo #6 shifted, and she righted it without looking. Her knee throbbed, and she palmed it to soothe the pain. Her mind reeled. Those eyes. She rubbed her wrists, clutching her hand to the opposite wrist.

"Everything okay?" the detective said.

"I think it's time for my pill," she said. "I need a sip—"

The door whooshed open so urgently, Shae knew it wasn't the nurse. Or the doctor.

A man strode in, wearing a suit jacket and nodding at Shae in greeting. In one assertive clip, he was at her bedside, ignoring the detective. He halted. Then did a double-take. Furrowed his brow. Blinked. Everything about him was certain. Sharp.

He thrust his hands out to the detective.

"*Lawrence?*" the man said to the detective, shocked. "What the hell are you doing here? What's—" His head snapped back to Shae. His eyes zeroed in on the folder on her lap, the photos. *"What the hell?* You took those off my desk?" His voice dropped, and he pivoted away from Shae as if to shield her from their discussion. He approached the detective, forcing him to step backward. "That's evidence. You know that. Wanna explain what's going on here, Lawrence?"

The detective shoved his hands in his pockets. His huge eyes flashed at Shae but quickly found the floor. He pitched his head down but didn't answer the man. He drew one of his hands to his nose and smelled it. He puffed out his shoulders and stood tall.

"Yes, sir. Of course. Just helping out. That's all. You've got a lot on your plate."

"Helping out?" The man's words were cutting. Shae wouldn't be surprised if they nicked the detective's skin. He straddled his feet sharply, like a scissor, and drew his hands to his hips.

"Lawrence—" He hurled the detective's name with such aggression, even Shae recoiled. Who was this guy? He looked at Shae. "I apologize, Ms. Wilmont. Please excuse us a moment. He faced the detective and pointed to the door. He then leaned toward Shae once more with a forced grin and said, "I'll be back in a moment, sorry for taking so much of your time." He followed the detective into the hall.

The hallway was only a formality because their voices were loud and clear.

"You're a fucking evidence custodian, Lawrence. And supply room attendant. *Not a fucking detective.* Are you a fucking idiot? It's against the law to tamper with or remove evidence from the vault. That includes photo lineups."

"I was taking initiative. Slackers are never crowned hero."

"What? What the hell are you talking about? Shut up, Lawrence. I've heard enough from you. What kind of fast one are you trying to pull? You log evidence. That's what you do. You stack photo copier paper. You order paper towels and tampons. For Christ's sake! That's it. Are you not clear on that?"

The detective—no, the *evidence custodian and supply room attendant*—began to speak but was interrupted.

"Don't answer that—I don't wanna hear your voice right now. You expect me to believe you don't know you're way out of line? I can demote you so fast you'll be cleaning toilets before lunch. What a dick move. What an absolute douchebag move. Stop smelling your hands. What are you doing? Stop putting those on. Give me those gloves. Enough with the fucking gloves! What's wrong with you?

"I was on your team, Lawrence. You know that? No one thought you should get that job. 'How does a mail clerk get an evidence custodian job?' I should've given it to Joanne. I took a lot of flak for not promoting from within headquarters. Instead, I brought you with me from NoDiv. People said I was crazy. But you know what? I thought you had what it takes. Hell, you dress the part. You're clean, you're confident. You've got presence. I wanted to give you a break. I never could understand what you were doing as a mail clerk. You seemed professional. Unless you're smelling your fingers. Or wearing these fucking gloves to file paper. But guess what? You're a fucking whack job!"

A heavy thump on the wall made Shae jump.

"Turns out Joanne's got a pretty good nose for things. She thought something was off about you. I didn't listen. Looks like she'll be getting the job after all.

"Now I need to worry about what else you've done. Jesus, I should've never let you take interview notes. I should've had the recordings transcribed like I used to. Now I need to worry about that. You listen to a few witness interviews, and you think you're a detective! Are you fucking delusional! You're making me look like a chump right now. Like I'm the fucking incompetent one. *That* shit ain't happening. I'll tell you right now, I've worked too hard and too long to be taken down by some peckerhead underling. I suggest you have a seat right there until I'm finished. Then we'll discuss what I'm going to do with you. Sit down. Right there."

"Excuse me, officer. Please keep your voice down." Shae recognized the nurse's voice. "And please, the expletives, we have patients—*Lawrence*?"

"Rita...what are you doing here?"

"I'm subbing for someone. What are you doing here? Are you on a case?"

"Oh...I'm..."

"No, he's *not on a case.* You know him? Friendly with the hospital staff, huh, Lawrence? Now I need to worry about how many times you've been here and what you've been telling people—or *asking.* Be sure I'll find out... Sorry about the language. I'm Sergeant Tramball, head of the Vista Verde Detective Unit. We obviously don't want to disturb anyone."

"*You're* the head of Vista Verde's Detective Unit?" the nurse asked. "How is that possible? Then what are you, Lawrence?"

"What is he? A *fired* evidence custodian and supply room attendant, and in a shitload of trouble for impersonating a detective—sorry about the language. I'd like to talk to you another time about what he's been telling the hospital staff. Lawrence is going to sit in that chair until I'm finished speaking with the patient. Don't move."

A moment later the door swung open, and Shae caught a glimpse of the nurse talking to the evidence custodian now exiled to the hall. "Supply room attendant, huh, Lawrence?" she said.

"*And* evidence custodian."

She sighed heavily. "Impersonating a detective. Why am I not surprised?" She folded her arms. "Welp, you did always want to look the part. You certainly have a nose for *that*."

"Hey Rita!" A man wearing scrubs strode past the nurse. "You're working here today?"

"Yup, until six."

"Great. Plenty of time for me to change your mind about having dinner with me!"

In walked the man in the blazer. He extended his hand. "Ms. Wilmont, Detective Lamar Tramball. Pleasure. Sorry to meet under these circumstances." He reached into the inside pocket of his jacket and presented Shae with his badge. Something the other guy didn't do, come to think of it. His name and photo were on the back. "Sorry about the confusion with...Lawrence. Very sorry about that. He meant no harm. Do you mind telling me what's been discussed...today...with Lawrence? You know, so we don't repeat anything and waste your time."

Shae wasn't convinced he didn't want to waste her time, but she told him everything that happened before he arrived, starting with Shae waking up to Lawrence smelling her armpit. Detective Tramball's face didn't even flinch when he heard that. "I see." He stood very still. He blinked once, and that was it.

"I think I should come back another time. This didn't get off on the right foot—" He quickly surveyed Shae's leg. "Excuse me. No offense intended." He raised his hands to apologize. "Let's start over tomorrow. We can go through the photos together to see if you know any of these women. Would that be okay?" It seemed like he wanted to collect the photos and leave, but he hesitated to retrieve them from her lap.

"Know them?" She didn't say that to herself as she had intended. "No need to come back. I understand time is of the essence. You want to make sure you didn't give the reward to—"

"No," he interrupted. "Is that what Lawrence said?" He looked puzzled. "We didn't give the reward to anyone. The informant didn't claim the reward. It was very unexpected. The information she provided led us directly to you. Therefore, she qualified. But she said the money wasn't the reason she came forward." He paused and stood there quietly. Watching Shae's face closely. "Not that it's pertinent, but maybe it had something to do with her receiving a scholarship for college. Dental school or something like that? I don't know." He waved his hand in the air as if to erase what he just said. "I probably shouldn't disclose that—" He studied Shae's reaction. "But sometimes it helps to jog the memory, you know?"

Shae stared at the detective. He didn't strike her as someone who disclosed information casually. She looked back at the photo.

"Still might be the abductor, obviously. We've seen this before. Denying the reward could be a sign of a guilty conscience. A lot of these guys are scammers. You wouldn't believe what they try to pull."

Shae wasn't listening. She was lost in thought.

"Obviously, we'll still go after her. Just as soon as you press charges."

Press charges? Shae looked back at the detective. She hadn't considered that.

Shae wanted this detective gone. She couldn't deal with all this. These emotions. This information. Having to reflect on it all. It was too much. Her head was spinning. Her ankle was on fire.

"I reviewed the photos," she said. "We were finishing when you arrived. I was on the last one."

The detective's eyes lowered to photo number six. Without saying anything, his eyes probed Shae's face. He didn't even move his head. He waited. Shae suspected he knew number six. Shae took one last look at the face in the photo.

From the bits and pieces Shae knew about the girl, she had no family, no money. A friend dead of an overdose—someone she tried to save from a tough life. She was scared of being arrested. That Shae remembered. The girl's mother went to jail for something she didn't do.

It all looked different now. Shae was petrified of the girl's dog. Of what the girl was going to do to her. She was scared of the neighborhood and the people who lived there and their circumstances. But in the Venn diagram of life, Shae recently discovered, they overlapped a lot. They were actually sisters of circumstance. The keepers of each other's secrets. With one big difference. Shae had the means to live comfortably without fear. Without judgement. Without sacrifice.

Shae looked at the photo again, at the girl's mouth and the dark circles under her eyes, a gash healing over perfectly shaped brows. A slim nose. Cheekbones dotted with fresh pimples. Long black hair. The girl's wig made her look severe, sullen.

"What about number six?" asked Detective Tramball. "Do you know her?"

Shae hadn't spent her lifetime having to convince people she was capable, smart, deserving, decent, honest. No one had ever asked Shae to prove who she was. And good thing, because she had spent most of her life not having a clue.

Shae's eyes locked on the eyes in the photo. Shae saw those eyes when they were hostile. When they were harried. Screaming and scared. Praying and pleading. She'd never forget those eyes. For the rest of her life, the girl's features would be implanted in her memory. She'd see them in her sleep. She'd see them on the street. She'd see them in magazines, on movie screens. She'd never not see them.

When do we know someone, exactly? When do we convince ourselves of who they are? Once we know their hopes and desires? Their regrets and failures? Their secrets? What qualifies us to make that conclusion?

She stared at the girl's eyes, and though she may have wanted to look brave, Shae saw fear in her eyes. She looked like a young girl stripped of courage. Knowing all too well how wrong things could go. And how quickly. By going to the police to save Shae, she put herself in the fire.

Shae felt something deep in her gut. She felt the same thing in her head and in her heart.

She gathered the photos and slipped them into the folder.

"No," she said, handing the folder back to the detective. "I couldn't possibly know her."

Acknowledgments

THE miracle that is completing and publishing a book marvels me again. Why does this process seem so fraught and fragile? Because anyone involved in the creative process hovers close to the edge. The edge of inspiration, invention, excitement, frustration, despair and resignation. We are bold and insecure, original and hackneyed, filled with passionate enthusiasm and crippled by all-encompassing self-doubt. Don't try this at home! No, try it. Really. It's exhilarating. Part of the time, anyway. But that's okay. If you can be exhilarated by anything for even a fraction of the time, I say go for it!

Keeping me on track and solidly away from surrender's edge are the people in my life without whom this book would be collecting dust on the hard drive.

An abundance of gratitude to my editorial team: Charlie Knight, Christie Stratos, Anita Stratos, and for their professional expertise and guidance, Guy Olivieri and Eliza Bryen. And to my cover designer, Bianca Bordianu for FOLLOWING YOU's stunning cover.

To my first readers, Rosanne Kurstedt, Lillie Bryen, Kathy Neumann, Lillian Duggan. What would I do without you? A big thanks and appreciation for your influence, support and friendship, the Westfield Writers Group, Marisa Mangione, Betsy

Laskaris, Wendy Murray, Cheryl Paden, Tom Butera, Kim Bongiorno, Emma Schwartz; Stephanie Karp and the members of Shut Up And Write. For words or deeds, Heidi Guest, Carrie Jacobs, Sophia Frank, Lori Kaplan, Dana Lopes, Sheila Valenti, Juliette Townsend, Starr Foster, Christine Grant, Arielle Eckstut, David Henry Sterry, Mimi Field, Jessica Collins, and Paola Fernandez Rana.

Thanks to Peggy Natiello, Anne Lesko, Denise DeBrocke for your affection and support. To Bob Natiello, in memory, whose wisdom and confidence continue to impact my writing every day. And to Joe, Margaux and Mark for not worrying about the voices I hear in my head.

Book Club Questions

To provide discussion topics, questions may contain spoilers.

1. Discuss how fear and panic drive Shae and Honey to presumptions about each other?

2. Shae says, "When do we know someone, exactly? When do we convince ourselves of who they are? What qualifies us to make that decision?" Discuss a time you thought you knew someone but discovered you were wrong.

3. One of the themes of FOLLOWING YOU explores how we believe certain people without judgement, and we judge others without believing. What are your thoughts?

4. Discuss the fascination we have with following people on social media to view their inner lives. When is the line crossed between curiosity and stalking, and specifically Lawrence's interest in Shae?

5. In what ways do you think childhood trauma contributed to the people the main characters have become as adults?

6. What do you think Shae's goal was in sending those letters to herself? Do you think she'll admit to it?

7. In the end, Shae and Honey know things about each other no one else knows. Why do you think they didn't reveal them?

8. Lawrence discusses how casual interactions with people in his youth—his aunt (by marriage) and his college roommate Charlie —shaped his life in important ways. Is there someone in your life who's done the same for you?

9. When Honey sees Shae's tattoo it triggers a memory of butterflies from her childhood. How does the butterfly symbolize different things to each of the main characters?

10. Discuss the phenomenon of intuition and times this sense has been right, or possibly wrong for you personally.

11. In what ways did your opinion of the characters change? How did your assumptions influence your first impressions?

12. Were you satisfied with the book's ending? What do you think will happen next?

THE MEMORY BOX

What if you Googled yourself & discovered something shocking?

In this gripping psychological thriller, the privileged suburban moms of Farhaven amuse themselves by Googling everyone in town, digging up dirt to fuel thorny gossip. Caroline Thompson, devoted mother of two, sticks to the moral high ground and attempts to avoid these women. She's relieved to hear her name appears only three times, citing her philanthropy. Despite being grateful she has nothing to hide, a delayed pang of insecurity prods Caroline to Google her maiden name—which none of the others know.

The hits cascade like a tsunami. Caroline's terrified by what she reads. An obituary for her twin sister, JD? *That's absurd.* With every click, the revelations grow more alarming. *They can't be right.* She'd know. Caroline is hurled into a state of paranoia—upending her blissful family life and marriage—desperate to prove these allegations false before someone discovers they're true.

The disturbing underpinnings of The Memory Box expose a story of deceit and an obsession for control and cautions: Be careful what you search for.

Get the book that San Francisco Book Review gives "5-STARS".

A NOTE FROM THE AUTHOR

Thanks for reading FOLLOWING YOU. I hope you enjoyed it.

I started writing this book many years ago, and it's evolved into a very different book than the way it began. It's interesting how life experience and the world shape our vision of things and the stories we want to tell. One of the themes of the book is identity, and for me one question remains. Who controls a person's identity? Do we control our own, or is our identity shaped by what others think of us?

If you'd like to leave a review on an online bookstore, Goodreads or BookBub, I'd be so grateful! If you select this book for your book club, I'd love to hear from you! Upload book club photos to the contact form on my website at www.evaleskonatiello.com, and they just might appear on my website or social pages! I'd be thrilled to join your book club discussion of FOLLOWING YOU, virtually, if I'm available, so do reach out.

To anyone who shares this book with friends, on social media, in book reviews and book clubs, or has asked for it at your town's library or bookstore—thank you! It means so much to me. Please tag me in your social media posts about the book!

I'm busy working on my next novel of psychological suspense and can't wait to share it with you. You can stay updated on news from me by signing up for my newsletter at www.evaleskonatiello. com. Stay tuned!

With gratitude,
Eva

Made in the USA
Middletown, DE
31 May 2022

66448547R00189